BEYOND THE EVER REACH

MORTALITY BOOK ONE

EVERLY FROST

For Ben

But Eve turned from the serpent
and did not eat of the fruit.
And for her obedience,
she was allowed to reach out her hand,
take from the tree of life and eat,
and live forever.

Evereach Origins, Second Edition

PEOPLE SAY that at the beginning of time, Eve made a choice. She turned away from the serpent and the tree with the forbidden fruit, and she left them both behind.

They say that her reward was to eat from the Tree of Life and when she did, we became invincible. Our bodies changed, our healing capabilities increased, and we could no longer be killed.

But I don't think it was when she swallowed the first bite or even when she told the serpent to get lost.

I think our world changed when Eve decided who she was.

And now, as this monstrous man pulls the ropes off my body and holds out his hand, offering me the one thing that can save me, the one thing that can keep me safe, now is when I'll make my choice.

Now is when I decide whether I'll fight or give in. Now is when I decide who I am.

PART I
FREAK

CHAPTER 1

I NEVER COULD watch anyone die.

Tricycle wheels flipped through the air. Brakes shrieked and metal crunched. The kid's trike rattled all the way across the road and hit my foot. I froze at the curb in front of my house, school bag sliding off my shoulder, vision filled with the spinning wheels. I told myself to walk away, pretend I hadn't heard the smash or seen the boy go under the vehicle. I should shrug it off like I was supposed to.

I should ignore the impulse to help.

I bounded around the broken bike and sprinted to the car in the middle of the road. A little arm extended from underneath the front fender, palm up, motionless. Biting my lip, I sank to my heels, wishing his fingers would twitch, fighting the tears that welled behind my eyes.

First death.

It always took one death to find out how fast someone was going to heal. The boy's fingers were flushed pink, regenerating, but the stillness of his hand told me he wasn't a really fast healer. I guessed it would be at least another half an hour before he was fully conscious again.

The silence was heavy after the squeal and crash. I hovered, not sure if I should pull him out.

I hated my brother for leaving me behind. If Josh had driven me to dance class like he was supposed to, I wouldn't be here now, staring at first death and not knowing what to do. I'd be going about my day like normal. No, I reminded myself. Today was not an ordinary day. Today was Implosion.

The driver emerged from the car with annoyance on her face. I flinched as she slammed the car door. Another woman ran from a nearby house, screaming into a phone. She raced to the driver and gave her a shove. "That's my son! I'm calling the Hazard Police. You'd better be insured!"

The driver threw up her hands and backed off, slumping against the side of her car, clicking her fingernails together, and tapping her heels against the pavement.

I knelt down to the boy as his mother continued to yell into the phone. She paced up and down the road, her voice shrill. "How long will it take to get a recovery dome here? What— you've got to be kidding me. I'm already late for work."

Wisps of his blond hair touched the side of the wheel like yellow cotton candy, all floating and soft. I wondered if his soul floated there too, inches above the hot road, waiting to get back to his body. I was glad I couldn't see the rest of his head.

Before I touched him, something zipped past my shoulder.

The drone circled up and back, swinging close to my ear. Shaped like a metal cross no bigger than my hand, it skimmed the air in front of the car. Beneath the hum of its four miniature rotor blades came the chatter of shutters. It was taking shots of the damage: the boy's hand, the wheel, a piece of tricycle jammed under there with him. Assessing the situation and relaying the information twenty miles west to the nearest Hazard Police station.

The drone flitted from spot to spot, whirring around the car straight toward the driver, hovering and clicking, transmitting her image back to the police. The kid's mother was next before the drone flew to me. A pinprick of light struck my eyes, and I stopped still, waiting for it to take the shot and move on, but the clicking stopped.

I frowned as the mechanical chattering died. Instead of taking my picture, the drone floated, paused for the first time. I stared back at it, waiting, a feeling of unease spreading through my chest.

Someone grabbed my arm.

My elderly neighbor, Mrs. Hubert, wrenched me to my feet, a pair of pruning shears wavering in her other hand. The camera clicked behind me—just once—and I imagined the blur of my body captured in the image. Before I drew breath, Mrs. Hubert's strong grip propelled me several feet from the car. Her long braid—a sign of her age—slapped against her thigh as she strode away from the accident, taking me with her.

"Come away, Ava. You don't need to get caught up in that." She flicked her head in the direction of the scowling driver who looked as if she wanted to strangle someone. I guessed she didn't have insurance, after all.

"But, he's still under there..." I threw a confused look at the boy's mother. She still hadn't checked him.

"Everyone deals with first death differently. You need to get used to it if you want to get through Implosion tonight."

Implosion. When I find out how fast I heal.

She tugged on my arm again. "Besides, the Hazard Police will be here soon. They'll take care of him."

Behind us, the info drone returned to the crash as Mrs. Hubert urged me further away from the accident. I picked up my bag and tried to forget about the child.

Mrs. Hubert opened her gate and went back to pruning her rose bushes as if nothing had happened. The shears snapped. Petals floated to newly mulched earth, bright red on brown. "Go on. There's nothing more to do here."

I forced myself to focus. If I didn't hurry, I'd miss dance class completely.

It took me twenty minutes to rush to the dance studio downtown, which made me ten minutes late. Dance was part of my schooling and counted as the first two classes of my day. Luckily, the studio was located just a few blocks up from the school. As I puffed toward the café below the studio, I slowed for a moment to breathe in the normality of people drinking coffee, the crackle of open newspapers, and the soft jumble of conversation. No more broken bike and tiny hand.

Approaching the corner of the building, I gave Lucy, the owner of the café, a quick wave. She'd offered me a waitressing job over summer holidays, which was perfect because I could head upstairs to dance practice after my shift. She returned the wave with a bright smile. With her olive skin and dark brown hair, Lucy had the kind of complexion that hinted at a Seversandian heritage. My own features weren't far off: brown hair, brown eyes, and skin that was a shade darker than pale. There used to be free movement between our country, Evereach, and the country across the sea, Seversand, but not anymore.

I took the stairs two at a time, raced past the poster I normally drooled over—an ad for the Conservatorium, the most prestigious dance academy in all of Evereach—and launched myself through the door.

Inside the studio, students were moving away from the warm-up bar into the center of the room. Ms. White towered at the head of the dance floor, her reflection tall and straight in the mirror behind her. "Hurry up, class! Selections for the Conservatorium are only six months away and I won't accept dawdling because summer's here."

I ran to put my bag down, searching the group for my best friend, Hannah. I caught sight of her pale blond head among the other students, shining like the first ray of sunlight that morning. She threw me a questioning look as Ms. White pointed me to the warm-up bar. I rushed through my stretches and positioned myself at the back of the room, focusing on the new routine, until Hannah maneuvered her way over to me.

"Where were you?"

"There was a car accident. One of my neighbor's kids got hit."

Her eyes glazed over. The boy's death wouldn't matter to her. It shouldn't matter to me.

"And Josh hates me, but what's new." I leaped, twisting my body mid-air and landing on my feet, to spring upward again.

Hannah dipped away, and when she moved back, she edged closer so we could talk. "Are you ready for Implosion tonight? My mom was all mushy about it this morning, it was embarrassing."

I forced a laugh. "Yeah, my parents not so much." Mom had taken me shopping for a new dress in all black so it didn't show the blood. Black wasn't compulsory and Josh had told me that some kids at his Implosion ceremony the previous year wore white, but those were mostly the religious kids, and they framed their Implosion clothes afterward to remind themselves about faith. I only had Josh's word for it, since only adult members of the family were allowed to attend the ceremony and it wasn't televised. Other than the dress shopping, my parents hadn't talked about Implosion much, as though it wasn't important that I was becoming an adult.

After tonight, I'd be allowed to grow my hair past my shoulders—but only about half an inch, since the length of our hair had to match our age. And I'd be allowed to drink. And move out of home, except only the really fast healers did that since they were offered paid Hazard training while they completed their last year of school. I figured I'd be stuck at home for the next year, but Josh was heading to college after summer holidays.

"So, what about Josh? He's going to the Terminal tonight? I heard it's going to be a massive fight."

My stomach clenched and I missed the move Ms. White was demonstrating. Josh had begged to go to his graduation party, but our parents insisted he come to Implosion with me. "Dad said no."

"But all the graduates are going. It's the last time they'll get to kill each other." The lightness was gone from her voice. "He *has* to be there."

I shrugged, but the nonchalant gesture was a lie. How could I tell her that the very idea of the Terminal made me sick? That my heart hurt every time I remembered the little boy under the car.

That the thought of Implosion—of being killed for the first time—made me shudder so hard I couldn't breathe. Hannah hadn't died before either, but I knew she didn't feel the same way.

I said none of those things as Ms. White's voice drowned out my thoughts, beating out a warning with a finger pointed firmly in my direction. "Concentrate, Miss Holland. Or I'll have to send you to school without your Extra-Curricular Pass."

Hannah flicked me a quick, apologetic glance and I ducked my head and willed my body to obey the music, to turn when it should and leap when it should. Finally, I lost myself in rhythm and movement and the quiet that always fell over me when I danced.

When we arrived at school, it was morning break and students crowded the halls. I pushed on the doors just in time for someone to release a wash of flyers advertising the Terminal.

A familiar giggle told me that Sarah Watson posed against the nearby wall. Her nail scissors glinted as she tilted her bleeding ear, showing off how her blood didn't even drip before her skin healed.

Fast healer.

I rolled my eyes and turned away before the inevitable face sucking with her latest conquest, but I was surprised when it was Michael Bradley. He had Sarah hanging off his arm as if she was an extension of his elbow.

"Remember when we said we'd never be some guy's accessory?" Hannah grabbed my hand with her eyebrows way up in her hair. "That's the one guy I'd make an exception for. Do you know he's never lost a fight at the Terminal?"

Josh didn't say how fast Michael healed at Implosion the previous year, but I'd heard he turned down Hazard training. I guessed, if my dad were part owner of the Terminal, I wouldn't bother with a job either.

Sarah caught my eye before I could pretend to look somewhere else. "Hey, Ava," she said, looking me up and down from my regulation-length short ponytail to my leggings. "Been to dance class? Seems like a waste of time to me."

She turned away before I could reply, but Michael gave me a nod, a strangely serious acknowledgment of my presence, and I wasn't sure how to respond. I frowned at him as Hannah pulled me along. "Pfft. She's just jealous. Besides, did you know she's a third child?"

"Truly?" When I turned twelve, Mom had given me "the talk." At the end of it, she'd told me that our bodies can only have one child, maybe two and that was a good thing because people lived for so long. Otherwise, the world would be over-populated.

Hannah drew me into the swarm of students. "Did you see how fast she heals? *She's* probably a Basher."

I glanced back at Sarah and Michael as they disappeared into the milling students. The Bashers were terrorists who hated slow healers and threatened to bury them alive. Members of the Basher gang were always fast healers. They went to extremes to keep their identities secret, always wearing full camouflage gear, and nobody knew who their leader was, but their message appeared in graffiti sprawled on the corners of billboards or across the sides of buildings: *Bury the weak.*

"Do you think it's true what they say about the Basher cells underground?"

"That they bury slow healers alive." She screwed up her face in disgust. "The police seem to take it seriously, but I don't know. Sounds like a scary story."

"I don't understand why they hate people who don't heal fast." I struggled to say the words "slow healer." It was insulting to label someone that way.

Hannah shrugged. "I heard they think slow healers make us look weak, vulnerable; everything we use Implosion to prove we aren't." She smiled and bumped my shoulder, trying to lighten the mood. "Hey, if I turn out to be a slow healer tonight, you've got my back, right?"

I attempted a smile as she pulled me down the hallway. Heading to class, I checked the steady stream of students for my brother. School was finishing early in honor of Implosion—I had only two classes left—and I didn't trust him to wait to give me a lift home.

As soon as the final bell rang, I raided my locker, hugged Hannah, and raced out to the parking lot.

Josh was already opening the driver side door as I ran up. "Hey."

He didn't answer, settling behind the wheel with his hair blending into the cracked black leather seat. He pointed at me and then to the passenger seat.

I raced around to the side and dropped into the seat, just as his best friend, Aaron Reid, appeared, his hair tousled and full of gel. He drummed his fists on the hood of the car and shouted at Josh through the windscreen. "See you at the Terminal, buddy!"

He signaled to Josh, put a finger to the underside of his chin, and pretended to pull the trigger. Josh mocked a slit throat in return. A ghost of a smile crept onto my brother's face as he revved the engine and slammed the car into reverse. Josh drove faster than the speed limit, but I picked my battles.

I chose my words carefully. "Aaron seems to think you're going to the Terminal tonight."

His jaw flexed and there were murky stains under his eyes that made him look hollow. "So what if I am?"

I took a deep breath. It wasn't because I didn't want him to go to the Terminal—as much as I couldn't stand the idea of people killing each other with swords or guns or drones, or whatever new thrill the Terminal came up with. I didn't want him to miss his graduation party either. But he'd been through Implosion before. He knew what was coming.

"Josh, it's my Implosion. You're my brother. I need..."

I don't want to be alone when I die.

I swallowed the words I couldn't say. I'd be surrounded by hundreds of kids. My parents would be there. But, somehow, the thought of my brother standing beside me gave me courage. Even if I regenerated straight away. Even if there was a chance I was a fast healer, I didn't want to lose myself to that moment of darkness. That moment of death.

The words tumbled out of my mouth. "I need you to be there."

He didn't look at me, his expression hooded and unreadable, as his hands tightened on the wheel. He was quiet for so long that exasperation bubbled up inside me.

"How can playing at the Terminal be more important than my first death?"

"Because I'd rather kill than watch you be killed." He glared at me as we stopped at an intersection, a deep darkness behind his eyes.

I struggled to understand. "Implosion's important..."

"You're a freak, Ava. It's a stupid ceremony that lets people sleep at night. Seversand isn't coming to kill us. Because we can't die. Nobody can."

He tapped his temple and pressed his finger there, his eyes boring holes into me. "The only war we fight is the one in our own minds."

I struggled against the burn of tears behind my eyes. A long time ago, our country, Evereach, was attacked by Seversand. At school, we'd learned about the old world war that was fought over control of Evereach's rich soil and water supplies. It lasted a hundred years while both countries tried to create weapons that could actually kill people. In the end, Seversand created a nuclear bomb, but when they dropped the bomb on Dell city—the city where I now lived—it didn't kill anybody. After that, world leaders drew up an international treaty: as long as each country's children regenerated at Implosion each year—as long as we proved we couldn't be killed—no country would go to war again. There was no point in wasting resources on a war that couldn't be won.

But it wasn't the past that bothered me. It was the look in my brother's eyes. I'd practically said aloud that I was scared to die and now he knew my deepest fear.

I didn't understand why I felt this way, why death bothered me so much.

Why am I like this?

It was a question I'd asked myself a thousand times and I still didn't have any answers. All I knew for sure was that I was alone. Alone and different. I couldn't stand to see the pity in Josh's expression. I slumped in the seat for the rest of the trip, until we pulled into the driveway.

Josh was out of the car before I had time to gather my things. I dragged myself toward the front door as the local neighborhood watch drone coasted by the house.

There was a happy shout behind me and the little boy who'd died that morning pedaled past on a shiny, new tricycle. His mom gave me a wave. I tried to smile as I headed inside, down the corridor, past the connecting door to the garage, and around the corner to the bottom of the stairs.

Mom was sitting at the computer, visible through the open door opposite the stairwell. She jumped out of her seat as soon as she saw me. "Ava?"

I was already part way up the stairs. "Yeah?"

"Get ready, sweetie. We'll have a bite to eat and then we'll go."

I dragged myself to the landing halfway up, pausing as the

air screen in Mom's study blared after me, the excitement in the female newsreader's voice palpable.

"Sixteen-year-olds all around Evereach are preparing for Implosion tonight. At exactly six p.m. in each time zone, young people of every nation have proven their ability to regenerate, including teens in Seversand." A hint of derision crept into the newsreader's voice as she mentioned Seversand, but she continued without pause. "In other news, Starsgard has refused to extradite the computer hacker known as Arachne…"

Starsgard. It was the only country that didn't take part in the world war or Implosion and its borders were heavily protected. On a map, the three countries reminded me of a set of lungs. Evereach and Seversand formed the lungs on either side, a wide sea between them, but they were joined at the top by a backbone of impassable mountains. Starsgard *was* those mountains.

The newsreader's voice faded as I made it to the top of the stairs, turned left, and headed to my room, passing Josh's closed door on the way. Further down the hall was the upstairs lounge. I wanted to run through it to the deck beyond, push open the sliding doors, and gulp fresh air. Instead, I turned into my room where I found the black dress, pressed and clean, lying on my bed next to a pair of dark stockings. Shiny black heels waited on the floor.

Next door, Mrs. Hubert's lights weren't on. Normally, her flickering television turned my bedroom into a disco, a kaleidoscope of moving lights. I peered out to see that her blinds were drawn and shuttered, and at the side of her house, the garbage can was overturned, spilling white plastic bags across the side path. I frowned as I headed to the bathroom across the hall to wash up.

Too soon, I was dressed and ready and Mom was calling. "Ava? Josh? Time to go."

Dad met me at the bottom of the stairs, dressed in a new black suit and Mom in a dress similar to mine. Dad held out his hands for me.

I didn't know what to say, so I blurted. "I don't feel like eating."

"That's okay, honey, let's just go. There's been a change of venue, so we have further to travel."

I followed Mom and Dad to the car and seconds later Josh thumped down the stairs behind us. Climbing into the autonomous vehicle, I tried not to crush my dress, smoothing it out in my lap. My parents were the first on the street to buy one of the new autonomous cars, but they were becoming more common.

Dad spoke to the navigation system and the serene female voice confirmed: *The Terminal.* I started, glanced at Josh, and he smirked back at me.

As the vehicle passed the darkness shrouding our neighbor's house, I said, "Mrs. Hubert's place is dark tonight. Is she out?"

In the front seat, Mom tilted toward me. "I'm sorry, sweetie. Mrs. Hubert had her final death today."

I stared at the window, frowning at my own reflection, as Mom said, "We mustn't be sad. She had a wonderful life. I'm sure all her descendants will come to the wake."

"She just didn't seem that old. I mean, her hair was longer than anybody's, but..." I remembered her braid slapping her thigh. Halfway down the back meant fifty years old. To the waist was one hundred. To the top of the thigh was two hundred and after that people stopped measuring as long as it stayed long.

Dad said, "There isn't always warning. Our bodies just stop regenerating. She must have been at least 350 years old."

Mom gave me a calming smile as the car continued out onto the main street. "I'm sure we'll be invited to the wake. Come on now, it's time to enjoy the evening."

Thirty minutes later, the entertainment precinct glowed ahead. Movie theaters, malls, and restaurants surrounded the massive Terminal skyscraper like ants swarming around a dirt mound. Once there, the car pulled into a multi-level parking lot and we got out and followed the complicated neon signs. A long, glass walkway finally opened into what looked like a living room, lined with plush leather couches and fine wooden coffee tables. A security camera drone floated in each corner of the room and on the opposite side, a big mahogany door advertised the entrance, with a touchscreen in the middle.

There was a short line, with other people dressed like us, all in black. Mom tapped in a code and tugged me through with Dad and Josh close behind. Moving across a walkway, we entered an enormous, dimly-lit room, with people already milling about. There were about 500 kids and their parents—all of the sixteen-year-olds in Dell city. The room was flat across the floor, but the sides curved up and over like a dome around us.

Surveillance drones hummed across the ceiling, recording what was happening for the eyes only of each country's highest authorities: Presidents, Prime Ministers, and monarchs.

Somewhere in the heart of Evereach, President Scott would be watching, flanked by the Head of the Hazards and the High Justice. The Seversandian President would be watching too. I'd seen pictures of her, standing at the head of an army amassed across shimmering sand dunes, her dark brown hair tied into a high ponytail and a row of jewels strung across her cheek from a ring in the side of her nose.

To one side of the room, a group of kids stood praying, heads bowed, all wearing identical white cloaks that made them stand out like glow-in-the-dark figurines.

I wished I could see the world the way they did—that our fate was decided by a woman in a garden who told a serpent to get lost and was rewarded for her faith with eternal life. Implosion for the faith community was a part of remembering and giving thanks. But the drones hummed and the room was like a crypt and it was impossible to think about new beginnings when the whole world waited for us to die.

"Hey, buddy!" Josh's friend, Aaron, appeared out of nowhere, fist thumping with my brother.

Dad looked surprised. "Aaron, I didn't know you had a sibling here tonight."

Aaron pointed over his shoulder and I noticed for the first time the Hazard officers standing at intervals around the room. They were covered from neck to foot in fitted green uniform, designed to allow them to move fast. Each wore a pair of drone-control visors, so transparent I could barely see them from that distance.

The man Aaron pointed to had the same color red hair as Aaron and a drone hovering at his shoulder. "My brother's with the Hazards, so I got to help set up."

As Aaron spoke, his brother's drone drifted toward us, and Mom wasn't the only one pointing at it. "That's new."

Smooth and sleek, the drone was striped gold and black and was bigger than any I'd seen before. Silver protrusions dotted its underbelly, tranquilizer darts masquerading as decorative studs. Its movements were calm, wafting close to the ceiling.

Aaron's response was indifferent. "It's a wasp."

I'd heard about them on the news. They were Weapons to Apprehend Suspect Persons—the latest police response to the Bashers. This one was the same black and gold as the other wasps, but it had narrow stripes all around its body, and I realized that each was decorated differently.

Aaron winked at me. "I'll be taking off now." He shook my father's hand. "Have a good evening, Mr. Holland. Mrs. Holland." A quick glance at Josh and Aaron was gone.

My skin prickled as Mom and Dad gave me a gentle push forward. Other kids were separating from their families and moving into the center of the room. Somehow, I ended up close to the front as we formed rows in rough arrow shapes across the floor. I hadn't even had the chance to look for Hannah. What was already dim lighting darkened so I could barely see.

I looked back for my family, frowning as Josh slid away from my parents, carefully angling his way toward the back of the room. He was taking his chance to leave and part of me sank to the floor. He could have stayed just this once.

The lights went off and the sudden silence crashed over me.

I flinched as sound boomed around the curved walls, an explosion in the air. A giant, orange mushroom billowed up around us: an air screen of projected images engulfing us in pictures of an inferno, as if we'd been dropped into the heart of a fireball. I gasped as the first exploding nuclear bomb splashed color across the height of the walls, swelling around us, a reminder to the world's authorities that it was our city on which the bomb had fallen hundreds of years ago.

The image of a woman appeared in front of me, kneeling inside the flames, her body cracking and roiling, separating and pulling together, trembling as she resisted the force of the explosion around her. I shuddered at the realization that I was looking at real footage of the day the bomb exploded.

The woman opened her eyes as words etched the air.

We are Evereach. We are invincible.

She struggled to her feet, her voice a whisper that may as well have been a shout. "We aren't dead. You didn't hurt us." Her braid swished around her body, flicking into the air under a force I could only imagine, lit up by flame and heat.

She reached to the ground and for the first time, I noticed there was someone at her feet: a teenage girl, her eyes big and dark, fissions forming across her skin and healing all at once like her body was a jigsaw puzzle fighting to stay whole.

The woman's voice rose. She threw back her head and shouted into the air, shouting at Seversand and all the countries allied with it. "Look at us! Our children are alive. You cannot hurt us!"

She gritted her teeth against flame and heat. There was an echo of her words as others appeared, others who'd fallen. They clambered to their feet and joined in her shout against the wind and fire, the dust of exploded buildings, shards of glass and wood whirling around them.

The people of Evereach roared. *"Our children do not die."*

Suddenly, my parents were beside me, each of them holding one of my wrists. I tried to pull away from them, and they shot me alarmed looks. Nobody else was trying to run. Nobody else was afraid.

They each held a knife in one hand, gripped one of my wrists in the other, pulling me close. I tried to wrench myself away from them, but the image of the woman and her daughter ghosted through me, leaving me cold and frozen. Above us, the drones swarmed, buzzing like a thousand insects, capturing the flash of steel, exposed skin, determined eyes.

When I died, I'd find out whether my soul floated or whether it left me or whether there was no such thing as a soul at all. I tried to take deep breaths, tried to stop shaking. We were strong. We had to show the world that we could never be broken.

The woman's voice whispered into the silent dark. "You will never defeat us, for our children do not die."

Blades bit my wrists.

CHAPTER 2

MY SKIN TUGGED and pain pierced me.

I screamed, yanking out of my parent's hold, desperate to get away from them, but suddenly there was another explosion.

This one wasn't an air screen.

With a mighty force, it shook the walls and smoke filled the room. A light in the ceiling flashed, a siren wailed, and then I wasn't the only one shouting.

Someone screamed. "Bashers! They'll bury us!"

People clambered and rushed around me, all shouting into the chaos, tripping and stumbling in the near dark and the flashing lights, the fear of being trapped alive driving them to the exits.

A second explosion rattled the ceiling and there was a ripping sound like the walls had come apart. Bashers in full-body brown camouflage gear appeared like dark shadows among the throng. To my right, the white-cloaked kids took up their parents' swords and slashed at the attackers while their parents fought with their bare hands. For a moment, there were blazes of white through the darkness, falling bodies, and then

Mom shouted my name. She grabbed my arm and my parents were beside me again.

A glowing shape flew near us and with it came the hum of a hunting insect. The Hazards and their wasps were fighting back. They'd clear a way through for us. But before I could blink, the wasp sped, not outward, but toward me and whipped to a halt. In the next second, it fired a dart at Mom and she dropped, a dead weight making me lurch.

Stunned, I reached for Dad, but he crashed to the floor as the rapid fire continued, two darts protruding from his chest.

Shock pinned me in place. The wasp's thin stripes were visible in the flickering light. It was the wasp belonging to Aaron Reid's brother. I couldn't understand why he would send his drone to tranquilize both my parents. Before I could move, it swung to me, still firing. In another moment, I'd be a lump on the floor.

An object flew past, smashing the whirlwind of sound and movement. Pieces of gold and black tore around me as the drone exploded. At the same time, somebody grabbed me up from behind, snatching me into a run.

A distorted voice spoke into my ear. "It's not your time to die."

My heart withered. My rescuer was a Basher.

A motley brown and yellow camouflage suit and a face mask concealed his identity. A voice modulator was fitted to his mouth so his words were intelligible but inhuman. Every instinct in my body screamed at me to struggle away from him, but he pounded across the room, taking me with him.

We were running straight for the wall. I tensed as I expected him to thrash me against it, debris crashing around us, burying me under the weight of wood and concrete. I was scared to die —I was worse than a slow healer. Once he buried me, I wondered whether I'd be strong enough to claw my way out or whether I'd be pinned, trapped in darkness where the Bashers thought the weak belonged. Because that's what I was and I knew it. Afraid of death. Agonized at the thought of people dying. Weak.

At the last moment, he heaved me up even closer to him and held me with one arm as he extended his other arm, some kind of device in his hand. He punched numbers into it as we moved. I tried to turn away, but his grip was made of steel. As I braced for the impact, an opening materialized.

We raced through as the door shut with enough force to take off a limb. The chaos in the Implosion room might have been miles away, it was so silent there. We were in some kind of short hallway, windowless, a door at either end. The Basher turned to the right and pulled me along again.

"Who are you?" I jerked away from him, but when that didn't work, I rammed myself against him, pushing us both against the side of the corridor.

I sensed the air leave his lungs, heard him gasp a breath, but he grabbed me up, not answering my question, dragging me along as I shoved and wrenched against him. "Where are you taking me?"

This time, he said, "Somewhere safe."

I stared in disbelief as we reached the door at the end of the hallway, a door painted blue with a touch screen just like the mahogany door at the front.

The screen said: *Please enter your code.*

He tapped at it and the screen went blank. Maybe he'd triggered some kind of alarm. I waited for the sirens to wail, but in the next instant, the screen flashed again.

Please proceed to the Mirror Room.

The Mirror Room. It was supposed to be a myth. Most rooms were open arenas with public viewing booths and video drones everywhere to capture the action. But there were rumors about private rooms, places people went to fight when they didn't want anyone watching. The Mirror Room was one of them.

Determination gleamed behind the strip of veil he wore

across his eyes. "I'm taking you where nobody can hurt you. Not the Hazards. Not the Bashers, either."

"But you're one of them—"

"I am what I have to be. For now."

To our right, there was a low grinding sound and a panel slid open, revealing another corridor beyond. I could run. I could fight him. But as much as I didn't want to admit it, he'd just saved me from my first death—and saved me from a hunter drone.

He said he was taking me somewhere safe and for some reason, I believed him. I didn't know why Aaron's brother would tranq my parents and try to tranq me when the walls were crashing down around us and Bashers had infiltrated the Terminal, but I put aside my questions and raced inside with the Basher, slowing down when we made it through and the door closed.

The corridor stretched out in front of us, curving in the distance. Lights dotted the walls, up high, but other than that, it was a blank walkway. No decorations, no other doorways. No drones, either. It seemed so empty, so *safe*.

Around the curve of the corridor, there were more doors, maybe twenty of them all along one wall of the massive corridor, spaced apart so that I imagined a combat room behind each one. Some of the rooms were supposed to be high-tech constructions. In some of them, the combatants didn't even fight people, but machines instead. Others were medieval, straight out of history, set up with thatched houses and muddy earth squelching underfoot.

Toward the end of the corridor, the Basher pulled me to a stop. He grabbed my wrists, making me wince, turning my hands up to the light so we could both see the damage: a cut on each, but only skin deep. One of the cuts oozed a little and I frowned at it, watching and waiting for it to heal.

Dismay filled me as I realized...I *was* a slow healer.

"Put your finger on it and press. It'll stop soon."

I did as he said, pushing away my humiliation and fear, avoiding his eyes. I'd deal with my new discovery if I made it out of the horror show I found myself in right then. I waited as he flicked his device toward the door. A flash of light caught my eye as the door clicked open and I put up my hand to block it. There was another flash, but I knew what it was this time, and I hesitated behind him.

It was the Mirror Room. Ceiling to floor, wall to wall, the reflections made even more dazzling by a silver ball turning on the ceiling. On one side of the room, the mirrors reflected rows of shiny weapons hanging from glass hooks. If there were video drones, I couldn't see them.

The Basher said, "We just have to make it through another couple corridors, but don't worry about the fighters. These rooms aren't scheduled for combat tonight. Just stay close."

I wanted to ask him again who he was, why he was doing this, especially when I was a slow healer. He had no reason to help me and every reason to leave me behind in the chaos, but he pushed the door open, filling the walkway with reflective light. As soon as he took a couple of steps, he ground to a halt, pushing me behind him, fixated on the other side of the room. Disappointment blossomed in the set of his shoulders and his sudden indrawn breath.

His indistinct whisper was garbled behind his voice modulator. "No. They promised."

The other person had frozen at the sight of us, a shout revealing his surprise as he rose from a bench seat placed against the far wall.

It was Michael Bradley. He was dressed in black, but the dark material couldn't hide the smears and rips, his skin perfectly healed beneath them.

He must be here for the graduation party and, despite what the Basher said about this room not being scheduled for combat, the surprise on Michael's face at seeing us indicated he'd expected to face one of his classmates in this room instead.

"Basher," Michael said, an angry curl to his lips. "Is that what all the commotion's about? If you're here for new recruits, you aren't going to make any friends by blowing up the Terminal." His eyes were on me and even at that distance, I could tell that a thousand thoughts went through his head.

The Basher suddenly grabbed me up against him, a knife at my throat. "You'll let us leave."

"Or what? You'll kill her?" Michael scoffed and the tension radiating off my captor shuddered through me.

The Basher shoved me a step closer to Michael—and the door on the other side of the room—as the silver ball above us rotated and cast our reflections a thousand times around the room.

In answer, Michael moved to the left, just a bit, revealing the sword resting down by his side as if he didn't think he'd have to use it.

Another step, and another. The Basher's chest rose and fell behind me, as though he was breathing his soul in and out.

Michael's hand tightened on his sword. There was blood on his fingers. He said, "Well, I thought I'd be fighting someone from the graduation party, but I guess you must be my last fight tonight."

The Basher's mouth was at my ear. "I'm sorry, Ava. I tried."

He shoved me aside and leaped forward, snatching a weapon off the wall—another sword—and springing at Michael with the sword raised. Michael's sword flashed to meet the Basher's and deflect the blow, but the Basher pushed, and the two weapons grated down each other with a metallic shriek, coming apart just before they chopped each other's hands off. The Basher sliced again, and again Michael deflected. Then again and again, so fast I could hardly keep track.

My feet had put down roots on the concrete floor. I huddled in a crouch, knowing I should move back to the wall, get out of the way, but I couldn't move, couldn't think.

The Basher whirled, slashed, his muscles pumped, his legs

crouching, springing. Behind his tight facemask, the lines of his face were severe.

They were evenly matched, neither giving ground nor missing an attack or a defense. The duel moved over to the bench and the Basher dashed up onto it, leaping down with a forceful cut that would have cleaved Michael's head from his shoulders. Michael dodged, crouched, and swung around to cut the other boy's legs out from under him. The Basher must have anticipated the move because his sword angled at the last moment. It cut through the air, headed straight toward Michael's eyes.

He dropped and flattened himself to the floor just in time, allowing the Basher to lunge over him. The Basher's sword struck the floor a fraction away from Michael's face with so much force that it twanged. He wrenched it out of the floor and Michael rolled to his feet.

Without hesitation, their weapons clashed, but something had changed. Michael wasn't defending anymore. He was attacking. He beat the Basher across the room, where the Basher rallied and almost caught Michael on the shoulder, but Michael kept on, pushing him around as if he was beating at a moth.

Then the Basher cursed. His sword flew through the air and landed several feet away. He lost his footing, stumbled, and in an instant, Michael had the sword to his throat.

Without a second's hesitation, Michael ripped off the Basher's facemask.

I jumped to my feet and Michael stumbled backward. "What...?"

My brother's pale face stared back at me.

"Josh!"

Josh looked right at me while I shook and trembled and tried to comprehend what was going on. He said, "Don't let them break you, Ava."

Michael lowered his sword, letting his weapon swing down by his side, letting Josh regain his balance, confusion swamping his face. He followed Josh's stare to me, his eyes wide and wild.

Before I moved, Michael roared with pain. His attention leaped back to Josh, breaking the contact with me. I wasn't sure if I shouted or screamed, only that some kind of sound came out of my mouth because, while Michael was distracted, Josh had thrust a knife into his chest.

The knife handle protruded right where Michael's heart would be. His face contorted, changing from shock to pain, and then to anger. He stumbled, his legs buckled, but he didn't go down. He wobbled, reaching out into the air as if he was trying to steady himself on oxygen alone.

Relief flooded Josh's face as Michael stumbled backward. Josh took a step toward me, ready to run, but his expression changed as he saw what Michael was doing.

Michael's whole body tensed. His eyes scrunched to dark slits. His right hand stopped clawing air and curled around instead. He took hold of the knife and levered it outward, freeing the weapon as easily as a needle through silk.

Josh's face took on the strangest expression I had ever seen —resignation, peace. He took a step back toward his sword, as though he was supposed to, but he seemed so slow about it. In an instant, Michael flipped the knife in his fist and plunged it into Josh's heart. Then he pushed Josh backward.

The air left Josh's lungs with an audible *oomph* as he thudded against the floor, half on his back, half on his side.

Michael closed his eyes and stood still. So still, I thought he'd really died.

I trembled all over, but I made myself move. I had to get the knife out of Josh and get him out of there right away. I'd never seen someone stabbed in the chest before, but if Michael could recover that quickly, then Josh could too. I'd drag him out of there if I had to. We'd get away and then I'd make him explain to me what was going on, why he was dressed as a Basher, and why he was taking me away.

I raced to him and crashed to his side. "Josh!" But there was something wrong with his face. When people regenerated, their bodies became flushed, glowing, circulating blood really fast. Regenerating. Josh's lips were pale, trembling, and his face was white.

I took hold of the knife, but it was slippery and when I pulled, my hands came up empty. I turned to Michael. He'd pulled the knife out of his own heart. He knew what to do. "Help me!"

Michael blinked at me and his eyes looked weird, all dilated as if he was in a dark, dark room. Not in this silvery place anymore. His voice was a whispered growl. "Give him a minute. He'll come back."

I tried to hold on to my thoughts as I turned back to Josh, to the pale stillness and the gray tinge spreading across his skin like a violent sea claiming every part of him. I tried to make sense of what I was seeing. Maybe this is what happened with hearts, maybe they reacted differently. But Michael hadn't reacted like this. He'd pulled out the knife and he was okay.

Josh would be okay too.

He opened his eyes and I breathed relief. He was back. Now he'd pull out the knife and get to his feet and we could find a place to answer the thousand questions racing through my head.

He didn't move. He gasped, breath gurgling in and out. He met my eyes. "Little sister." My arm stung as he gripped it, fingers pressing, pushing me, as though he wanted me to get away from him, as though he wanted me to run away.

I shook my head at him. "Josh…what…"

His eyes closed and his hand dropped away. I waited for him to speak again, to move like he should. I shook his shoulders, but he didn't respond. Confusion threatened to overwhelm me.

I needed to help him, but I couldn't do it alone. I searched the room for some kind of emergency alert system. There'd been a big deal about it when they opened. It was all over the news. The Terminal was totally safe, they'd said.

I found the emergency intercom on the far wall, a black rectangle in the center of a pink-tinged mirror, and I ran to it and hit the button. "Hello? We need a recovery dome! Now!" No clinical voice came out of it, telling me to stay put, that help was on the way. "Hello? I need help! Oh…"

The button wasn't glowing. I ran desperate eyes over the box, wondering if it was switched off, but the only button was the one I'd struck. I screamed into the plastic grill. "Answer me!"

The silence was horrifying. When I turned back to Josh, Michael leaned over him. I ran over, meaning to push him away, but he stepped back before I had the chance and shook his head.

"Ava. He's…I've never seen anything like this before. I think he's…"

Dead.

"This isn't possible. It's not possible." I shoved at Michael, glaring into his eyes, the eyes of a monster. "You killed him!"

He put his hands up, but didn't touch me, backing away.

As I watched him, all the panic in my body slid away. The fear and horror were gone, and I knew that this time, when I bent over Josh, I'd be able to pull the knife out; his heart would let it go.

The knife slid out and I willed Josh's chest to rise and fall, to breathe, but it was too late. I clambered to my feet and stabbed at Michael with all my strength. He stood there, letting the knife fall. And fall again.

The slash across his face healed in an instant. The gashes I left on his chest and arms turned pink with new skin and faded. I raised the knife again as tears slid down my cheeks. He reached out and pushed my arm away. Really gently. His guarded face and stern mouth blurred as my vision turned to water. I pressed my eyes shut and clutched the knife so hard I was in danger of cutting myself, but I didn't care. What would it matter?

His hand covered mine, tugging at the knife, trying to make me let go, but I heaved at him, pushing as hard as I could. "Get away from me!"

When I opened my eyes, he was gone. The mirror-plated walls reflected only hundreds of me, back and forth, around and around, standing alone with the weapon in my hand, each drop making a larger puddle next to my black heels. A puddle that threatened to slide across Josh's Basher uniform.

I had to get it off him. If anyone found him like this, they'd know what he was. They'd hold him responsible for the explosion at the ceremony and all that property damage. In the last year, I'd heard of only one other Basher being caught. He was tried for hate crimes against slow healers and sentenced to life in prison. If Josh lived…No, not *if*. *When* he came back to life, they'd lock him in solitary for the rest of his life for being a member of the gangs. He may as well be buried under rubble.

I snatched at the brown suit, using the knife to rip it at the seams, not caring whether he had other clothes underneath, but he did: his collared shirt and tie, black for Implosion, hiding the blood pooling across his heart. I ripped and tore the Basher uniform from his arms and legs and rolled it into a ball, running to the door and throwing it down the corridor.

Back inside the room, I slipped and buckled. Once kneeling on the splattered floor, I couldn't get up again. I put my head into my hands, curled over my knees, and closed my eyes. I didn't feel anything. Not the wet tiles, not my wild hair, not my empty, useless hands. I didn't try to reach for the emergency intercom again. The lights in it were dead like my brother. Out of order. Like me.

I hated Josh.

I hated him for leaving me in his dust. I hated him for calling me a freak. Most of all, I hated him for being a Basher, for dragging me in there, for getting himself killed.

But he was my brother. And death was not a possibility. Not here. Not now. Not until we were hundreds of years old.

It must be a mistake. I glanced at him, thinking that any second now his arms and legs would start trembling—enter the pre-healing phase—like they should have already.

Running footsteps brought me to my feet, and a man I didn't recognize raced into the room with a large pack slung across his back.

Relief surged through me. He'd brought the recovery dome. Now he'd bring Josh back.

CHAPTER 3

"OUT OF the way, girl." The man skidded to a stop beside Josh, dropping to the ground and swinging the giant pack off his back.

An oxygen mask came out, followed by an enormous needle filled with dark fluid that the man thumped into Josh's chest and compressed. He spoke into his mouthpiece, calling for a full recovery transport. "We need it now."

He shoved at Josh, half rolling him over, and ripped at the material across Josh's right shoulder. Beneath his shirt, there was a section of puckered skin, white and warped, about an inch in diameter. The man paused and cursed at it. He cursed again, shaking his head.

Then he whipped into action, opening out his pack and throwing it upward so that it snapped mid-air into a rigid dome shape. It reminded me of one of those clear umbrellas that stockbrokers in suits always seemed to carry, except without a handle. He pulled it down to the ground so that it encircled Josh's whole body. He tapped the console and the dome sealed itself to the floor.

"Stand back," he said, and I obeyed.

Only then, I realized that Michael stood at the door. He

hadn't run after all. I'd expected him to be far away by then, but he'd come back with the medic.

He leaned against the archway as if he was waiting at a bus stop. Bored, uncaring, ignoring the gore adorning his chest and neck—a tattoo of death. I wondered, if I looked closer, whether I'd see signs of strain around his eyes, maybe a tight jaw, frozen shoulders, fear, and uncertainty hidden well.

The recovery dome flashed, spilling bolts of organic energy into Josh's body, and I waited for him to respond. Any second now, my brother would gasp, the blood would stop flowing from his chest, and he'd come back to himself.

The dome was alive with electricity, jolting Josh's body. The energy inside the dome reached out beyond the umbrella cover, making my skin prickle. I didn't look at Michael again or watch the medic. The only important thing was Josh's face. I waited for his eyelids to flutter, his mouth to draw in oxygen.

The man stood up. He lifted the microphone toward his mouth. He stopped, started to speak, and stopped again. Another curse left his lips and hung in the air. He ran his hand over his eyes and shut them for a moment.

He lifted the console in his hand, pressed a button, and the silver disco ball stopped spinning, the dimmer lights went up. He pressed something else. "Permission to turn off the recovery dome."

Silence. Then, "Because he's dead." He put his hand over his eyes. "You heard me."

"No." This wasn't happening. I contemplated Josh's body as if it was far away, and not a real dead person. The first I'd ever seen.

"Miss?"

The man's face blurred. I put my hand to my heart, checking that it was still beating. My brother…no…

"Miss?" When I didn't answer, he looked to Michael.

"She's Ava Holland." Michael pointed at me and then at the ground. "That's Josh Holland—her brother."

The man's shoulders were tense, his eyes blazing at Michael. "You'd better get home to your father before the Hazards get here."

Michael hesitated and the man strode over to him, seized his arm, and said something I couldn't hear. Michael met my eyes over the man's shoulder. I tried to read his expression, but I couldn't. He nodded and left the room through the corridor that I'd snuck in through.

The man came back to me. "Ava? I need you to listen very carefully. You need to get out of here. They'll already be calling it in, and they won't send the usual officers for this one, do you understand?"

I didn't understand. Not at all. I tried to see his features: hazel eyes, round chin, a receding hairline and a braid halfway down his back—the same age as my dad—but they were all mashed together. I felt as though I needed to remember who he was, as though it was important, but all I wanted to do was slide to the ground and cover myself with darkness. "I'm not leaving my brother."

If he heard me, he ignored me. "You need to get yourself to a recovery center. The nearest one is on Delaney Street, back through the tunnel. When you get there, tell them to call your parents, but don't leave. Make sure they keep you there."

I reached for Josh, wanting to shove the recovery dome away, wanting to stay with him. "I'm not leaving him here."

The man shook me. "There's nothing you can do for him."

"But—"

His voice rose to a commanding shout, his eyes blazing at me. "Ava! Go! Now!"

My legs moved even though I didn't want them to, obeying the man. I fled the Mirror Room, out through the walkway with a hundred doors, and shot out through the open panel. There was an open door at the end of the short corridor and when I ran through it, I found myself in the waiting room at the front of the Terminal. Lounge chairs had been ripped apart and one wall was blackened and cracked. I'd expected it to be swarming with people, but the place was deserted. They'd evacuated everyone already.

Only then, I realized I had no way of knowing where Mom and Dad were, how I'd even get to the recovery center. I turned to go back—I shouldn't have left Josh—but the panel closed. I didn't know how I was going to get anywhere, but the only way was forward, so I took off at a run toward the parking lot.

The car was still there. When I got to it, I banged on the window because I didn't have keys. Or a phone. I couldn't even call someone for help.

My hand went over my mouth. How was I going to tell Mom and Dad that Josh was dead? Not first death. Not second death. Final death. For the first time, tears burned behind my eyes, my shock turning to grief. I tried to gulp back the sob that choked my throat as I remembered his last words.

Little sister...

I curled downward, trying to press the pain of losing him out of my body.

A screech around the corner of the parking lot made me jump and twist, flatten myself against the side of the car as a sleek blue sports car squealed to a halt in front of me. The engine revved and the window slid down.

"Get in," Michael said.

I swiped at the tears in my eyes. "I'm not going anywhere with you."

"Looks like you aren't going anywhere without me." Michael leaned toward the passenger side window. He paused when he saw my face.

I glared, summoning all my will to stop my tears, pushing back against the heartache. "I'm not getting in a car with you."

Michael left the engine running and jumped out of the car. He strode straight over to me but stopped before he touched me. "I know you have no reason to trust me right now, but you have to get out of here."

I shook my head, scooting along the vehicle. "Get away from me."

He moved to grab my shoulders. "Ava—"

I kicked him hard in the shin. I meant to kick him somewhere else, but I couldn't get my knee up. He bent, reflexively, just a little bit, but it was enough for me to hit out with the palm of my hand, straight into his nose.

He backed away from me, holding one hand up and wiping his streaming eyes with the other. "I'm trying to help you."

"Well, don't. I don't want you near me." I should've grabbed the knife and brought it with me. I caught sight of someone moving at the other end of the lot. I shouted and waved my hands. "Hey! I need help!" I slid around the car, away from Michael. "Help me! Please!"

Whoever he was, he came at a run, and Michael backed away even further.

It was another man dressed in black, except this one had a shiny badge and a tranquilizer gun resting at his waist. The guard slowed to a jog, one hand on his weapon and the other held toward Michael. "Back off, son."

Michael obeyed, taking wary glances between us.

"He's trying to make me get in his car."

"I can see that, miss." But something on the guard's face changed. "Michael Bradley?" There was a click and Michael squinted as a flashlight flooded his face. The guard lowered the torch. "What are you doing here, son?"

"Her car's broken down. I was offering her a lift, but I guess she took it the wrong way."

The guard relaxed and laughed. "Got a way with the girls, don't you?"

Michael shrugged as the guard turned to me. "What's your name?"

Before I had time to answer, he shone the flashlight in my face. "Wait a minute…" I sensed another change in his stance as his voice became harsh. "Are you Ava Holland? You need to come with me."

There was a clank of metal as he procured a pair of hand-cuffs and grabbed my arm.

He didn't say anything else.

The light dropped, making a lazy swirl in the air around me and then a sharp plunge. I looked up from the human crumple on the ground to Michael standing behind him. He bent over the prone guard and shoved the tranquilizer gun back onto the man's belt.

I stared at the guard and the glinting handcuffs. "I don't understand. Why would he arrest me?"

Michael's fists clenched. He swore several times. "Your brother just *died*. Here, in the Terminal, the worst place it could possibly happen. You can't stay here. Not if you want to see daylight again. You just can't."

I stared at him. "What are you—?"

He said my name and his voice was loaded. Loaded with words he didn't seem to want to say—or couldn't. I could see his mind working over it, sifting through his thoughts. He said, "The Terminal isn't just a games facility. My dad works here."

"So?"

"He's a scientist, Ava."

"What are you trying to tell me?" I pursed my lips at him, running his words around my head. "That there are secret experiments going on here? That there are people lurking in basements creating potions or monsters or something?"

"I know you don't believe me, but you need to leave." He ran a hand through his hair and his voice lowered. "I just tranq'd a guard. I'm in it so deep ... I don't even know why I'm trying to help you."

He strode over to the car, which was still purring in the middle of the parking lot, but he paused before he slid into the driver's seat. "No. I do know." He didn't look at me as his voice became hoarse. "This is my fault. If it wasn't for me, you wouldn't be standing here and Josh wouldn't be back there … I'm not going to force you to get into the car, but I really think you should get out of here."

The guard began to stir.

"There are more where he came from," Michael said.

I ran over to the car, but not the passenger side. "I'm driving." I glared into his shocked face. "It's the only way I'm getting in a car with you, Michael." I poked his chest as hard as I could, right where he'd been stabbed, hoping it would hurt.

He didn't even flinch. "Okay, if that's what it'll take…"

He ran around to the passenger side as I slipped into the driver's seat, scared out of my brain. A guard had just tried to arrest me, and Michael shot him. I couldn't control the volume of my voice as I shouted. "Where's the parking ticket? Unless you want me to drive straight through the boom gate, you'd better have paid already."

He flicked me the small plastic square. I shoved the car into first gear and compressed the pedal, zipping forward and around the curve, praying there weren't any cars coming in the opposite direction or we'd all be totaled. Finally on the lower floor, I zoomed toward the boom gate and passed the ticket over the reader. I accelerated out of the parking lot and down the road, slipping the car into fourth gear. "How do we get out of here?"

He stared at me as if he was the one in shock. "Um. Left up here. Watch out! That was a stop sign, Ava. Who taught you how to drive?"

I bit my lip. "Josh did."

He didn't say anything and I asked, "You're directing me to the recovery center right?" It was all clicking into place. The images flashed through my mind. "That man—whoever he was —back in the Mirror Room. He told you to take me, didn't he?"

"Neil Cheyne. He's my godfather. And yeah, he told me to take you somewhere safe. Somewhere away from the Terminal.

He said…" Michael turned his face away. "He said it was the least I could do."

We twisted and turned our way out of the Terminal Precinct and entered the tunnel. The headlights from another car jabbed my eyes. I tried to blink away the black spots left behind. I tried to forget about my brother's body. I'd left that behind too.

Josh had been trying to convince Mom and Dad to let him fight at the Terminal for as long as I could remember. But when I'd watched him fight Michael, it was as if he'd been there before —or somewhere like it. There'd never been any self-defense classes or martial arts lessons or anything like that. Josh played soccer and video games and drove his car like a lunatic, nothing else.

Except for all the times he disappeared.

I ran a hand over my eyes and then clenched it around the steering wheel.

Michael said, "You need to be in the right-hand lane."

"What?"

"The Delaney Street exit is on the right. You'll miss it if you aren't in the right lane."

Hysteria set in. "My brother just died and we're talking about lanes." I choked on a sob. "Do you know what the stupidest thing is?" I glanced at him, his face flickering as the tunnel lights whizzed past. "I always wanted to drive one of these cars."

I started to cry, even though it was a dangerous thing to do. Crying while driving. I tried to sniff the tears back. I blinked hard as my vision blurred. I expected him to shout at me, tell me to pull myself together, but he stared through the windscreen at the passing lights as if he didn't care anymore.

He said, "Why did Josh die? He was at Implosion last year. He healed almost as fast as me. The Bashers only want the strongest. If he was one of them, how could he die?"

Michael's words traveled around and around my head, spinning in their own little hurricane, all tangled in with my own confusion and sadness. And anger. I said, "I bet they tried to recruit you, too."

Michael's jaw ticked. A flash of rage was quickly replaced by an expression that reminded me of something ripped apart. "I'd never join them."

But Josh had. I wondered if I would ever know why. Our parents had never made a big deal about healing and they'd never taught us to hate people who didn't heal fast. Josh had never said or done anything to make me believe that he would ever try to hurt anyone or take part in destroying homes and workplaces. In fact, I remembered when we were kids and Josh had come to the defense of a boy others were teasing because he'd cut his leg and he didn't heal for a whole minute. Disappear on me, yes. Hate, no.

Through my tears, the Delaney Street exit loomed up ahead. I thought about driving on. Just driving and driving until we left Dell city and ran out of gas and ended up in the middle of nowhere. I wondered if everything would make sense once we got to the end of that road.

Instead, I turned the wheel and took the exit. A big blue sign announced the recovery center with arrows to the entrance. I pulled the car to a halt in front of the wide doors and stared straight ahead as the silence enveloped me. I spoke to the windscreen and didn't look at Michael. "I don't ever want to see you again."

He didn't say anything.

I jumped out of the car and raced away into the bright lights.

<h1 style="text-align:center">CHAPTER 4</h1>

THE RECOVERY NURSE told me to wiggle my fingers. "All right. That looks fine. Show me the cuts again."

I turned my wrists up.

"I'm going to turn off the lights to have a look. Okay?"

I nodded. She pulled the blinds and the room went dark before she flicked on the ultra-violet overhead lights and examined my arms.

Turning the light back on, she pursed her lips at me. "You're a slow healer."

On another night, I would have flinched at the insult.

A small smile touched her face, as though she hadn't meant to be so harsh. "Well, you've certainly got quite a bit of blood on you, so I'm sure I'm just seeing the final closing of a deeper wound."

I sniffed, blinked. There was a hot well of water behind my eyes, but I was determined not to cry.

She patted my arm in an awkward gesture. "You've been through a lot. Those Bashers have enough to answer for, let alone ruining Implosion for you." She busied herself with flicking open the blinds again. "You'll need to stay here until we can locate your parents."

I nodded, intertwining my fingers to stop them shaking so much. The medic at the Terminal—Cheyne—had told me to stay at the recovery center, not to leave. I didn't know why and it was all starting to feel wrong. My brother was dead and I was supposed to skulk around the center, waiting for my parents. Recovery centers were for people who needed a recovery dome or who were still regenerating—or if they got in the way of a police pursuit and were accidentally tranquilized. Sometimes doctors had to dig bullets or shrapnel out of people who healed too fast, but I had no reason to be there. Hysteria rose again, pushing up through my chest, rushing to my mouth, and I was sure I was going to scream.

The door crashed open and Mom rushed into the room. "Ava!"

Relief slammed through me. "Mom."

The next thing I knew, I was smothered in the comforting scent of her favorite perfume. I closed my eyes as she hugged me. If I stayed right there, with her perfume surrounding me, maybe everything else would disappear, but she pulled away too soon.

"They won't tell me what's going on. Dad's still in a recovery dome—they said he was hit with a tranquilizer by mistake—and I woke up just now. What happened to you? How did you get here? Did the Hazards bring you?"

The feeling of comfort fled. "They haven't..."

My voice choked up. She didn't know about Josh. I put my head into my hands. The nurse watched us both, her pen hovering above her clipboard. She looked as if she was going to speak up. I'd told her everything the minute she walked me into the examining room. She'd listened without speaking and then she'd made a single phone call. She'd had a look on her face as if I was a case for a mental health clinic.

"Mom…" My voice broke. I wondered how I'd make my mouth form the words. *Josh is dead.*

A knock at the door stopped the sound in my throat.

"Mrs. Holland?" The man wore the typical green Hazard suit, close-fitting around his body and up his neck, a sharp contrast to his red hair. My breath seized and my heart constricted. It was the same officer with the wasp that shot my parents at Implosion: Aaron Reid's brother.

The image of the wasp firing tranquilizers at my parents and then coming for me dashed through my mind. I glanced at Mom, but she didn't seem to remember anything, just looked blankly at him. He had a slim face, high cheekbones, and piercing eyes. He looked like the kind of guy others underestimated. The kind of wiry fighter who could move fast, light on his feet like a dancer.

"I'm Officer Douglas Reid, ma'am." He flicked open his ID. "I'm sorry, Mrs. Holland. They said it might be better if you had a familiar face right now. Can you come with me, please?"

Mom was trying hard to keep it together. "Yes, of course, it's nice to see you again, Douglas. It's been a long time. Of course, we see Aaron a lot, but…" She still hadn't moved.

He took hold of her arm, prompting her to her feet. "I've been away at training in Chasm. But it's good to be home. Could you come this way, please?"

The nurse had stood as soon as the officer knocked. For the first time, the expression on her face changed, draining pale. She looked at me and then at Mom. Her mouth opened as if she was about to drop to the floor. I read her expression: maybe she wasn't dealing with a mental health case after all.

Mom's face turned fragile, ready to crumble. "What's going on? Nobody will tell me."

"Ma'am, if you'll just step outside with me, I'll explain everything." His hand on her arm tightened visibly and it was clear she didn't have a choice.

Mom kissed my forehead. "I'll be back in a moment, sweetie. Just sit tight, okay?"

She left with Douglas Reid and he shut the door. They stood outside the room and I watched them through the window. Mom was really still like one of those mime artists pretending to be a statue. Officer Reid spoke, but she just stood there, and then her legs must have buckled because suddenly she slipped out of view and he reached out to grab her and I heard her screaming all the way through the cold window glass.

The doctor leaned toward Mom. "Mrs. Holland, have you ever suffered a serious injury?"

Tearstains gouged streaks through Mom's makeup, dark smears where she'd tried to clean up her mascara. Her hand clamped over mine, so hard that it hurt, but I didn't say anything as we sat together in the doctor's office. I needed her to hold me together as much as she needed to know I was still there.

Officer Reid stood outside the door, a slim line of green through the misty glass.

"Um." She bit her lip. "Yes, when I was young. My eye." She gestured. "A kid at school poked me with a stick."

The doctor gave her one of those calm, medical smiles. He'd told us that he didn't usually work at this recovery center, which was generally staffed with recovery nurses. His specialty was surgical removals. They'd called him in because of the Basher attack, but it was lucky he was there in the circumstances.

"Was your sight affected in any way? Did you have any trouble healing?"

"No, of course not. They didn't even have to call the Hazard Police. They had a recovery kit at the school. I look okay, don't I? Why are you asking me this?"

The doctor gestured at me. "What about your daughter? Has she ever been in an accident?"

Mom looked at me and back at the doctor. She shook her head slightly. "No." She shook her head again as if she couldn't stop shaking it. "Ava's never been hurt." Her hands fluttered to her face. "Well, maybe she sprained her ankle once dancing, but it stopped hurting straight away, just like normal, right sweetheart?"

She barely glanced at me and I was glad because I still remembered the sprained ankle, how long it had throbbed, and how much that still confused me. I'd been extra careful since and I'd made myself strong. Strong muscles didn't get hurt.

Mom rushed on. "And then there was Implosion tonight, but I don't really remember…" Her eyes clouded over. She touched her temples and rubbed her skin.

The doctor leaned away. He wrote something down. "Mrs. Holland, we can't find any evidence that your daughter suffered more than superficial cuts tonight—which are taking an extremely long time to heal. I'm afraid I'm going to have to order tests for her." He handed Mom the clipboard. "I need your signature on this."

"Why?"

"It authorizes the Hazard Police to carry out the tests."

"The police? No. I—" She looked at me. Her hand tightened as though she'd never let me go. She glanced at Officer Reid standing outside the room, her expression suddenly alarmed. "No."

The doctor exhaled and there was finally something human in his demeanor. "Mrs. Holland, if your daughter has the same condition as your son, she could be in very great danger. We need to know what's going on here. The Hazard Police can help with that. I can assure you, the tests won't hurt. They just need to scan her and take a little blood, that's all."

He rubbed his eyes. "It's very important we understand what's happened. There are so many questions about your son's death. We don't know if it was caused by genetic factors or something external. If we're dealing with some kind of biological hazard, then your daughter might have been exposed to it."

Mom gasped. "You mean because of the Bashers at the ceremony? You mean they could have figured out a way to kill people?"

The doctor shook his head. "We don't know right now, but your daughter's best chance is to be checked and tested."

I glared at the mottled carpet, trying not to look at the stains on my shirt. I tried not to think about Josh's body. I would never tell Mom that Josh was a Basher, just like I could never understand why he was one of them, not when the last thing I saw in his eyes before he died was a fierce protectiveness…

Mom was watching me, her eyes filled with tears. "Sweetie, I know you're scared right now. I am too, but I need to know that you're safe. Okay? Don't be worried. The police will take care of you."

One of her hands left mine. The pen dipped. She scrawled her signature in big, curvy lines across the authorization. She handed it back to the doctor, squeezing my hand over and over as though she was desperate to make sure I was okay. "I won't lose another child. I won't lose my daughter. Please make sure she's safe."

As soon as Mom said the words, Officer Reid sauntered into the room like he had supersonic hearing. I watched him approach, blood pounding in my ears. *Safe* was the last thing I felt around him.

As he surveyed the room, his stance was offensive—I could tell by the way he held his arms, the angle of his shoulders. He assumed the same position a dancer did right before lunging. The blood drained from my face. I remembered him now, a few years ahead of me at school. He'd killed five of his classmates the day he graduated—picked them off one by one and locked their bodies in different parts of the school so they missed the ceremony. Nobody ever said why.

He took hold of my shoulders and pulled me upright with his strong hands. "Come with me, Ava." He smiled at Mom. "Don't worry, Mrs. Holland. We'll bring her back before you know it."

I told myself he wouldn't hurt me. He was a Hazard. They helped people heal, dug people out of damaged buildings. He'd probably just take some blood from the cuts on my wrists and that would be all.

But the way he looked at me, not like a Hazard at all, turned my stomach into acid. I suddenly remembered what Michael's godfather had said to me back at the Terminal. *They won't send the usual officers for this one.*

Officer Reid had been at Implosion. He'd sent his wasp after Mom and Dad and then me. He was there for a reason, I just didn't know why.

I looked to Mom as the panic spread. She couldn't let me go with this guy. But she'd dropped her head into her hands and didn't see the gleam in his eyes, her shoulders shaking as she sobbed. The doctor patted her hand, leaning between us, blocking my view. My legs wobbled and would have given out except that Officer Reid clutched my upper arm.

The door closed behind us, and my imagination went wild as he propelled me down the corridor. "What are you going to do to me? Really?"

He didn't answer until we reached the end of the hall and he punched the down button at the elevator. Once inside, he said, "Tests. Just like the good doctor said."

"What kind of tests? Blood tests? What?"

He clasped his hands behind his back, all casual looking. "Don't you want to know if you can die?" He looked at me with a strange twinkle in his eye as if he'd just told a joke and I was supposed to smile and say, "Good one." He had the same eyes as his brother, wide, oval, green. I pictured Aaron that afternoon mocking a gun at his chin and pulling the trigger. I pictured Reid dragging his dead classmates into the storage room, the broom cupboard, squishing their bodies in before they woke up.

The elevator descended, but my stomach remained on the upper floor. "Everyone dies."

He paused before he nodded and spoke. "Eventually." He shifted so he was half-facing me. "You know, the easiest way to figure out if you can be killed would be to slit your throat right now and see if you heal."

His eyes were shining gems. I looked away from him and clamped my mouth shut. I stared at the doors as the elevator descended even more. The button he'd punched looked like some kind of sub-basement. He'd inserted a security key as well. As we passed the lowest level, the elevator continued to descend, new numbers flashing on the display at the top of the door. A small panel extended from the wall and Reid tapped it a couple of times before it slid away, seamlessly disappearing into the side of the elevator again.

I heard myself mocking Michael about scientists lurking in basements.

The light blipped above the door. Reid pulled me into an entrance room, lit with green fluorescent lights. On the other side of the small entryway, a steel door gleamed. When the elevator doors shut behind us, he seemed to relax, and I guessed there was no way I could escape.

"Where are we?"

He beat a tattoo of numbers into the control panel and went through a series of identification tests: fingerprints, ocular, and voice recognition.

"Not many people get to see this place. In fact, it doesn't exist." He chuckled. "Like Eve and aliens."

I pressed my lips together. "You're not really a Hazard, are you?"

"They prove useful at times."

"That would make you—what?—special forces? Central intelligence?"

He raised a derisive eyebrow as if to say that I was way off the mark.

Worse then. "Black Ops." Another supposed myth. Like the Mirror Room at the Terminal.

He smirked but didn't answer. The door slid open and another corridor stretched away into the distance. It reminded me of the Terminal's corridor with all the doors. We stopped at the second one. It was steel too, except that there was an uneven patch in the middle, as though someone had taken a hammer to it.

He saw me looking at it. He nudged me in the ribs, making me flinch. "The last one tried to escape."

He was suddenly really close to me, so close I smelled the new plastic scent of his suit like an artificial skin encasing his body. It took every ounce of strength in me not to step away. I said, "I just want to get this over with."

No sooner were the words out of my mouth than he grabbed me, locking his arm around my neck and forcing me over, knocking my head into the warped steel. I tried to scream, but his arm compressed my throat. My whole body froze up.

He pulled me back and propelled me forward again, dinging the top of my head into the door. "Knock, knock."

CHAPTER 5

I STRUGGLED, tried to grab his hands, rip his fingers off my throat. When his hold didn't budge, I kicked out with my feet, attempting to connect with his shins, his feet, anything to make him let go, to make it stop. He squeezed harder, crushing my windpipe until I gasped and struggled to breathe.

The door swung open. My eyes glazed, the room swam, and my stomach churned. It smelled like … copper.

Reid pulled me into the room at a half-crouch, not letting me up. He pushed me into something hard—a chair I realized—and fastened something around my neck before I could flinch. I grabbed at it—some kind of leather, too tight against my lacerated skin—before he wrenched my hands down one at a time. I tried to scream but the strap around my neck wouldn't let me draw enough breath and the sound became a pitiful squeak. Straps whipped around my wrists and ankles and locked into place. Something tickled my forehead.

"Look what you did." Reid shook his head at me. He grabbed a cloth and dabbed at my forehead. He showed me the coated rag, blood smudged black in the weird green light. He gestured around at the room. "It's emerald light. Even better than ultra-violet. We can see everything in it." His eyes finally left my forehead and ran the length of my body. "Bones, muscles, ligaments. Everything."

I wanted to turn my face away, not give him the satisfaction of seeing how much I was shaking, but the constraint around my neck was too tight. He leaned closer and poked his finger at the skin around my neck. "Bruising." Then my forehead. "Still bleeding."

The corner of his mouth twitched up before he stomped away from me. I followed him with my eyes, but metal plates jutted up on both sides of my face. All I could see was in front of me. The other side of an empty room: a wall with something splattered on it. I didn't want to know what. And up: a ceiling made of tiles like the ones in an office, all perforated and bumpy looking.

Something rattled. I shrank inside. I'd seen this kind of thing in horror movies. The metal tray with the medical instruments on it and the villain saying, *just because you can't die doesn't mean this won't hurt.*

I tried to ignore the throbbing in my forehead where he'd hurt me. I needed a wall inside my mind. Something to protect me from what was about to happen. I needed a wall of steel and iron, the toughest substance I could imagine, or I wasn't going to survive.

His face popped into my vision again, a syringe filled with black liquid in his hand. "Hold still."

My eyes widened. "Wait. No. What is that?"

He smiled before his face disappeared. "We call it *nectar.* It's like…" He popped back into view and cocked his head, thinking. "It's like a little bit of immortality. We want to see what it does to you. Probably, it will help you survive what we need to do. Possibly, it might kill you. We'll see."

I rasped, wanted to shriek. "You can't give me that."

"Sure I can." He patted my arm as if it would console me

before he continued, "Don't worry, you should be really happy in a minute. Or else you'll be really dead."

I struggled, yanking on my restraints. "You can't do this!"

My arm stung. There was pressure, fluid being forced into my muscle, and my body warmed as if someone had let in the sun. Like boiled sugar and kaleidoscope candy. It spread through my arm, to my shoulder, up my neck, into my head.

The throb in my forehead stopped. The sting from the cut went away and it wasn't just numb, it was more than that, as though it had instantly healed. If only I could touch it, I would know for sure.

My vision blurred, swayed, and sparkled at the edges. The splatter on the opposite wall melted into the shape of a rose. A red rose blooming just for me. The green wall sprouted vines and leaves, twisting and twining from floor to ceiling, a backdrop of life behind the rose. It was calm, tranquil, a perfect picture of serenity and something else...

There were flashes of gold as a creature the size of my hand emerged from behind a vine. It was a scorpion. Not black or brown like a real one, but made of gold. It scurried to the middle of the rose and stopped there, gleaming against the deep red. Its stinger rose, ready to strike the center of the flower, but it paused, hesitating like some kind of warning...

The budding rose was wrong. The scorpion was wrong. None of it was real.

A ball of heat wound up from my stomach, burning me from the inside out.

Really happy?

No.

I pressed away from the morphing splatter on the wall, wishing I could press myself out through the back of the chair, out of my restraints. My ears rang with the roaring buzz in my head, and the burning sensation scorched my skin. I was going to die. He said it could kill me. If I didn't breathe, if I didn't find myself, I'd burst inside my own skin.

I sagged—retreated behind the wall of iron I'd created in my head, forced myself to relax, fighting the urge to yank myself upward, to scream against the pressure building inside me, willing my arms and legs to go limp.

"That's the way, Ava. Just relax. You're still with us. That's good." Reid's blurry form shimmered toward me. My vision was vague, muddled. I couldn't see him properly, the nectar had done something to my eyes, but I made out the shape of wide glasses resting on his face. He bent and pushed up the hem of my jeans, examining my ankle.

When he spoke, it wasn't to me, glancing past me as though there were people there, watching. "The old ankle injury is confirmed." He rose to my face, peering at my neck and forehead. "Bruising vanished. Head wound healed. Nectar has caused rapid regeneration." He separated my eyelids with two fingers. His words were a sharp whisper over the hurtling pain in my head. "Pupils dilated. She's restful."

He wafted around me, undoing my restraints, one after the other. The leather strap around my neck released my windpipes and I gulped in air. I tried to focus as he crooned at me, putting a hand on my arm, beckoning with the other. "Come with me, Ava. We'll do the tests now. It will all be over soon."

Instead of taking the hand he offered, I lurched at him. All the heat inside me burned back to the surface. Air filled my lungs.

I screamed, a sound that tore around the room as wild as a shrieking wind.

I paused like the scorpion.

Then, I smashed my forehead into his.

His mouth parted in shock, eyes wide, no longer hazy, but severe and piercing.

The impact stopped the roaring in my ears, the room turned silent, the thud of our heads knocking together eased the pressure under my skin and turned the room clear, but only for a moment. I wanted to do it again. I needed the release of contact, of energy traveling out of me. I kicked him in the chest, sensing the crunch of bones underfoot, and the force inside me eased up again—for a second.

Reid crashed to the ground, curled up, head in his hands, while panic and chaos swarmed around me.

I jumped away from the chair, crouched, bent my legs, preparing to launch myself forward as people teemed inside the room, all of them grasping at me. Struggling to get away from them, I threw myself at the rose on the wall, my entire body connecting. The flower burst against me and the scorpion slipped away. The collision fed every nerve along my side, releasing something inside me, something that had to get out.

The sound died down around me as though I'd startled them with my crazy jump. One of the watchers threw an arm out, stopping the others as they rushed toward me, herding them back to where they floated in my blurry vision as if they were waiting now, to see what I'd do next.

I struggled to think, to reason. To see clearly beyond the haze, the shadowy edges of my vision, the sloshing room, and the energy shrieking through me. I fought the nectar pulsing my veins, beating at me, and thumping with every beat of my heart, pounding around and around my body. The green lighting came back into focus. So did the door.

If I could get to it, maybe everything would stop. Maybe I'd be okay.

In and out of view, the room around me blurred and cleared, showered in light and dark and shadows everywhere. I forced my legs to move, lurching across the floor, footsteps compacting the ground, jarring deep into my bones.

The trolley with the scalpels and syringes was in my path and I heaved it aside. It bounced against the wall and rebounded, spraying instruments around me, cutting my face and arms. I flinched, trying to stay focused on the silhouette of the door handle.

Someone grabbed at me and I shoved him, both hands

connecting with Reid's torso. He crashed backward, rammed into the wall. I stared at his crumpled body while I swayed on the spot, nausea bearing up through me. I didn't know how I'd pushed him so hard. All I knew was I had to get to the door. I took a step, jerked at the cold steel of a knife under my foot, biting me. I jumped, stumbled. Slipped on another instrument.

The floor came up at me, pebbled with sharp knives and cutting things—things that would slice me in a thousand places. I tried to regain my balance, reaching out into the air with nothing to stop my fall.

There was a shout. A struggle somewhere beyond me.

Suddenly Michael was there, an outline stretching toward me. I crashed into his arms, and he punched us backward and away from danger. We landed in the corner of the room where it was quiet.

His body cushioned the impact, his arms tightened around me, smothering the roaring and crashing, pulling me in to the shadows where I was safe. Where I could breathe again for the first time.

I tried to see his face. I started to speak even though I didn't know what I was going to say, but someone else lifted me up and wrenched me away from him and I started screaming.

"Tie her down. Do it fast. Don't let her get you."

There was a flurry of movement. My back hit the chair. Black-clad figures rushed around me, tugging my arms and legs as I tried to fight them, kick them, scratch them. Scissors flashed, ripping through my clothes, material falling away and air rushing in. I searched for Michael, but he was gone. It wasn't really him, just somebody trying to grab me and stop me getting to the door.

"Get off me!" I yanked at the new holds they'd tied to my wrists and ankles, pulling and shoving, jerking upward as hard as I could.

Reid's voice was close by, and I craned to see him, imagining that he rubbed his chest where I'd shoved him, that there was a wince in his voice. "Sir?" he asked. "What should we do now?"

"Give her another dose of immortality." This was a new voice, combined with a person-shaped shadow across the floor.

There was a pause, and the surprise radiating off Reid hit me. "I don't think we should, sir. Her reaction already—it's incredible. She's amazingly strong. We don't know what another dose will do to her."

"Reid. That's an order. Give her another dose. We're breaking new ground here. I want to see what she does."

Reid slammed a syringe into my arm. The nectar burned under my skin.

No rose this time. No honeyed sugar warming me.

The wall blistered, paint rising in welts. The wall in my head blistered too, burnished iron glowing hot. I sensed a prickle against my legs and looked down just in time to see my bare calf glowing.

I turned my hands over, palms up, and puddles of heat shimmered in them. It couldn't be real. The volcano trapped inside me. Even if the leather restraints around my wrists crinkled and contracted as if they'd been thrown into an oven. But the strength in my hands was real. The horrible pounding of my blood was real.

I screamed with effort as I pulled my wrists upward and the bands around them stretched. The arm of the chair lifted. The leather frayed even more, giving me hope that maybe I could get out of this. Get away from these people and all the craziness.

With a rip, the bands warped and stretched, shrieking apart. The arm of the chair came with it, separating with a groan and a *snap*. I flexed my fingers, feeling the strength in them. My ankles wrenched free. I didn't really know how, but I stood up and walked off the chair.

To my right, Reid froze, hands splayed out as if he was warding off the heat waves rising around me. His Hazard suit shone, drooping at the wrists as though it was melting off him. I crouched, just a bit, the way I'd seen Josh do, right before he leaped at Michael and almost took his head off. Except that I didn't have a weapon.

I snatched the broken arm of the chair, lifting it into the air and hurling it across the room. It struck Reid in the shoulder and his face flashed pain before he cried out, grabbing at his arm. I didn't think I'd thrown it that hard, but his arm flopped as if I'd dislocated his shoulder. I wondered what would happen if I pitched the whole chair at him. I spun, ready to wrench it off the floor, but I didn't realize that the other person, the shadow, waited behind me. His drone hummed as it rose, its black and gold body brilliant in the light.

Crack.

The dart was a prickly weed in my side, and I plucked it out. I half-turned before the drone got off another one, this time in my neck. It pulsed there, forcing me to my knees. I reached out, heaving fire out of my mouth, feeling it spread from every pore in my body as if I'd turned into some kind of girl-dragon.

Forget dragons. Forget Reid. I was going to throw the chair at the guy with the drone.

A third dart hit my chest as I managed to turn. My knees scraped the floor as I finally saw his face. It was the medic from the Terminal. The man who'd administered the recovery dome. Cheyne. Michael's godfather. The man who told me to come to the recovery center. His big body blocked the light, blocked the door, drone control visor masking his eyes.

"Well done, Ava," he said, right before I fell onto my face.

Boots ran past me and fire extinguishers hissed, surrounding me in clouds of foam, killing my hope of escape.

The room shifted. My cheek dragged the floor, skipping over every little groove in the concrete as they each took one of my feet and pulled me along. A silvery trail followed me, but it took me forever to figure out it was made of tears.

CHAPTER 6

THEY HEAVED ME onto a white bed in a white room. My head lolled to the side as they maneuvered me onto my stomach on the plastic covered surgical bed. I tried to move my eyes. There were metal domes and glaring lights. Drones floated around me, chattering and zooming in and out.

Cheyne shouted orders, and I guessed we weren't alone. "Take her blood, measure her hormone levels. We need to know what happened in there and why."

Someone else said, "Her heart rate's off the charts, sir, and so is her brain activity. Her thought patterns are segmented. Look at this. Her frontal cortex—it's out of step with the rest of her brain."

Cheyne leaned in with a sudden laugh. "No," he said. "It's not out of step. It's in control." He smirked at me. "She's compartmentalizing her brain to protect herself. But we need to know how."

"We'll find out soon enough. We can't give her anything else until we get the bone marrow. It could mess up the results."

Cheyne grabbed the top of my head with his thick fingers and tilted it so I looked up at him. "It seems that the more nectar we give you, the stronger your reaction. Given your response just now, we can't give you any more. So, I'm sorry, but this is going to hurt after all." He paused and added, "Of course, the paralytic we shot you with might help a bit. But not much."

As if he was sorry. The smirk on his face told me that he didn't care. I couldn't believe I'd fallen for it—his panic at the Terminal, as though he was trying to look after me, help me. I couldn't believe I'd let Michael drive me to the recovery center, the very place I should have stayed away from.

Something pressed on my ankles. I couldn't sense much of it, but I assumed they were clamping restraints on me. I discovered I was right when they hefted my arms and clipped my wrists to the side of the bed. My finger twitched. The paralytic might be wearing off, but I wasn't sure if that was a good thing or not.

They talked among themselves—medical jargon I didn't understand. More talk of hormones, molecular structure, pituitary-something-or-other. Recalibrating nectar dosage to achieve equilibrium, whatever that meant. At one point, Reid sauntered into the room with a bunch of vials and Cheyne greeted him with, "We can regulate the dose. It should still work."

Reid nodded and said, "Yes, sir. Just like before?"

Then they receded out of view, and somehow that scared me more. I was sure I was going to die. They'd never let me go. They'd tell Mom that something happened to me, that I didn't make it. Like Josh.

Reid poked his freckled face into mine. "We're going to take the bone marrow now. Try not to move." He laughed at his own joke and disappeared again.

I shut my eyes and tried to breathe, tried not to be afraid, but as the needle pierced my hip, a scream formed in my windpipe. A scream that never came out. Was never heard. But lasted too long.

～

"Almost done now, Ava."

Somebody dressed in white moved at the edge of my vision. I cracked open my eyes, desperate to see where I was and who was speaking to me. No more green-lit room and steel chair. No more white bed and sharp lights. But the pain lingered in my lower back and hip, a dull throb.

"It will take a while for her to become fully conscious." The same quiet voice said, "Can I get you anything, Mrs. Holland?"

Mom's voice murmured something, and Dad's joined hers, a rising growl that drew me further awake.

"Yes, very soon, I think. She'll be perfectly fine."

Dad's sharp words cut through the haze. "Don't lie to me! She's not fine. She'll never be fine." There was a pause and a sob. "I can't believe we almost killed her at Implosion."

The white figure tensed and retreated from the room.

Somebody leaned in and stroked my hair. I recognized the ring Dad gave Mom for her fiftieth birthday the year before. "She'll never be fine again."

"Mom?"

"Hush. Don't try to talk."

"Mom, they did stuff to me."

"They ran the tests, honey."

"They put me in a chair and stuck needles into me. They had this stuff and it was black and they called it nectar. Michael's godfather was there and they took my clothes. And then they pulled out my bones."

Dad leaned in. I smelled his aftershave. I frowned because Dad only shaved in the mornings, making me wonder how much time had passed. Worse, I wondered what had happened while I was unconscious. "It's all right, honey. The doctors explained … The drug they gave you to administer the test causes hallucinations. You're okay. It wasn't real. Whatever you thought happened, it didn't."

"Hallucinations." I said the word slowly. "Drug. You mean nectar. The black stuff."

My head ached. I tried to see them better. They had their foreheads together—Mom's tilted toward the crook of Dad's neck as he stroked the shoulder of her favorite blue cardigan. She'd had time to go home and change. My neck was stiff, but I attempted to see the window to figure out whether it was night or day.

"Nectar? I've never heard of that. No. They told us what it was..." Dad frowned toward Mom. "What did they call it?"

Mom said, "I don't remember. One of those drugs."

Hallucinations? The green light, the leather straps, the cut on my forehead that healed as soon as they injected the nectar ... the terrible heat that filled my body after the second dose, the terrible strength. My parents shook their heads, the certainty on their faces irrefutable, brushing away the possibility that anything had been done to me other than a harmless blood test.

I started to speak, to tell them that they were wrong, but Mom's hand touched mine, trembling like a butterfly. She said, "The results came in, sweetheart. And it's..." She sobbed and covered her mouth.

Dad took over, his face grim. "It's not good news, Ava. You and Josh, they told us you have a gene they've never seen before. It's one in a million. It's really unlucky, but, sweetie, it inhibits regeneration."

I thought it through. I went over it in my head—a gene, regeneration. I had a gene that nobody else had, except for Josh, he had it too. And it killed him. Whichever way I looked at it, it led to only one question. "So if I'm killed ... I'll die?"

"Yes." He dropped his head into his hands. "You'll die."

The room filled with silence the way that the last rays of the setting sun wink out when the light is gone and all that's left is heavy quiet.

I'd die. I wouldn't regenerate like other people. I wouldn't heal. If I were shot, I'd bleed out. If I were strangled, I'd suffocate. If I dropped to the bottom of a pool and never came up, I'd drown.

I was drowning right then. "How long have I been here?"

"Just the night," Dad answered. "They said we can take you home this afternoon."

"All right." I had a gene that meant I would die. Just like Josh had died.

Josh was right—I was a freak.

I woke to the sound of Mom screaming.

I tried to sit up as movement blurred in front of me. I caught sight of Mom's blue cardigan, flung across the top of her chair. Then Dad's brown hair flying as he dashed across the room to where Mom grappled with Reid. She grabbed him by the shoulder and tried to gouge out his eyes.

The sheets tangled around me as I scrambled to get to my feet. As I sat up, the room swam, sunlit windows slid across my view, the white light angled. I skidded across and touched my feet to the floor, pressing back against the bed to steady myself as the room stopped slipping, the threatening speckled dark receded, and I righted myself.

By then, Dad pulled Mom back and blood trickled from Reid's cheek and nose, dripping onto his uniform.

Mom's voice grated in the sudden silence. "You promised we could bury him."

I tried to breathe as Mom's words sank in. They weren't going to release Josh's body. There wouldn't be a wake. We wouldn't be able to say good-bye...

Reid touched a finger to his cheek and frowned at the blood. "Mrs. Holland. It's an offense to strike a Hazard Officer." As he spoke, tiny blue blood vessels became visible on his cheek and the side of his nose. In another moment, the wound zipped itself up, the skin sealed and the bleeding stopped.

"Where's my son?"

Reid's hand went to the tranquilizer gun at his waist and I

waited for the wasp to arrive, but he just looked past Mom to Dad. "Mr. Holland?"

Dad pulled Mom further away, talking quietly into her ear. She struggled and tears streamed down her cheeks, grief pouring from her words. "But they said we could bury him. I need to bury him." She pulled away from Dad, who struggled to restrain her.

"Mrs. Holland," Reid said. "I won't forgive you twice."

Dad yanked Mom back and she howled like a wounded animal. She collapsed against him, submerging her face in his shirt.

It was Dad's turn to become angry. "You said there was no biological hazard. You said it was genetic. Surely, we have the right—"

"I'm sorry, Mr. Holland. As I explained to your wife, there is a serious public health risk associated with your son's body. There are any number of diseases your son could have carried and we simply don't know what his remains will do now that he's dead. We aren't able to anticipate what kind of contagions his body might produce—or already contain. He must be quarantined at all costs."

He took a step forward, a quiet threat, and Dad pulled Mom further back, keeping a distance.

Dad's face was pale. His words were soft, an attempt to stay calm. "You're saying that his body could endanger others. That his mortality could ... spread."

"Well, it shouldn't, of course. We've always resisted viruses and bacterial infections. We know they exist—we've seen the deadly effect on animals of cancerous cells and bacterial infections—but no virus or bacteria has succeeded in harming a human being. Yet." His face twisted in an expression close to disgust and he held up a warning finger. "Combined with a death gene, there's no saying what could happen."

Dad's voice was worried. "What about Ava? Will she be okay?"

Reid shrugged. "There are theories that the first humans were mortal, that regeneration evolved over time. Some people believe mortals lived alongside us a long time ago." He glowered. "Until we wiped them out."

I tried to remember back to history class, or maybe it was biology when the teacher had eyed the religious kids sitting in the back row and declared that the curriculum required she teach at least two lessons on the theory of regeneration. She said that, according to the theory, we'd started out as microorganisms, slowly evolving into inferior pre-humans—just animals really, with primitive instincts—finally giving way to the smart, strong human beings we were today. Mostly, I remembered the kids interrupting and arguing that the theory was wrong: humans were given the gift of regeneration when Eve made her choice—Adam had lived for 930 years and that was even longer than we did now.

Reid smiled for the first time. "Mr. Holland, your daughter has existed in society without any consequences so far. So did your son. We have no reason to suspect that she is a threat to the community." His smile broadened. "As long as she stays alive, that is."

Dad glared at Reid and took a step in my direction, placing himself between my bed and the officer. He froze as his gaze slid from the empty bed to the floor where I crouched.

Mom and Dad's faces were gray, and a smirk twisted Reid's expression, as though he knew I was awake the whole time and he was just waiting for my parents to catch up.

Dad turned even paler. "Honey. We thought you were asleep. We didn't want you to hear…" His jaw clenched. He rounded on Officer Reid. "Thank you for the information, officer. We've taken up enough of your time already."

"Of course." Reid reached inside his suit and pulled out a card. "You know where to reach us if you have any concerns."

I tried not to sag with relief when he was gone. All I wanted was to go home, leave the recovery center behind me, do something normal. Like calling Hannah or dancing or even loading the dishwasher. I had to get away from this place. I had to get away from that man pretending to be a Hazard and the memory of a green room that wasn't supposed to exist. Then maybe I could get it out of my head, the feeling of Reid's arm crushing my neck, pushing me into the chair, dragging me across the floor. Maybe I could convince myself that it was all a hallucination like Mom and Dad insisted.

I waved my arm in the air, flapping the IV line around. "Can I get some help with this, please?"

Dad raced to me, pressing the buzzer for the nurse, helping me back to the bed.

Within moments, the nurse reappeared, but she didn't meet my eyes as she removed the IV shunt. This time, she wore gloves.

"Where are my clothes?"

"We brought you new ones from home." Mom looked as if she was about to burst into tears again.

I snatched up the bag and raced into the bathroom, pulling on fresh jeans and a t-shirt.

In the bathroom mirror, my eyes had dark rings under them. My skin was stretched out, strained. If only Josh was still alive. I had so many questions for him: why was he with the Bashers? Why was he trying to take me away? How did he survive his Implosion, only to die at mine?

I pushed through the door to find Mom and Dad waiting. They gathered me up between them, Dad supporting both of us with his big arm reaching across my back, his fingers curling around Mom's arm. Out of the room and down the corridor, the recovery nurses at their station watched us go. It felt worse than falling in the middle of a performance. Even in the spotlight, I could pretend it was deliberate—bounce right back—but there was no escaping this.

I was too busy watching my sneakers to notice the people

crowding the front doors until Dad pushed them open and the shouting hit me.

Lights flashed. News drones hummed and hovered, broadcasting video live into people's homes, my face splashed across air screens everywhere. Reporters rushed toward me, pushing at each other.

"Ms. Holland! Ava!"

One of them shoved a microphone into my face, hitting me on the chin. My hand flew to my face, aware that it cut me. There was a flash of red as I checked the blood on my fingers before a stranger's voice intruded.

"Ms. Holland! Is it true you can die?"

I opened my mouth to speak. *No comment.* That's what I was supposed to say. That's what everyone said when they had something to hide. But it turned out I didn't have to speak because the crowd was suddenly silent.

Only Dad moved, pulling closer to me, still hugging Mom. He squashed me against him, ramming his body between me and the reporters while the guy who'd hurt me gaped at me.

No. Not at me. At my chin. They all were. Waiting for the cut to prove them right or wrong.

I sensed the warmth where the blood continued to pool.

"She isn't healing."

"Oh, my God."

"Is the drone getting this? We need this footage."

Another reporter shoved in, right up in my face, his voice an accusation. "Is it true that mortality is contagious?"

Then he paled, staring at the blood on my skin as though he'd just realized how close he was to me. He went from white to red as he backed away. "Let the drone get the footage." Suddenly they all were looking at each other and then at me, their determination to catch the latest headline turning into something else—caution.

Dad crushed me against him, right next to Mom, and barreled sideways through the reporters. They scattered as drones buzzed and swarmed around our heads, trying to wedge between us. My face ended up pressed inward so nobody could see my chin. Except for Mom, whose eyes were filled with tears. She didn't stop staring at the smears on Dad's shirt as though there was a scream in her throat that wouldn't come out.

Finally, security arrived and cleared a way for us. All I wanted was to disappear into our car and wind up the windows. If only I had a hood, I could pull it over myself and hide behind it. I sank into the back seat as the security guard slammed the door.

A horrible, sliding, sick feeling filled my chest cavity. What if the crazy reporters followed us? What if we had an accident trying to get away? What if Bashers blew up my house or my school?

What if I died?

I wasn't ready to die. I had too much to do yet. I wanted to dance. I wanted to make it to the big league—all the way to the Conservatorium in the northern city, Glade. Hannah and I would go together. I wanted to travel, to leave Dell and see the other cities, maybe even go to the central region and see Evereach's capital city, Chasm. And some day I wanted to kiss somebody—somebody who cared. But there wasn't a boy in the world who'd come near me now.

We reached the tunnel and I closed my eyes before it made me remember the ride in Michael's car. At least, so far, there weren't any news vans performing stunts of insanity on the road with us. Instead, it was awfully quiet. Mom and Dad didn't say anything and for an eternity, all I heard was the *swish-swish* of the tunnel.

When we finally pulled into our driveway, my chin had stopped bleeding, and I couldn't believe how normal it looked. Josh's car was parked out on the street as if he was at home. Not dead after all.

By the time I made it up to my bedroom, my heart was about

to crack. The sight of my black dress confronted me. It was folded neatly on the top of my bed, washed and ironed.

I quietly gathered it up, took it to the bottom drawer, and placed it beneath everything else, hiding it away from sight, until I could imagine it didn't exist anymore, that Josh hadn't died, that I wasn't mortal, that there hadn't been fear in the eyes of the reporters when they looked at me.

I crawled into my bed and let go of the well of tears.

CHAPTER 7

THE DARK HUE of dusk pervaded the stairwell as I trod carefully on each step. My eyes were red and blotchy and my legs wobbled with the exhaustion of crying myself out. There was a hollow in my stomach that might have been hunger, but no amount of food would ever fill the empty space inside me. I'd passed Josh's room on my way, and I couldn't bear to look inside it.

Turning left into the open plan kitchen and living area, I sighted across the dining area to the windows on my right and further down to the lounge with the double-width windows at the end. I half expected them to be barricaded against hordes of reporters camped out around the house, blinds drawn against drones seeking new footage, but everything was quiet except for the air screen and Mom chopping carrots close by in the kitchen. She had a bag of them on the table and a stainless steel bowl full of precise carrot chunks.

As soon as she saw me, she flew to me and gathered me up in a hug. I kissed her cheek, but a fresh stream of her tears washed my kiss away.

Then I heard the screen.

"Urgent diplomatic meetings are being held around the

world tonight after the confirmed final death of teenager Joshua Holland, who was stabbed in the heart by fellow student, Michael Bradley, last night at Dell city's Terminal games center."

A picture of Josh appeared on the right-hand side of the screen as if he could have been standing there in front of us. I leaned against the table, holding my breath, feeling like I was outside myself, looking in.

Mom pulled me closer, shaking her head, her hands trembling in mine. "They've been running the story over and over and I can't seem to turn it off because every time they show him..." She tried to breathe. "It's like he's still here."

The reporter ran a hand over his pale forehead. "President Scott will travel to Seversand tomorrow to speak directly with Seversandian President, Elissa Vale, about these events. The Delaney Recovery Center is refusing to release Joshua's medical records for privacy reasons. These scenes are from outside the center today, as Joshua's sister, Ava Holland, left with her parents."

There I was, lurching backward as the microphone hit my chin and the reporters hushed. The footage zoomed in on my face, onto the blood on my fingertips. A reporter right next to the drone whispered, "She's still bleeding," and then Dad barged in front of me and scooped me up out of view.

I sank harder against the table. At least they didn't know Josh was with the Bashers. Or, if they did, they weren't saying so.

The newsreader reached for a glass of water and the footage swiveled to a woman with fine blond hair. She said, "The Attorney-General will announce tomorrow whether the city intends prosecuting Michael Bradley for Joshua's death. It would be the world's first murder trial." Her eyes grew wide as if to punctuate her words. "The Terminal is refusing to confirm whether or not there's footage of the death. No doubt they're hoping for a favorable decision, not only for the sake of their shareholders but also because Michael is the son of Robert Bradley, scientist and Vice-CEO of the Terminal."

The first newsreader shook his head. "The Terminal has cautioned against panic, insisting that the games facility is completely safe."

I couldn't stand it. "It's not safe! The intercom was broken. I couldn't even call for help. It was only because of Michael that anybody came..." My voice broke since Michael was the one who killed Josh in the first place.

Mom's face crumpled.

"Mom ... I'm sorry."

"Oh, sweetie." She brushed the hair from my face. "You didn't kill him. None of this was your fault." She exhaled as though she was struggling to speak, as though there was more she wanted to say, but couldn't.

The newsfeed continued with a panel of guests, and suddenly their words broke into our conversation. A woman with wiry hair wrapped around her head in plaits said, "They're saying it's probably a genetic disorder, but what if it isn't? What if it's a disease carried in the blood of these people? I mean, can it spread? Are we really safe? What is the President doing to protect us from this?"

"He's rushing off to Seversand to try and stop a new war," another panel member interjected. "Our economy can't take another hundred years of destruction at the hands of those Seversandian savages."

The third panel member vigorously nodded his head. "International peace agreements have been in place for hundreds of years and it's all very simple—every year each country proves that its children can regenerate and no country goes to war. I'm just going to come right out and say what every other person in Evereach is thinking: that girl is a threat to national security and she should never have been allowed to leave the recovery cen—"

Mom's hand shot to the control panel and switched the air

screen off.

I stared at where the images had been.

"It's okay, sweetie." Mom tried to smile, but she was very pale. "Just … go back up to your room. Okay? I'll bring your dinner to you really soon."

Her face was a maze of sadness and, behind it, something else. Something scared and full of regret. I wished Dad was back already, although I didn't know where he'd gone since he said that his work had given him the week off.

When I reached my room, I dialed Hannah's number. As I listened to it ring, I stared out of my window. Mrs. Hubert's house was still pitch black, but lights flickered down the street. Somebody drove into their garage. Somebody else walked their dog past the end of the street.

I'd give anything to be normal again.

Hannah wasn't picking up and neither was her message bank. I checked the number and tried again, but with the same result. I paced and paced beside my bed until I wanted to drop to the floor like the carpet could suck me up and twine around me and I'd cease to exist.

I couldn't stay in my room anymore, but Mom and Dad wouldn't let me out of the house. There had to be somewhere I could go. Then I remembered—the dance studio would be open late for practice. Only the hard-core dancers went on Saturday night and they wouldn't pay any attention to me. I could blend in, melt into a patch of dance floor, and dance all my pain away. Maybe that's where Hannah was right now. I'd give anything to talk to her, to tell her everything, help me figure it all out.

I threw my hair back into a bun and checked the cut on my chin. It had closed and was just a pink line now. I wondered if it would always be there or if it would go away. At least it didn't hurt anymore. I slapped on makeup to cover the effects of crying until I didn't recognize myself. Shoving my purse and phone into my dance bag, I pushed open my window and grabbed the fire stairs that lay flat against the side of the house, giving them a shove until they reached the ground. Just as I was about to head out across the garden, headlights turned into our street and shone toward me. I ducked behind the nearest garden bed, recognizing Dad's car as it pulled into the driveway.

Guilt rocketed through me. They'd be so worried if they discovered I was gone, but I couldn't stay in the house. I had to get out.

The garage door opened and closed.

I ran for it down the street, my sneakers slapping the footpath. I didn't breathe until I turned the corner, and even then I kept running. The cold air on my face felt good and so did the sense of movement. I could finally control something, even if it was just my feet. The studio's neon sign gleamed ahead and I raced up the steps, pausing to catch my breath at the top.

Ms. White had plastered a new poster of the Conservatorium on the wall outside the studio. It was a vibrant picture of a dance platform surrounded by trees, an open air auditorium. Deep in the distant background were the mountains of Starsgard. I peered at the image and the outline of the majestic Starsgardian towers rising into the sky. Each tower was built on top of a mountain peak and they seemed so serene, so mysterious. I wanted to reach out and touch them, as though I could soak up some of that calm and transport myself there. Away from here.

I shook my head and made my way into the studio. It was brightly lit and soft music played. Two ballroom dancers practiced lifts over to one side, and a ballet dancer warmed up at the bar. I padded to the bench at the side and began a brief warm up, since the run had done most of that for me already, then I pulled out my music and turned the volume up, starting into an old contemporary routine that I'd performed several years before.

Finally, everything blurred. The pain of the last two days disappeared. No more crazy rose buds, scorpions, and medical tests. No more mortality. Josh could be alive again. He could drive off and make me late for class as many times as he liked and I'd forgive him every time. As I danced, my body finally did what I wanted, moved the way I wanted it to. It wasn't my enemy anymore. It wasn't going to kill me.

Without realizing, I spun into Ms. White and lurched backward, yanking out the earbuds. "Ms. White! I'm sorry, I didn't see you."

I reached out to steady us both, but she jerked away from me.

"What are you doing here?" Her eyes reflected shock as she twitched away from my touch.

"I-I'm practicing."

"You shouldn't be. I told your parents already. You can't dance here anymore."

The fear on her face consumed my whole vision.

I shook my head, my chest heaving. "I'm one of your best dancers."

"Not anymore, Ava." Her expression softened to deep pity. "You're … different."

I sucked in a breath and hurried to argue with her. "I still heal like everyone else. I do. Really. Just slower, that's all."

"No, Ava. You're mortal. What if you cut yourself…" She glanced around. The other dancers had stopped practicing and were staring at us. She lowered her voice. "You could be contagious."

"It's genetic," I said, not believing what I was hearing. "I have a gene, not a disease. I can't hurt anyone. You have to believe me." I reached out to her, but she shrank away from me. I stared from her face to my hand, hovering in the air, and let it drop.

"I'm sorry, Ava, it's not me you have to worry about. Nobody will dance with you. Every single parent has rung me already, threatening to pull their child out of my class."

"I can't believe it…" I met her eyes. "You really want me to go."

Ms. White nodded, her braid flapping behind her waist, her mouth forming a resolute line. "I need you to go. Please."

I looked past her to the door and caught my reflection in the mirror. It all crashed down on me—the Mirror Room at the Terminal, Josh's body, Michael pulling the knife out of his own heart and plunging it into my brother's. I whirled, and my reflection whirled with me. For a second, the knife was in my hand again, dripping his blood onto my shoes.

I rushed past Ms. White and scooped up my bag on the way to the door. I fled down the stairs and around the darkened corner, pounding the pavement as fast as I could.

Nobody would let me dance. Nobody.

A clawing pain jabbed in my chest as if she'd ripped out my heart. How could I not dance? The thought terrified me. It was all I wanted to do. It was everything. It was *me*.

I gasped, pumping my arms, wondering what else they wouldn't let me do now. Where else they wouldn't let me go. The voices of the panel members on the air screen echoed around and around in my mind.

They never should have let her leave the recovery center.

My head spun so hard I didn't see the road or the streetlights, or the cars going past, or the stars in the sky. I almost missed my house. It looked so dark and sad.

I wished I could run on and never stop. I struggled not to collapse, but I had to get inside and crawl under a blanket and try to breathe. I made it to the window, kicked off my shoes, and dropped my bag onto the floor. My bed waited for me like a magic cloud that would suffocate the world. As soon as I pulled the covers over my head and curled into a ball, I heard the door open.

"Sweetheart?" It was Dad's voice. "Are you awake?"

I didn't want to answer, but maybe Dad would understand. Maybe I could tell him what Ms. White said. When I was little, he'd come to all my dance recitals, he'd even hired a drone to record all my practice sessions. He'd called me his moonbeam, and he'd looked so proud of me.

"Honey? I'm sorry, but you have to take this medicine. The doctor said it would help after the tests."

I pushed the tips of my fingers out of the covers, trying to get hold of myself long enough to talk. Sliding the covers to the side, I sat up, everything screaming inside my chest. "I'm awake."

Dad gave me a small smile. He held out a cup of liquid while Mom hovered behind him, grasping her cardigan around her as if she was cold.

The mug was full, but the clear liquid didn't taste like anything, and it made me realize how thirsty I was. I handed the glass back to Dad and he nursed it in his hands.

"Okay." He cleared his throat, chewing on his lip as if he wanted to say more. For a long moment, he stared into the bottom of the empty glass. Then he dropped beside the bed and took my hand, searching my eyes. His own were red from tears he wouldn't shed in front of me. "Have a good sleep, moonbeam. We love you. Always remember that."

I blinked, trying to focus through my own tears. He hadn't called me that for years.

Mom knelt next to him and kissed my forehead, pressing her cheek to my skin, leaving damp tears behind. "We love you so much, Ava."

I was so tired all of a sudden. Her words slurred in my ears.

She leaned over me and whispered, "Trust your instincts." Then she said something else that sounded like, "Goodnight," and I slipped back under the covers as they closed the door. My arms and legs were numb, as though they'd disconnected from me. Maybe my body wanted to belong to someone else, someone who was allowed to dance, someone who hadn't watched her brother die.

I woke once, thinking that people crowded around me, blurry faces and vague voices, black-tinged at the edges. I'd only been asleep for a minute, but when I tried to open my eyes, the pressure of my eyelids bore down on me.

I surfaced long enough to see Mom's shape, her blue cardigan. I made out Dad's form, but there was something wrong with my room. It looked as if plants had grown up inside it, standing tall against the walls, swarming my parents. It reminded me of the people watching in the strange green room that had sprouted a rose and vines—the room my parents said was a hallucination. I tried to focus on the people now. One of them was right behind Mom. For a moment, there was a flash of gold before the other woman's figure blurred again.

Mom's voice was a whisper, a hush in my ears. "Isn't there another way?"

There was a murmur from the person standing behind her, something I couldn't make out.

Dad's response was quiet. "We have no choice. We can't let them use us."

"But they'll use Ava, instead." Mom's hand was pressed over her heart.

The other person drew closer, not so close I could make out her face, but her words were audible. "With you both, they could have an endless supply of mortal girls. The damage would last millennia. Far beyond what they could do with Ava alone."

"Can't we take her with us? Please!" Mom's voice was like cracked china, breaking apart.

The other person shook her head, receding. "This is the only way."

Mom gasped. Dad wrapped his arms around her, holding her upright. She said, "I can't bear it. How will she survive?"

"I don't know." Then Dad sounded certain, strong for the first time. "But she'll understand. I know she will."

Mom sobbed. "I can't do this—"

Her blue cardigan blurred and her voice was sucked into a void. They were gone in a whir of movement, a vague memory.

I descended into darkness again.

A *tap-tap* at the window cut into my sleep. I squinted gritty eyes against the brightness shining into my bedroom. I'd forgotten to close the blind and the summer sun cast a painful glare onto my bed. I struggled to my feet, teetered my way across the carpet, and grabbed the cord. The tapping bird balked and took flight, soaring out over the street and up toward the sun.

I puzzled over how bright it was. It looked like midday out there. When I checked the alarm clock by the bed, it read 3:00 p.m. How could it be the afternoon already? I stumbled over to the door, headed across to the bathroom, and faltered down the stairs. Something squishy had replaced the bones in my legs. I grabbed the railing and tumbled down the last steps.

The first thing I noticed was Mom's study opposite the bottom of the stairs.

No desk. No computer. No bookshelf. Just dents on the floor and marks on the walls where the furniture used to be. I forced myself to rush into the living area. Same thing there: no dining table, no couch, no coffee table. Just more empty space and indents. Turning left into the kitchen, I rushed around the table and threw open the cupboards. A few cans of food, pasta, spices, a couple pots and pans, they were still there, but all the kitchen appliances were gone, even the toaster. Mom hadn't gone shopping for a few days and the fridge was half empty. I leaned against it, trying to draw breath.

"Mom? Dad?"

Then I realized what I needed to check. I ran from the kitchen, back past the stairs and Mom's study, around the corner to the connecting door to the garage, sliding it open with my heart up near my voice box. The empty gray concrete garage glared at me and the contents of my stomach heaved. My legs were numb as I made it to the front window to see that Josh's car was gone too. My head was going to split open.

Stumbling back to the kitchen, I finally focused on the charge card lying on the table. A note rested under it. Mom's handwriting was a faint scribble: *For food*. I stared and stared at those two little words.

They'd packed up the house and left me behind. They'd

taken everything with them except food and some plates. And me. I tried to remember waking up in the night and my room had been full of blurry shapes standing watch. People snatching my parents away, and now Mom and Dad were gone.

Then I realized, the night before, when Mom leaned in and gave me a kiss, she hadn't said goodnight.

She'd said good-bye.

CHAPTER 8

MY HEAD DROPPED to my hands. My temples pounded. I slid to the floor in front of the kitchen table, staring at the empty space around me.

The drink that my parents gave me before they said goodnight must have had something in it to make me sleep.

But … had they chosen to give it to me or had someone forced them?

They'd both been crying when they kissed me goodnight. They'd said they loved me and the looks on their faces told me they needed me to believe it.

They would never leave me willingly.

Someone must have taken them. Whoever it was could have been in our house when Mom and Dad gave me the drink. It could have been Reid or someone working with him. Maybe he arrived after I snuck out to the dance studio and threatened to hurt me if my parents didn't do what he wanted. But, if it was Reid, I wondered why he would leave me behind and not take me too.

And why would he want my parents?

I tried to remember what I'd heard when I woke up in the night. Mom asked if I'd be okay. Dad said I'd understand. I tried to, desperately. Mom and Dad had two mortal children, despite being normal themselves. That made them different, and if they were different, then maybe people would think something was wrong with them too.

I gasped at a new thought: had the Bashers taken them? I was the very definition of weakness, so maybe they'd come for my parents as a way to get to me … but that didn't make sense because, like Reid, there was no reason they would take my parents and leave me behind.

I rubbed my eyes with my hands, trying to make sense of it all. I had to get rid of the after-effects of whatever I'd taken and water was my best bet. I needed to flush it out of my body so I could think.

Determined to make myself move, I grabbed a glass from the cupboard and filled it with water. My head swam like the bubbles from the aerator tap.

I didn't know how much money my parents had left me or how long it would last and what would happen when I couldn't buy food. Maybe Lucy would still let me waitress at the café under the dance studio. Except that my face was all over the news. I wondered if she would be afraid of me like everyone else.

The glass overfilled in my hand, water gushing over my knuckles. I gulped down the whole cup and filled it again.

After my second glass of water, I sat on the floor with a third clutched in my hands. The decorative strip in the tiling above the stove was visible and I started counting the little tiles.

I told myself: *By the time I get to the end of the row, I'll be okay.*
Bang! Bang!

I jumped so hard that my head hit the edge of the table. The sound echoed from the front of the house. It was the front door, thudding with the force of what sounded like someone trying to knock it down. I peered around the corner of the table, seeking the dining room window on the other side of the room.

The vertical blinds were only partly pulled and there was a

flash of color and movement, followed by another. Quiet foot-steps, lots of them, and I knew what they were doing. Surrounding the house.

I leaped to my feet, dumping the glass into the sink, crouching and desperately seeking a place to hide in a house emptied of furniture. The bare walls stared back at me. There was another flicker of movement and I ducked behind the table again, hoping beyond all hope that they hadn't seen me. But I'd seen them.

Green uniforms and wasp drones.

The person at the front door shouted. "Ava Holland! It's the Hazard Police! Open up for your safety!"

I gave myself two seconds to consider the risks. If they were really Hazard Police, and not operatives like Reid in disguise, then they could be there to protect me and take me somewhere safe. The reporters outside the recovery center, people on the air screen, even people who knew me like Ms. White were all scared of me—afraid of my mortality. They'd looked at me with disgust and fear, but I wondered if fear could turn to hatred and violence. Could they be so afraid that they'd try to hurt me? Was it that kind of hatred that fuelled the Bashers? The mere fact that I was different, that I could die, could cause people to not only shun me but to take their fear out on me.

But if Reid was among the Hazards outside my house, then they wouldn't take me somewhere safe. Nowhere was safe with him. And right then, that threat was more real than the chance someone might attack me in the street.

The knocking stopped and there was more movement around the sides of the house.

My hiding place wouldn't last long. The house was open-plan with wall-height windows at intervals along the dining and living room walls, and most of the blinds were open at an angle. Mom used to boast about how "light and airy" it was. It was the first thing visitors would say and Mom would gush about it, all "I know, don't you just love it?"

If the men took the time to peer inside—if a drone stopped to assess the windows—they'd see me.

All that light was going to get me killed.

I tried to remember if I'd passed any open windows, but I'd stumbled straight down the stairs into the kitchen. I didn't know about Mom's study or any of the upstairs bedrooms.

All it would take was one open window and the drones would swarm inside.

It was now or never. I scooted along to the far end of the table and scrambled left around the corner, headed for the laundry, only a few feet away. It was tucked at the back of the house past the kitchen and the downstairs bathroom. It was the only place in the lower house with frosted glass windows—and a broom cupboard.

I slid around the corner, not daring to close the laundry door in case it banged behind me and attracted attention. The broom cupboard was in the far left corner another ten feet away. Just as I propelled myself toward it, there was movement outside, and I ducked and pressed myself against the laundry sink under the windows, right next to the back door. I told myself to stay calm. As long as they hadn't seen me through the glass, I was safe.

I held my breath, waiting for a shout that would tell me I was discovered. I was about to crawl across the floor to the broom cupboard, I was already on my elbows, when I heard voices and I almost choked.

"Is this the only back door?" It was Reid. Cool and in control. He was using them to get to me. He'd take me back to the green room, back into the underground, and everyone could forget that my brother had died and get on with their lives, knowing they were safe, that my mortality couldn't affect them anymore.

"Yes, sir. This is the only exit on this side of the house."

"Break the window. But keep the drones back."

"Sir?" Doubt and concern plagued the other officer's voice.

"Our orders are to bring Ava Holland in safely for her protection. I'm not sure that this is the best—"

"Your orders are to do what I say! Break the window. Now."

The next moment, glass shattered and sprayed. I hadn't made it anywhere near the broom cupboard and now I had no choice but to curl my head into my knees, protecting my face. Pieces of glass landed on my head and my shoulders, and wedged behind my back. They settled in my hair and between my neck and the collar of my polo shirt. I tried to shake them off and shuddered as they prickled my skin.

If the other officers thought they were there to help me, to take me somewhere safe, Reid knew the truth. He said, "The next one, too."

There was a second crash, and another shower of glass shards, this time larger. They clattered and cracked against the cupboards against the far wall. Something dropped directly onto my neck, a late shard, and I bit my lip to stop from crying out as it stuck in my upper back. I stayed still for as long as I could bear. Outside, there was silence.

If I moved even an inch forward, I'd be outside the concealment of the laundry tub and he'd see me. Then the drones would come after me.

Reid sounded perplexed for the first time. "Guess she's gone."

I closed my eyes, hoping the officers would go away now. If they thought I was gone, then surely they would leave.

He continued. "Let's check anyway. Break the door. Search the premises. If she's here, I want her brought out. You, check the perimeter. I don't want anyone disturbing us."

Obedience this time. "Yes, sir."

I jumped with the force of the door being kicked. It was followed by a loud crack. My head whipped upward to see the door handle hanging loose.

The bullet must have missed me by a sliver.

I had seconds to move if that. But with the now-gaping

windows, it would take a miracle for the drones to miss me. And where would I go? The broom cupboard may as well have been a mile away because I'd have to get across the floor. Even if I tucked myself into the cupboards on this side of the room, I'd have to veer out into the open, and then they'd see me. That plan had only worked while the windows were intact.

I glanced upward and caught sight of the air duct in the ceiling. Again, I'd have to move into the open. Even if I made it up there, they'd follow me in and I'd be cornered with nowhere to go.

But up was the right way to go. I knew it was. The sky could protect me.

The men thought I was gone, and the drones would only go where they sent them. If I went in the least likely direction, there was a slim chance I'd be safe. Very slim, but it was the only option I had. I judged how fast I could get back through the door to the living area, past the kitchen and to the base of the stairs.

The door rattled again. It began opening, pushing glass in my direction.

I shot to my feet, head down, and catapulted through the door to the living room. Drones hummed as I made it through. They'd take a couple of seconds to assess any risk to the incoming Hazards. Seconds I could use.

Halfway through the living area, a flicker of movement at one of the windows made me leap behind the kitchen table. There was a guard standing to one side of the dining room window, but he seemed to have been placed there to survey the street because he kept looking out and around, rather than inward. Through the gaps in the blinds, I could see his wasp floating at the top right of the window. I plotted a path to the bottom of the stairway directly opposite Mom's study.

The sound of crunching glass in the laundry told me the Hazards were inside the house. A wasp sailed through the laundry door, facing outward. As soon as it turned, it would see me.

I had to move. Now.

Ducking my head, I zipped through the galley kitchen and rushed around the corner to the base of the stairway. This time, I didn't stop to hear whether I'd been spotted. I took the stairs two at a time, grateful that I was barefoot—until I saw the trail of blood spots I left behind.

My whole being sank to meet the smears on the floor. I vaguely registered the glass in my feet. The cuts in my arches and toes. I didn't have time to check them. The humming drones drew closer, the sound rising and falling as though they were flying in and out of rooms, checking each one, and I hoped it would buy me precious seconds.

Making it to my room, I snatched up my sneakers. Then I ran over to the window ledge and placed my bloody fingers on it, hoping they'd think I'd gone down the fire escape, before I yanked the shoes onto my feet. Ignoring the pain and avoiding the blood spots, I raced back into the hallway.

The drones were flying up the stairwell and the Hazards would see the blood trail and know that I was in the house.

I ran right, tearing toward the retreat at the back that opened out onto the deck. Once there, I turned the lock on the sliding door and let it close, locking myself out. It wouldn't delay them for long, but it would stop the drones for a moment, and even a second could make a difference.

The guttering at the corner of the house, at the edge of the deck, was attached to one of the steel pilings used to support both the deck and the roof over it. Josh and Aaron used to shimmy up there when they were in second grade, dangle their legs over the edge of the roof, and dare each other to jump.

I wasn't even half sure that the pipe would hold my weight, but I'd rather fall to my death than let Reid take me in to run more tests.

Taking hold of the pipe, I levered up onto the balcony railing. Between the railing and the roof, there weren't any other footholds or anything to push off. I'd have to use my legs and arms to wriggle the six feet upward. I couldn't afford to have sweaty palms right now. I tried to calm myself, picturing myself in the dance studio, mimicking the climbing of stairs. It was an act, a dance move, something to carry out with strength and elegance, something I could control and achieve. Holding the image firmly in my mind, I forced my body upward. It was harder with sneakers on my feet, but I couldn't afford to leave a blood trail.

They were probably about to rush into my room to find the smears all over the carpet leading to the window and the fire escape.

Right on cue, a shout rose from deep inside the house. They'd tear apart my room, trying to find me, expecting me to be hidden in a cupboard, under the bed, even leaping from the window. They wouldn't look out this end of the house. Not yet, anyway.

I glanced down once to check that there were no men patrolling the garden underneath me, but I couldn't see any. That didn't mean they weren't there. If I made it to the roof unseen, I'd consider myself lucky. I sought purchase on the edge of the roof, scrabbled one hand on the steel roofing, trying to find a notch—anything—that I could use to latch onto when I released my other hand. It was smooth and impossible to grip.

The pale green roof blurred and I realized that I had tears in my eyes, or sweat, I couldn't tell which, but either way it made me mad. I wasn't going to get this far and then fail.

Then, to my surprise, I found it. Right there in the perfect place to lever my hand—a hollowed out crescent with a soft pad around the edge. I used all my strength to wrench the rest of my body up and onto the safety of the roof.

I rolled away from the edge, panting, the sun beating down on me, burning steel under my back, and the deep pressure of a glass shard that I'd forgotten about. I jerked upward and yanked it out, crunching my jaw to stop from crying. As the relief of having made it onto the roof flowed through me, so did the pain.

Once I was safe, I'd find out how badly I was hurt. For now, my wounds would have to wait.

There were voices, closer below, standing on the inside of the door to the deck. They'd be trying to decide whether to come out, and I wasn't about to give them any reason to. The neighborhood watch drone never traveled this high, but it would only take one curious Hazard to direct a wasp skyward and I'd be discovered.

I crawled along to the main roof, where there was a crevice formed between two decorative peaks—a place to hide and wait for them to leave. I couldn't hear their voices anymore so I didn't know what they were saying. I hoped they thought I'd gone down the fire escape from my room and through the garden. That would make sense, especially as my bloody footprints stopped there, although the guard on that side of the house would swear I never got past him.

Sinking into the only shady area of the crevice, I felt around for the coolest place to sit and, as I did so, I touched a flat portion of roof, only a hand width high and wide. I pulled back to study it and found that it appeared to be a small door with a lever.

The mechanism clicked and the opening released. I ran my hand around the rubber edging that would seal tightly against all kinds of weather.

There was something inside, and I reached in to pull it out: a box marked with a big red cross. I racked my memories for a moment, wondering if I'd seen it somewhere before, coming up with nothing. All I knew for sure was that somebody had been coming up there from time to time. They'd carved out the handholds on the deck roof to make it easier to climb up and they'd left the box there.

As I levered open the lid, the items that fell into my hands were as strange as the cross on the lid.

Thin rolls of soft white material, small strips of perforated plastic, needles labeled as hygienically sealed, spools of thread also sealed in plastic. Then there were things I did recognize: safety pins, tweezers, and syringes. Last of all: two vials of black liquid that had to be what Reid had called nectar.

There were rough drawings made in gold marker on the outside of each, and I frowned at them, realizing that they were pictures of scorpions. Gold like the one I'd seen when Reid gave me nectar.

I rocked back on my heels with the objects clutched to me.

It was some kind of medical kit.

There was only one person that it could belong to. Only one person who could come up there regularly—who would have something to hide—something that needed needles and, of course, bandages, that's what the rolls of material were.

This stuff belonged to Josh.

He knew.

Josh knew he could die.

CHAPTER 9

I REMEMBERED JOSH'S face that night at the Terminal, the way he'd looked at Michael—intense, on edge, as though he was fighting for his life, as though it meant so much more to him to win. Michael hadn't cared; he'd known he couldn't die. But Josh knew. He knew his life was at stake.

The day he died, he'd pointed to his temple and told me: *The only war we fight is the one in our own minds.* He'd told me he'd rather kill than watch me be killed.

Sobs rose up in me as I clutched the bandages to my chest.

Josh knew that I could die, too.

That's why he'd snatched me away at Implosion. That's why he wanted to take me somewhere safe. He'd said he was a Basher because he had to be, and maybe being a Basher was the only way he could figure out to interrupt Implosion and stop my death.

He'd saved me.

But how had Josh survived his own Implosion? Michael had told me that Josh healed almost as fast as he did, which was impossible, unless... I stared at the little vials of black nectar in the medical kit. When Reid injected it into me at the recovery center, the cut on my forehead had healed immediately. He'd called it a dose of immortality. If Josh had carried nectar with him, ingested it somehow, he could have survived the Implosion wound. It was the only way he could have healed so fast.

I ran my thumb over one of the scorpions, wondering if Josh had seen the same crazy things I had when he took nectar.

There was a sudden concentration of sound at the corner of the house. Footsteps battered the ground and I pictured the soldiers gathering at the side of the garden. I wanted to scoot to the edge of the roof and see for sure, hoping they were going away. Instead, I lay still, trying to quiet my own breathing so I could hear their voices and listen for the approaching hum of drones.

"Why would she run? Doesn't she know she's in danger?"

"She's hurt now, too." That was the officer who'd questioned Reid. "Well, at least we know the Bashers haven't got her. That blood trail was fresh."

I sucked in a breath at the mention of the Bashers. I was the weakest of the weak and unlike the slow healers, I'd be easily erased. I clutched the vials of nectar harder, pressing the scorpions to my chest. How careful Josh must have been to fool the Bashers. I shuddered at the risks he must have taken. But he'd had an advantage that I didn't have. The Bashers already knew the truth about me.

The men at the side of the house sounded like normal Hazards. Like they really had been sent to take me somewhere safe and they had no idea why I'd run away from them. If only Reid wasn't with them...

I shimmied toward their voices, ready to call out. Maybe they could help me. Maybe I could tell them about Reid. I paused because if Reid was Black Ops, then I couldn't predict what kind of control he had over them. He'd said he was in charge and the other officer had obeyed him.

I had no choice. I couldn't trust them. I couldn't trust anyone.

I lay still as Reid's voice cut through the conversation, pausing directly below me in the side garden. "Get me a list of all the places she frequents and get the surveillance drones out there. We need to find her before the Bashers do."

Their voices dimmed, vehicles roared to life and sped away, but I still couldn't move, clutching the medical kit to my chest, shaking from the pain in my back. Too scared that someone would see me climbing down, I waited until nightfall.

Finally, the sun descended and shadows and pockets of night grew. I opened my eyes, my body stiff and unbending, a headache pounding from the back of my head forward into both of my temples. I rolled onto my side, expanding my lungs with air for long moments, knowing I had to get inside, find food, and rest, even though the thought of falling asleep, being vulnerable, made me shudder. My home wasn't safe anymore.

I tied the medical kit inside my shirt and made it down the pipe, using the hand-holds that I now knew belonged to Josh, and dropped to the balcony. I'd locked myself out, so there was no use trying to get in through the glass door. I took a moment to rest and then made my way over the railing, holding on with my hands and working my legs around the top of the steel post until I was sure I had a good grip. Shimmying down it was somehow harder than climbing up. My legs kept tugging, my clothes jamming, my arms shook, and I dropped the last few feet and crawled along, grateful for the simple feel of ground beneath my feet.

The back door hung on its hinges, standing in a bed of glass. I supposed that at least anybody trying to get in that way would make a lot of noise. When I rounded the corner into the kitchen, I set the medical box on the table and grabbed the tweezers out of it, ripping off my sneakers and dropping to the floor, twisting my feet toward me.

With the blinds open, there was enough light to see without

turning on a lamp. It took forever to tug each splinter and shard out. A couple from my arms caused me trouble and I finally plucked a stubborn one from my hand. I eyed the needle and thread but couldn't bring myself to use it. I couldn't reach the wound in my back anyway.

I considered the vials of nectar. If I used them, I could heal straight away, but when they'd given it to me at the recovery center, I'd burned so hot, I'd started a fire. That would be the worst way to draw attention to myself. I put them away and left the kit on the kitchen table.

Climbing the stairs was easier than before, and I headed to the bathroom and splashed my face with cold water, hoping it would bring some sense back to my world. A dark patch of blood spread across my right shoulder when I looked in the mirror, and I tried to shake off my dread as I dressed in clean clothes.

Despite the risk, staying in the house for the night seemed like the best option. If I ran for it, I'd be out on the streets and who knew where Reid would look for me, not to mention all the usual CCTV drones. If the Bashers were looking for me too, then chances were high that they'd hear my family was gone, that the Hazards had found my home empty, and they wouldn't look for me at home. But I couldn't stay there any longer than one night. I'd have to take off tomorrow.

In the meantime, I had to make the house as safe as I could, but I didn't know how I was supposed to protect myself when it was empty. It wasn't as if there were any heavy cupboards to board up windows. Then I remembered Dad's outdoor shed. It might have some tools I could use.

I detoured to my bedroom, pulled open my dance bag, and filled it with anything I thought would be useful: jeans and t-shirts, nail scissors, tweezers, pens and pencils, sturdy shoes, a pair of costume glasses—which led me to my costume bag where I found two wigs and performance make-up I'd used in dance performances. If I had to disguise myself, at least I had somewhere to start.

Then I raced downstairs where the gloom hit me. I remembered it all over again, the door rattling behind me, the glassy rain on my head. My back still ached, the cut stung, and so did my feet. I shoved on the laundry door, working it open just enough to slide through.

Satisfied that I was alone in the yard, I jogged over to the shed to find the latch ajar. Which probably meant Dad had taken his things with him, after all. I levered the door open, wincing when it creaked, finding it hard to see anything more than vague shapes. I knew I'd regret it if I turned on the fluorescent light, but I wasn't sure what else to do. There could be any number of life-saving items in there—or none at all.

I stumbled inside, shuffling my feet so I didn't trip on anything. A few steps inside, it was pitch black, and I prepared to shut myself in the dark and flick on the light.

There was a flash of light moments after the crunch of soft footfalls. I froze in my tracks. Torchlight pooled at the door to the shed, a circular glow like an artificial moon on the grass. "Ava?"

I grabbed the nearest object—a coiled up hose—and stepped out into the light, surprised when the torch clicked off, leaving us in darkness.

"Stay back," I warned, thinking that a hose wouldn't do much, but it was heavy and I could throw it, and at least it was *something.*

"Ava? It's me. Michael."

Oh no. Not him. He was the last person I expected. "Stay away from me."

"I'm not a wicked witch." The smile in his voice made my face burn as my eyes adjusted to the dark. A stupid hose wasn't going to protect me from Michael Bradley, the guy who took a knife and cut my life into pieces.

"I don't melt," he continued. The corners of his mouth

tugged up, his shoulders relaxed, and I saw a glimmer of the guy he was at school. "Even around you."

My hand went slack around the garden hose. It thudded against the side of the shed when I threw it away.

Michael's grin was short-lived, replaced by a narrowing of his eyes. "There's glass all over the back porch. Was it Bashers or Hazards?"

When I didn't answer, he stuffed the torch behind his back. "I'm amazed you escaped them." He held up his hands as though it would make me feel better. "I'm not here to hurt you. Seriously, Ava. I'm not."

"Right." He was the one who stabbed Josh to death. The one who drove me to the recovery center where Reid tortured me. His godfather was some kind of high-ranking officer. Of course he was there to hurt me. It was probably his job to lure me somewhere so they could capture me.

"Look. Can we go inside? It's not safe out here."

"Like I'm letting you in the house with me."

I stepped toward him, and he took a step back, still with his hands placating in the air. "I'm not one of them. I'm really not."

"There's no way you can convince me of that. Your godfather—Cheyne—the one who was supposed to be on my side. He's part of this." I gestured at the shattered glass adorning the back porch. "So are you."

"Really? Maybe we have more in common than you think."

"You can't die. I can." I spat out the words and advanced on him with my fists clenched. "We are so far apart from each other it's not funny."

Again, he took a step back, and I wondered if he was as afraid of me as Ms. White had been. No matter what they said on the news, I knew I couldn't hurt him—even though I wanted to, so badly. I wanted to take away from him what he'd taken away from me. My brother. My parents. My safety. My whole world.

I sought the coiled shadow of the hose again and realized

that I could use it, that it could buy me time. I lunged for it, and he must not have anticipated me at all because he just stood there, preparing to speak, as if anything he could say would convince me to listen.

The hose gripped in one hand, I landed a punch on his startled face with my other. It was a wimpy hit, but he stumbled backward, surprise etched on his features. As soon as he was on the back foot, I shoved him, as hard as I could, so he lost his balance.

Before he recovered, I snapped the hose around his neck, jerked on it to force his head down, and catapulted onto his back. I yanked the ends in opposite directions, crushing the resistance of his neck, straining my forearms. He fought me, leveraging his elbow to jab me lightly in the chin, so lightly I wondered why he didn't clobber me like I knew he could.

It wouldn't kill him. But if I could get the hose tight enough to crush his neck, render him unconscious, he'd take a few minutes to recover: a few minutes for me to get back to the house and escape.

My chest heaved. Sobs wracked through me. My arms burned and my heart choked.

I gripped harder, arm muscles boiling, kneeing him in the back to keep him down, trying not to think about what I was doing. Especially when my own timid voice in the back of my mind told me: *this is wrong.*

He wasn't struggling that hard. I was sure he had more strength than this. He could have turned the tables on me, wrenched himself out of my grip, thrown me off him, and then charged at me.

All he did was try to speak. One word, over and over. His voice gasped for air, trying to be heard and it finally edged into my consciousness.

"Out ... cast."

He strained to say it again, and again. My eyes widened.

That's what I was—an outcast. But why would he say that to me —insult me—unless he meant … *just like him.*

A cry tore out of me and my hands shook, the hose slippery with my sweat and tears. I stumbled away from him, catching myself before I tripped and fell, hovering off to the side as if I was the wounded one, staring back at him with my heart in tatters.

He hunched on the ground, a crumpled mound, one arm hidden under him, the other trying to hold himself up. His torso shook so hard his arm gave out and he dropped his forehead to the ground, coughing into the dirt and grass.

"Outcast." He heaved out the word and then there was silence, broken only by his rasping breath in the frozen air.

For the longest time, he huddled on the ground, and for an eternity I stared at him, hearing that word inside my head and thinking about how it applied to me so completely. I wasn't part of the world anymore. I was outside it all. I tilted my head back and even the stars seemed that much further away, as though they couldn't stand to be near me.

That's when it hit me how quiet it was, how dark. None of the neighboring houses had lights on. There hadn't been any headlights all evening, cars shining their way down the street into garages. No people walking dogs. No familiar clatter as neighbors took out the trash. No doors opening and closing or kids playing in backyards.

If I walked down the street right then and peered inside the houses, I knew they would be empty. Relocated. *Evacuated.* Away from the worst threat of all: me.

I could only imagine what they'd been told. Biological hazard. Contagion. Risk of final death. For your safety…

I wondered if Michael was the last person I would ever look at.

It took an age for him to shuffle up to his knees, his face down, his hands planted on the tops of his thighs as leverage. I dreaded what I would see in his face when he looked up.

He finally raised his eyes to mine. "We're outcasts now. You and me. Nobody will ever look at us the same way, treat us the same way. We're *different.*"

I didn't shake my head this time, didn't try to deny it.

"You're the first mortal, Ava." His expression was dark. I didn't think I'd ever seen anything so raw as the look on his face. "But I'm the first murderer."

CHAPTER 10

ICHAEL SAID, "I can't go home."

I couldn't hide from the look in his eyes, the look that said he had nowhere else to go and he couldn't leave, even though I'd just tried to strangle him.

Worse was the realization that he wanted me to. He wanted to die, but he couldn't.

"The way everyone looks at me." His head dropped, mercifully, and I didn't have to face the ripped look in his eyes anymore. "I'm the one who tore the world apart."

I remembered the drive to the recovery center. He'd sat there, staring at the tunnel lights as though he didn't care whether we crashed or not.

He looked up again, pinning me. "Do you know I can regenerate faster than anyone else? It takes me three seconds to restart my heart when the average is thirty. The other guys are always coming at me because if they can beat me, then that means something. That night at the Terminal, some idiot chopped off my arm and it didn't even hit the floor. Dad says I'm one of the…"

He must have seen how pale I'd become because he stopped.

"They should be charging me, but they aren't going to. The Attorney-General said there was no intent to kill. And then he told Dad we should change our name and move to another city —maybe one of the country towns in the western region where they don't get the news so much. Yesterday when I went to buy milk, a little girl started screaming when she saw me. She thought I was going to kill her dead. People won't come near me because if I killed someone, then I can kill them too. They're saying the same thing about you on the news already. That it could be catching. That people should stay away." He chomped his lip, sucking in a breath. "I'm sorry. I don't know why I'm telling you all this."

The stars were so bright above us that his words didn't seem to matter anymore. The night sky sparkled without the usual house lights obscuring it. I focused on the constellation of the Milky Way, thinking about how soft it looked, how radiant. I wondered how amazing it would look from the top of a Stars-gardian tower. All those stars swimming through the darkness, shedding their light like shedding skin.

"Why aren't you afraid of me too?" I asked him, the words slipping from my mouth in a dizzy haze. "Don't you know I could kill you just by looking at you?"

He choked. "Don't *you* know I could kill you just by touching you?" He swallowed, his eyes suddenly glassy, his voice hoarse. "You're no more deadly than moonlight, Ava Holland. I'm sorry I'm the only one who believes that."

As he spoke, the curtain of night tilted. The ground suddenly tipped, and I was cushioned in something as nice as cotton candy.

"Ava!" Michael's face was close to mine, hovering above me, his chest next to my cheek, one arm cradling my head.

I tried to speak, but my mouth was hollow. At least my head had stopped spinning and I felt safe for the first time all day.

He broke eye contact, looking past me to his other hand, the one that had caught me, turning it back and forth. "Your back's bleeding. I'm taking you inside."

I was propelled along in the air before I knew it, and it was at that point that I understood how much he'd allowed me to hurt him before, how much he hadn't fought back.

I felt it, in every part of my body that touched his.

"Energy," I said, and he gave me a curious look.

He shoved the laundry door open with his back, and I found the will to grab his arm. My entire hand tingled. I wondered if Sarah Watson had felt like this when she hung off Michael's side that day at school. I considered whether normal girls could feel the energy zipping through him. I'd danced with boys in dance class and none of them had ever felt like this.

It was like touching a live wire. I wondered briefly whether it would kill me. There was a part of me that didn't care.

Then I remembered about the floor. "Watch out for the glass!"

"I saw it. Don't worry. I've got boots on."

I bit my lip. "I'm getting my voice back. That's a good sign, right?"

"Yeah, you had me worried for a minute there. Looks like you've lost enough blood to make standing a bad idea right now." He gave me a perplexed look, and I realized that he'd stopped moving. "So they're really gone."

"My parents? You say that like you knew they were leaving."

"I heard Cheyne talking. It's why I came here. He told Dad you'd disappeared and they were looking for you everywhere. I wanted to find you, make sure you were okay." His arms tensed, one shoulder lifting as if he'd shrug if he could. "Look, that doesn't matter right now."

I followed his gaze around the empty living room. "Just put me on the floor. Mom's not here to stress out about getting blood on the carpet."

He was about to rest me down in the middle of the living

room—the back of my calves prickled on the woolen fibers—when he yanked me back up again.

"It's covered in glass. Those idiots must have tracked it all through the house. You got anywhere better? It's not like I can clean up and carry you at the same time."

I managed a smile. "I dunno. You could fling me over one shoulder and vacuum with your free hand. I'm sure you could manage."

The serious look on his face changed into a sudden grin. "Don't tempt me." Then, "Seriously, Ava, I can't put you down on that, and it'll take too long to clean up. We need to figure out what's going on with you."

I sighed. "Upstairs. To the left. My parents left my room intact."

We were there in what felt like a couple of seconds. Too soon for me, although I wondered what I feared most. Part of me didn't want him to let go of me, as though the buzz was all that was keeping me alive. The other part of me didn't want him to step foot in my room. It wasn't like a boy had ever seen it.

He pushed open the door and rested me down on the bed. The softness of my butterfly quilt replaced the warm tingle from his body.

"Do you have a spare blanket?"

I frowned at him. "If they've left Josh's room alone, there'll be one in there. Why?"

He was already gone and returned in seconds with the quilt from Josh's bed in his hands.

It meant they'd left Josh's room intact, and I felt a sense of peace about that as Michael pulled the blind closed, tucked the blanket over it, and then flicked on the lamp, snatching up one of my t-shirts from the floor to fling over it, dulling its brightness.

He shrugged when he found me staring at him. "I don't want the light to be a beacon for every Basher around." He gestured at my back. "Let me take a look." He said it like an order, but I heard a question.

In answer, I turned onto my side and flicked at my shirt, giving him permission to lift it. "How bad is it? No. On second thought, don't tell me."

There was a pause. "What did you do to yourself?"

I almost cried. "What did *I* do? It wasn't me—it was *them*. All that flying glass. And that bullet, I swear it missed me by nothing. What do you think I did? Broke out my favorite dance routine for them? What I did was hide in the corner. And then … and then…" I didn't want to remember it, running over glass, climbing the roof, finding out Josh knew all along he could die…

Michael was quiet. I listened to the silence, hearing nothing outside, slowly becoming aware of the damp on my back, the deep ache of the wound.

He finally spoke. "I, um … I kind of don't know what I should do. There's a lot of blood and it's not going away. Wait a minute." There was another pause, and I sensed movement. I turned just enough to see him move toward the dressing table and pull open the top drawer.

"My underwear isn't going to help."

He jumped away from the drawer and went bright red, and his reaction surprised me since I figured mine wouldn't be the first he'd seen. Or, at least, that was my assumption, but I realized there was a lot I didn't know about him. All I had were assumptions, and the more he spoke to me, the more I realized none of them might be true.

He said, "I need something to wipe your back clean. So I can see what's wrong."

I pointed, and the pain between my shoulder blades made me wince. "Try the second drawer. I've got some old cotton tops in there."

He came back with a white singlet, and I tried not to shrink away from him when he touched the wound.

"There are two pretty big flaps of skin here. They're each about three inches along, but only a quarter inch deep. You were lucky the glass didn't puncture your lungs." I turned again to catch sight of him run his hand through his hair.

He met my eyes and shook his head at me.

I sighed. "I think you have to stitch me up. With a needle and thread. You took Home Studies, right?"

"Yeah, I know about stitching. But what if it doesn't work for you?"

"Well, it's all I can think of!" I took a deep breath. "I'm sorry, it's just that you get to zip yourself up, but I don't. I need a bit of help doing that."

He took a deep breath. "Got a needle and thread?"

"There's a kit downstairs. On the kitchen table." I bit my lip, hoping he wouldn't ask where I got it. "It's got medical stuff in it. Stuff that can be used by someone like me."

He pressed his lips together, his eyebrows drawing down. I waited for the difficult question, but all he said was, "Okay."

He was gone before I could say anything else and I dropped my head back onto the pillow. The pain in my back had deepened. I wondered how dirty the glass was, whether I was getting sick. Every now and then there'd be a story on the news about someone who got dirt in a wound that closed up too soon and they had to have it cleaned out. What did they call it—infection? One time there was a kid who healed too fast around a bullet. His brain started to go funny, so they got a bunch of hot-shot surgeons in to operate. Nobody ever said whether the kid was okay afterward, but the surgeons were all over the news.

My face was clammy. Sweat pooled under my chest. Something wasn't right with me, I knew that much. I stuffed my face into the pink butterfly that covered most of the pillow and waited for the next disaster.

A tap on my shoulder made me leap off the bed, slamming into Michael.

"Ava!"

I registered his face and the tingle where one of his hands rested on my shoulder, stopping me from startling further. He was half on the bed, half off, and he seemed to be waiting for me to relax. "Sorry. You were asleep." His hand moved to my forehead. "I was kind of worried."

"What? That I'd died or something?"

He removed his hand and I missed the cool tingle as he shrugged. "I brought up the box." He gestured to the dressing table and the blue container sitting there wide open. Then he lifted his other hand to show me the contents.

A vial of black liquid rested in his palm, the golden scorpion partly visible.

He wasn't smiling and there was something tense about his jaw. "Where did you get this?"

I couldn't tell him because then I'd have to tell him about Josh, but the truth was I didn't really know where it had come from, where Josh had got it. I bit my lip, trying not to remember the green room and the needle filled with black liquid and how I'd thrown myself against the wall after they injected me. How I'd *cracked* the wall after they injected me. I said, "You know what that stuff is?"

"Do you?" He said it carefully, as though he was saying one thing and asking another.

I narrowed my eyes at him while uncertainty and wariness warred against each other on his face.

He said, "It's my dad's research. He's done a lot of work for the government—tranquilizers, nanobots, tracking technology, but this..." He eyed me. "This is seriously classified. It's called nectar, and it's still experimental. Only a handful of people know about it, including Cheyne. It's supposed to speed regeneration, decrease rehabilitation time, completely remove pain from the dying equation. It's supposed to make everyone like me. And more. Stronger. Faster." He looked down at the bed. "Dad's still testing it."

They'd tested it on *me*. "So it makes normal people heal faster?"

"Way faster." Then his expression changed, and I knew what he was thinking.

"No." I shook my head and scooted away from the little bottle, right over to the opposite edge of the bed. "I'm not drinking that."

"If you take this, you might not need stitches. I mean, I don't know for sure, but it's worth a shot, right?"

I stared at him, knowing that what he said was true. After they'd injected me with nectar in the Terminal, the wounds on my forehead and neck had healed. If I drank it now, the rip in my back might heal, too. But I shook my head because of what else it did to me: blurred vision and uncontrollable strength, so much energy inside me that I burned from the inside out. "I can't drink it."

I'll set fire to the house.

"Stitches are really going to hurt. You need to try this first. Drink it. If it doesn't work, then … then I'll stitch you." He leaned over and pushed the vial at me. The scorpion seemed to leap out at me.

I shoved his hand away and pressed my lips together.

"Please drink it!"

I shook my head, glaring at him.

In response, he ran a hand across his forehead and studied the ground for a moment. His fists clenched and unclenched as if he was trying to control himself. His next words were quiet. "I need you to drink this because I can't … I can't do this—stitch you up—if I know it's hurting you."

I stared at him, stricken, biting my lip. I didn't know what he would say or do if I told him what happened when I drank nectar. That I became someone—something—else. Something fiery and uncontainable. That we wouldn't have to worry about lamps because *I* would be the beacon drawing the Bashers to my house.

"I can't drink it. They gave it to me at the recovery center when they tested me and it … it does weird stuff to me. It won't just heal me."

A wary look replaced the frustration on his face. "What do you mean—weird stuff?"

I struggled to find the right words. I remembered what it was like at the recovery center when Reid gave me the first injection of nectar. I'd healed and the pain had disappeared, but then the splotch on the wall had turned into a rose and the room had filled with things that weren't real—vines and a scuttling scorpion like the one on the vial. Everything had shimmered, I couldn't focus, my vision had been so bad I'd even thought one of the guards was Michael.

I looked into his eyes, begging him to understand. "It changes me. It makes me strong—unbelievably strong—but I can't control it. It's like having all the fire of the sun trapped inside me, and it has to come out." He was about to speak, so I hurried on, not sure if I was making sense. "And I can't stop it. It forces itself out of me. It makes me do stuff. Crazy, insane stuff, and it's really not good."

How could I tell him I'd burned so hot that I'd breathed fire?

I tried to draw breath, the words tumbling out of me. "I'm sorry. I'm really sorry that you have to stitch me up. If I could do it myself, I would, but I can't reach, and I know it's going to hurt, but I promise I won't cry."

I stopped and stared at my hands in the sudden silence. If I was really honest with myself, it wasn't the nectar I was afraid of.

It was what Michael would think. I had no idea what would happen if I drank it. I only knew what happened the first time: that I broke a metal chair with my bare hands and crushed a man's chest just by shoving him. I wasn't going to drink it in front of Michael and scare him away. Or worse—hurt him somehow. Not that anything I did could probably hurt Mr. Restart-My-Heart-In-Three-Seconds. "I'll be brave. I promise."

He sat down, studying the vial in his hand. It looked as if a million thoughts raced through his head. "Dad said nectar is like immortality trapped in a bottle. I don't think it's meant for people ... like you." He looked grim, his face ashen. "I'm sorry they gave it to you. I won't make you take it if you don't want to."

He crossed to the cupboard, put the bottle into the medical box, and firmly closed the lid. "Okay. You'll need to hold on to something."

I turned onto my stomach and pulled my hair out of the way. I exhaled fully. "Just get it done."

I sounded a lot braver than I was. I turned my face away from the needle and thread he pulled from sealed packages because I didn't want to look at them.

The needle entered my skin and I was not prepared at all. There was nothing to save me from this pain. I couldn't even stamp my feet or thump my fists. After the first involuntary twitch made the pain intensify, I had to stay very still.

So I shouted instead. "I'm not brave. Not at all. I lied. I am going to shout. A lot. Until you're finished." I yelled each word like I wanted to yell at my parents for leaving and at Josh for dying. Like I wanted to yell at every person in my street who left silence around me, and every person who would look at me like I was an outcast. But I stayed still—for the ten thousand years it took Michael to stitch me back together.

I knew it was over when his hand rested on my shoulder again, soothing vibrations on my trembling skin. "Sorry, Ava."

"Sorry for helping me? Don't be." I bit out the words, my teeth chattering. I wiped my palm across my sweating face, ready to sit up.

"No. Sorry for this."

The wash of liquid across my back preceded a bone-deep sting, so sharp that the sensation burned all the way through my lungs and out the other side of my ribcage. I launched myself off the bed in reflex and found myself crouched on the floor under the window, facing Michael. He stood very still on the other side of the room with an uncorked vial in his right hand and a stopper in his left.

It was the bottle of nectar.

CHAPTER 11

"WHAT DID you do? Michael, what did you do?"

He didn't answer, but his alarmed expression hardened. "I'm just trying to help you, Ava."

I drew myself up, clenching my fists. I waited for the weird to start—the pounding in my head, the blistering heat. I waited for his face to change when he saw the freak I was about to turn into. I stepped away from Josh's quilt because the last thing I wanted was to burn anything that belonged to him. "If you gave me nectar, I swear..."

His expression cleared. He shoved the cork back on the bottle and held it up for me to see. It had writing on it and the glass was brown, not clear like the nectar bottle. "It's methylated spirits. It'll stop any infection."

"Methylated spirits?" I marched over and snatched up the bottle, reading the label. I realized he was telling the truth when the inner monster didn't make an appearance. "Why would methylated spirits stop infection?"

"It's pure alcohol. Everyone knows alcohol kills bugs. They use it on animals." He said it so matter-of-factly, as though he was telling me something a child would know.

"Well, I didn't know that. And it hurt!"

"It's supposed to. That's the way it works."

I wondered how he knew that stuff. I certainly didn't have a clue what would help me and what could equally kill me when it came to chemicals. Doctors and nurses specialized in recovery domes—the administering of organic energy and hydration so the natural processes worked faster—and they dug things out of people who healed too fast over foreign objects. But I'd never heard of anyone worrying about killing bugs. Vets probably knew more about that stuff, since animals got sick and died all the time. I wondered if that's what I was now—some kind of animal.

I scrutinized his face as I lowered my voice, pointing at the bottle. "How do you know about that?"

"I, uh…" His expression changed again, and I wished I was given a life for every time he scowled at me. His jaw ticked. "Does it matter?"

It did to me. He seemed to know a lot more about my mortality than I did. Even when he'd shrugged his shoulders as though he didn't know a thing about stitching me up, he'd still done it. I backed away from him, shuffling my feet through the mess on the floor, pressing up against Josh's quilt hanging over the window, wishing my suspicions would go away because he was there and he seemed to want to help me when nobody else did. "You've stitched someone up before, haven't you?"

He put down the bottle, keeping his eyes on mine. "I don't know what you're talking about, but you need to rest because that wound doesn't look so great."

"How would you know how to stitch someone up when there's nobody else like me? Or am I wrong? Are there others like me?"

"Just sit down, okay? I don't want you pulling those stitches."

"Or what? How do you even know that's a bad thing?"

He got a patient look on his face. "Because it makes sense. The stitches keep the wound closed so it can heal itself. You said that yourself. If you rip them open, you'll tear your skin even more."

"Yeah?" This time, I took a step toward him. I reached behind my back. "Why don't I just give them a tug and see what happens?"

"You're nuts."

"Tell me how you know this stuff. Tell me how you know how to stitch people up and torture them with spirits."

His jaw clenched and he didn't answer.

I raised my eyebrows at him. "Tugging now."

"Go ahead."

I glared at him. Heat flashed through my skin the instant I touched it. I jerked away from it, knowing I'd failed. He'd called my bluff. My hand dropped to my side and I tried to ignore the pain for long enough to make sense of the jumble in my head. "Michael, you can't turn up at my house, out of nowhere, and suddenly expect me to trust you because I don't. It doesn't matter how much you think we have in common—I don't trust you. I don't think I ever will."

"I know." His voice was quiet, small. He looked across the room at me for a really long time before he exhaled and his shoulders sagged. "I had a brother too."

"*Had* a brother?"

His eyes snapped to mine. "It's not what you think. He's not dead. Mom took him with her when she left. He was a slow healer."

I sucked in my breath, but Michael went on. "If he hurt himself really badly, then I helped him. And yeah, I stitched him up a couple times so he'd heal better. But he wasn't like you."

His jaw clenched and his fingers closed around the bottle. "Mom took him away because the Bashers found out about him. They started threatening us. Mom wanted to leave, but Dad wouldn't agree to go. He didn't try to stop her leaving, but Cheyne did. He said she knew too much about their research. So one day I woke up and she'd left in the night. My brother's the reason Dad started working on nectar in the first place. He went searching for a cure—disappeared for months sometimes when I was a kid. But now I don't know what he's doing or why, and he doesn't tell me anything anymore." He turned away from me, put the bottle back in the kit, and leaned on the dresser, shoulders slumped, not looking at me. His hair fell over his face in the mirror.

I stared at the floor, thinking that I shouldn't have pushed it so far. I didn't want to talk about my family either. The fact that Josh had known he was mortal was a secret I wouldn't ever share with anyone. That he'd died trying to save me...

I looked everywhere but at Michael and noticed the smears of blood on the carpet where I'd walked earlier. Wanting to change the subject, I asked, "Do you think we should clean up the glass?"

"Not you. You should rest or you're never going to heal." He exhaled and turned around. "I'll make us something to eat."

He turned to leave and I thought about the near-empty kitchen downstairs. I remembered the charge card that my parents had left for me, but it wouldn't be safe to use now. I may as well cut it up with my nail scissors.

"There's not a lot of food," I said.

"It's okay, I brought some with me, just in case."

"Oh, yeah?"

"Eggs, cheese, sun-dried tomato. Do you like omelets?" He sounded wary, as though he'd asked me whether I preferred guns or swords.

"Yeah. I do." I chilled all of a sudden, hollow. My stomach was a black pit. I rubbed my forehead. "Thanks."

He gave me a nod and that was all before he disappeared from the room. As soon as he was gone, I crawled under the blanket. A short while later, the automatic garage door rolled up and his car grumbled inside, muffled by the walls downstairs.

I tried to decide how I felt about Michael being in the house. More than that, I wondered how long he'd stay. Having him there made my heart kick as if I was about to perform on stage. My skin still tingled from where he'd touched me. My reaction to him was like being even more alive than I already was. I rubbed my eyes and poked my head over the edge of the bed to see my duffel bag still on the floor, full of my things. I'd planned on leaving and I figured that was still a good idea. Just because Michael was there didn't change the fact that the house wasn't safe anymore.

My head had stopped ringing by the time I smelled cooked eggs and melted cheese. I pushed back the covers and couldn't believe how much my mouth watered.

He didn't say anything as he put the plate down in front of me, juggling a glass of juice onto the bedside table. He hadn't brought up a second plate, and I asked, "Aren't you having any?"

He tilted his head toward the stairs. "Mine's in the kitchen."

"Oh." I blinked at my plate, not wanting to eat alone. I tried to read his expression, guessing that he either didn't want to eat with me or he needed my permission. I didn't know which, but I decided to take a chance. "You can bring it up here if you like."

For a moment, he scrutinized my face. Then he shrugged and left, and I didn't know whether or not he planned on coming back. Footsteps on the stairs a moment later answered my question.

As he entered the room, his eyes went from my face to my untouched plate. "Why aren't you eating?"

"I was waiting for you." I bit my lip as he perched on the edge of the bed like an awkward gorilla. Satisfied that he wasn't going to leave, I took the first mouthful and the savory flavors burst between my teeth. It practically knocked me over. "Mm-mmm. This is good." I stuffed another huge forkful into my mouth.

The corner of his lips tugged up. His shoulders relaxed and he looked more like he belonged at the end of my bed.

I said, "You know, I honestly didn't believe you could cook."

He shrugged. "Since Mom left, I cook all the time—"

"Really? I figured you'd have a housekeeper. Staff. You know."

"Dad doesn't like strangers in the house. He likes to bring his work home."

I was too busy eating to see his expression. "But *this*." I poked my fork at it. "This is really good."

"I can't figure you out, Ava."

The seriousness of his voice weighed on me and I dared to glance up—but only after cramming in another forkful. "Oh, yeah? That makes two of us."

"I wasn't joking."

I swallowed. "Neither was I."

He shook his head. "I killed your brother and you're letting me eat with you."

So that's what he was thinking. I stared at the last piece of omelet. He had killed my brother. And I *was* letting him eat with me. I guessed on some level it didn't make sense—sharing a meal with my brother's murderer. But then, not a lot of my life made sense at that point. "He killed you first."

"You know what I mean."

"Okay." I put my fork down and met his eyes, hoping I wouldn't see images of Josh falling. "You didn't know he was going to die."

"It doesn't matter. I meant to kill him."

"Yes, you meant to kill him. But you didn't mean for him to die." My voice sounded so matter-of-fact, so sure of itself, as though there wasn't any part of me that disagreed—no sneaky, angry thoughts in the back of my mind questioning his motives. It was true that I didn't trust him, but I realized that I didn't blame him anymore either. Not in that moment, with the two of us perched in my room. Maybe tomorrow would be different, but right then all I wanted to do was eat and forgive.

He shook his head. "It must have been the first time I ever felt like that. When he turned up in that Basher uniform and he stabbed me, it made me so mad. I completely lost it. I've never..." His eyes flickered as if he was going over it in his head. He dropped his fork and it clattered onto his plate, but he didn't seem to notice as he put his hand to his chest. "When I died, there was just—nothing—in my ears. This silence. Just ... impulses. It was like my arm moved on its own, my fingers closed on the knife, and pulled it out, and I wasn't even in control." He suddenly focused on the fork, snapping back into the present. His eyes sought mine. "I talk too much."

My plate was empty. Somehow I'd finished the last bite without noticing. I avoided him as I studied the leftover swirl of melted butter. "What are you going to do now?"

He said, "I'm going to make amends."

I bit my lip and wondered what that meant, but I let him finish his meal in silence.

He put his fork down. "I'm not going back home. If you don't want me here, just say so and I'll leave. But I'm never going back there. I don't understand what my dad's doing and I don't want to be part of it. I can't go back to my old life anyway."

"I know." I nodded toward my bag. "I'm leaving tomorrow. I guess you can come with me." I thought of his car. "Actually, I guess I could do with a ride. But that's up to you."

"Okay." He cleared his throat. "I'll clean up dinner. You should get some sleep."

His hand brushed mine as he reached for my plate, and I wondered if making amends meant waiting on me hand and foot. I dared to meet his eyes for a second. No, it was something else, but I wasn't sure I wanted to know what.

He disappeared into the hall and part of me wanted to call him back, ask him how long he was going to stick around. Just tomorrow? The next day? The words stopped in my throat. I glanced at my bag again and grabbed a pair of pajamas, heading across to the bathroom.

When I got back, I was surprised to find a sleeping bag unrolled at the base of my bed, but its owner was nowhere to be seen. My eyebrows went right up. "Taking liberties." But I found I didn't really mind. I didn't want to be alone.

I jumped as my phone rang, feeling my heart bang against my ribs. I checked the caller ID. "Hannah!"

Her voice was a whisper. "Ava! My parents will kill me if they find out I'm calling you. I've spent the weekend at the recovery center. The nurses keep whispering about viruses and bacteria—and cancer. I thought only animals got that. You wouldn't believe how freaked out my parents are. But I had to call you. Are you okay?"

I almost started to cry. "Yeah. Yeah, I'm okay. I mean. I'm not. Not really. But I am. You know what I mean."

"Yeah. Ava, I'm sorry about Josh. I can't believe it. Nobody can. We're all in shock."

I didn't know what to say. My best friend had finally called me back and I was about to turn into a blubbering mess.

"They said on the news that you were back in the recovery center. There are reporters everywhere. I was hoping I might bump into you here."

"No." I shook my head, even though she couldn't see it. "I'm not at the recovery center. You should never believe the news, right?"

She paused. I sensed her fidget on the other end of the line. "So, where are you? I want to see you. I want to know you're okay."

"Um." My head whirled. "I'm at home, but don't come over…" I struggled to think of a lie that would keep her away—and safe.

Her voice went quiet. "Wow, I didn't think they'd let you stay there. I heard they evacuated everyone because they think you're contagious. People are totally freaking out about this mortality thing."

I took a deep breath and a plan formed in my head. "Look, I'll meet you somewhere."

"Dance studio?"

"No." My response was too sharp. I tried to soften my voice. "No, I can't go back there. How about behind the café though? You know, at the bottom of the studio, in the alley. I really don't want the reporters in my face."

"Yeah. Okay."

"And Hannah, can you do me a big favor? Can I borrow some money?"

There was a pause.

"I promise I'll pay it back. It's just … everything's kind of … I just really need your help."

Her voice softened. "You can count on me, Ava. Tomorrow morning? Ten o'clock?"

I breathed a sigh of relief. "Great."

"Take care, Ava."

I clicked off the phone and sagged onto the bed, ready to sleep and forget.

The darkness lifted beyond my eyelids and a sudden rush of awareness took over. Blood on the carpet. Glass in my back. My eyes shot open, but with the quilt over the window, I couldn't tell what time it was. I slipped out of bed and padded across the floor, tripping over an arm flung around the end of my blanket.

Michael was asleep on the floor, his head resting on the rolled up butterfly quilt. He must have dragged it off the bed and over himself. No wonder I'd been cold in the night.

I watched his face, how calm he looked while everything churned inside me. Maybe if he stayed there, asleep, there would be one part of my life that was under control, one part that was peaceful. I glanced at the door where he'd wedged a chair under the handle and I could pretend—just for a moment—that my room was safe.

Then I came upon the kit and the bottle of methylated spirits resting on my dressing table, a nasty reminder. I backed away from it, running my hand over my eyes as I crept over to the window. I pulled aside the quilt and cracked open the blinds, peering down at Mrs. Hubert's low-set, brick home. Dark gray settled over her roof, a first brief glint off the solar panels she'd had installed two weeks before. I guessed she didn't have any idea then that final death was only a couple of weeks away.

A shadow passed behind her window. I frowned down at her living room, thinking that something moved there. That wasn't possible. She was gone. Everybody was.

Unless...

I rolled my shoulders, trying to ease the sudden tension in them. I was about to turn away from the window when there was a *crack*. The sound crashed through the air moments before glass and wood shattered over me.

I HUNCHED MY BODY, curling downward and away from the falling debris. The quilt came with me, sliding to the floor, and something bit my ear.

I followed the object as it flew through the air and lodged in the wall. Then I jumped to my feet and leaped over where Michael was still asleep.

He lurched up, groggy, driven awake by the crash. "Ava!"

We collided and one of his arms came up around me, his eyes meeting mine as he pulled me against his bare chest. In one swift movement, he twisted us around, his back to the window, blocking me. My eyes widened. A shout surfaced in the back of my throat as the next bullet hit him.

Michael braced. There was another bullet—and another. With each, he pushed me away with rigid arms, spitting blood, still holding me so his body protected mine, but not so close that the bullets might speed through him to me.

"Get down." His voice was a rasp, a bare whisper.

With a shock, I realized that he was going to take as many bullets as he had to until I was out of range. His words from the night before rang in my ears. *Make amends.* I knew it from the look on his face and the way he held me so tightly, right where I wouldn't get hurt.

I dropped to the floor and squashed myself against the carpet and he followed me down. At the last minute, he punched off the floor as if he was about to bash out a round of push-ups. Something bronze slipped out of his mouth.

"No." I put my hand over my mouth as I realized that the first bullet had lodged in the back of his head. "No, no, no. Are you okay?"

His face contorted in concentration.

"There are two more," I said, wanting to help, but not knowing how. He shoved my hand away, balancing on one arm as if it was the easiest thing in the world. I guessed, compared to spitting out a bullet, it was.

"I … can count." He ground out the words as his whole body shuddered, his eyes squeezed shut. Something dropped from his shoulder. Another bullet. He flopped over and reached into the wound in his stomach, snatching out the final bullet before his skin closed. Dropping it onto the carpet, he ran his hand over his face. "I almost healed over it."

My stomach turned. I tried to get closer to him, but he shook his head at me. "Just give me a moment. I'll be okay, and then we have to get out of here."

The blind hung in tatters at the window. There was no cover now, nothing to conceal us other than the bed. I couldn't believe a drone hadn't soared inside the room already. I looked from the exposed opening to Michael. He was only wearing blue boxer shorts and my face went red. I glanced away, but he raised his eyebrows.

I rushed to speak before he could say anything. "They're using bullets. Not tranquilizers. And where are the drones?"

"Yeah, I noticed." He grimaced. "It's not Hazards."

My heart pounded. "It's Bashers, isn't it?" They were out there.

As I spoke, another bullet bashed out the remaining glass

from the window and knocked off part of the wooden surround. He grabbed my hand, urging me forward, and the shock from his touch stung all the way up my arm, so sharp my eyes watered. I crawled as fast as I could toward the door with Michael close behind me.

"I'll get the door," he said. "Stay down and cover your head."

I wasn't sure how he was going to get the chair out from under the door handle without eating more bullets. When he reached it, he crouched, poised against the wall. His hand shot out. He snatched the chair, angling it out from under the handle and flung it—one-handed—up into the air. The chair fragmented as a round of bullets cut through it. I face-planted on the carpet, throwing my arms over my head as Michael shot up into the path of gunfire, curled his hand around the doorknob and threw it open. He ducked, just as another bullet tasted the bedroom wall.

"C'mon, Ava. We have to move."

But I remembered the medical kit on the dressing table. I'd happily leave the methylated spirits behind—even the bottles of nectar—but I needed that kit, the bandages and needles and thread. It may as well have been on the other side of the world right then.

Michael followed my line of sight and shook his head. "No, Ava. Don't."

I shimmied across the floor as he scooted out and tried to grab me to stop me from committing suicide. I readied myself, took a deep breath, and then launched myself toward the blue kit, into the path of gunfire.

Michael shouted and I caught his swift movement. As my hand closed around the kit, he leaped up and out toward the bed with something in his arms. In the next instant, he propelled himself off the bed end, flinging out the butterfly quilt. The giant pink creature spread out like a flag of war, blocking out everything around me. Bullets whipped through it and cotton filling floated like snow. One bullet hit my shoulder, but I didn't have time to think. I scooped up the kit and plummeted. The blanket engulfed me and Michael with it, the two of us crashing to the floor, wrapped and twisted.

I heard a voice at my ear. "You'd better not be dead."

"I'm okay. My shoulder hurts, but I think it only grazed me." I checked and confirmed. "It nicked me."

His arms trapped me so I couldn't move. "Are you going to do anything else insane? Tell me now, all right?"

I shook my head, not sure if he could see it. I guessed he did because, in the next moment, we rolled out onto the floor. Clutching the kit to my chest, I shuffled forward, but before I dumped it into my duffel bag, I snapped open the lid and removed the two little vials of black liquid nestled inside, shoving them across the floor. With all the side effects, they were no use to me. Then I dragged my bag around the corner where he propelled me.

"Listen, we have to head downstairs to my car. And then we're getting out of here."

I tried to focus on his eyes and not the shooting tingle where he gripped my arm. "They're waiting for us out there. There's no way we can get past them—"

"Getting in the car and getting out of here is the only plan we've got."

I tried to rid my mind of the image of him spitting out a bullet. There was still blood on his chin. I wanted to wipe it away. I reached out—almost touched him—but he grabbed me and pulled me after him.

Turning right past Mom's study, we headed through the hall to the internal garage door.

He said, "Your parents took the remote control, so I'm going to start the car, press the button and jump in. Okay."

"I'll do it," I said. "I'll press the button. You start the engine."

"No way, Ava. They'll have guns trained on the door."

I couldn't argue with that. I raced to the passenger side and threw my bag behind the seat. Michael opened the driver side, turned the key in the ignition, and raced to the back of the garage.

His chest rose in a deep breath. Then he thumped the button with his fist and ran back to the car. I expected to hear the chatter of gunfire. The door was already a third of the way up when he hurtled in, slammed the door, and revved the engine.

I waited with my heart pounding in my throat as the metal door rose. I stared out the back of the window. Michael revved the engine, inching backward without getting too close, waiting and looking, arm tensing on the gear shift, ready to gun it out of there as soon as the gap widened.

The door rolled up high enough, and I gasped.

A single figure stood waiting, covered tightly from head to foot in motley brown and beige Basher cloth so I couldn't see her face, but her figure marked her clearly a woman. She stood very still, all alone, but she held what looked like a bomb launcher.

Michael saw it too. "What the—" He froze for a split second.

I wondered how many pieces I'd explode into. I wondered how Michael's body would heal itself. Whether he would fragment and then pull himself back together like the people who were hit by the nuclear bomb. I wondered how that would work. By his expression, he didn't exactly know himself.

We both knew I'd be dust afterward.

His jaw clenched and the car roared backward, straight toward the figure.

"You're going to hit her!" I shouldn't have cared whether we ran her down or not. She was a Basher, which meant she was a fast healer. Being pummeled by a car wouldn't keep her down for long.

"It's too late." Michael's face turned white. He heard it too. The *whoosh*.

As the car escaped the garage, flying down the drive, the bomb zipped toward us. Michael's foot came off the accelerator. He let go of the wheel. In the second before the bomb hit, he threw his body across the gap between us, shoving me hard up against the passenger door, and at the same time reaching for the handle.

I dropped as the door gave way.

"Michael!" I screamed for him as I crashed toward the concrete driveway. Trying to shield my head, I threw my arms up as I thwacked the ground.

Michael leaned halfway out of the car, trying to get out, tugging at something.

The missile hit.

Flames burgeoned. Windows cracked open. Metal tore apart. Somehow, I was clear of the explosion, but heat scorched my face, my arms, my legs, more heat than I could bear, and all my thoughts ripped apart. Michael was so close, yet so far. I'd made it out of the car, but I wasn't far enough away to miss his expression.

A second explosion burst across us. Michael's face floated in flames for a split second. He found me, saw that I was clear, that I was safe.

Then, with a faint smile, he shattered.

PART II
TERMINAL

A SECTION OF METAL frame zipped past my curled up body, hurtling beyond my vision. I sought the place where Michael had been, the center of the explosion close by, a giant burning hole that glowed in the middle of the white-hot carcass of his car. I wanted to see movement, to see him stand up as though nothing had happened. Part of me believed he would.

My whole body hurt from the fall. I was still lying half on the concrete driveway, not present enough to roll away from the flames. Even when I thought about moving, I couldn't make my arms and legs work, kind of like they didn't belong to me anymore. As if they'd become somebody else's.

As if they weren't there.

The sickening suspicion made the world turn. My eyes ran toward my arms, reassuring myself. My hands, too, and each of my fingers. Maybe, if I concentrated really hard, I could feel them, even if they were full of tremors. I watched them twitch, forcing myself to at least try to control the shaking, although I knew it wouldn't do any good. I didn't have time to check my legs before pounding vibrations broke my concentration, drawing my eyes up and beyond to the figure coming toward me—not Michael, but our attacker. I stared up the barrel of a gun.

She nudged me onto my back with the tip of her boot. She spoke, but it was a buzz in my ringing ears and all I did was frown up at her, feeling like she was too far away to hurt me. She said something else through the warbled voice modulator and the gun moved closer to my face. The weapon shook.

"...misery."

I didn't understand, could barely hear her, but I figured it didn't matter what she was saying. She was going to kill me—that much was clear.

Something moved at the edge of my vision—another person. I froze, hoping with all my heart that it was Michael, but it was another disguised figure. He ran into my field of vision, grabbing the girl with the gun and snatching it away from her. His words rasped through the buzz in my head.

"You idiot! What are you doing? They need her alive!" It was a guy. I could tell that much from the set of his shoulders, even though his voice may as well have been the beat of a moth's wings.

The girl yanked away from him. The way her mouth moved told me she was shouting, but her words were a mere whisper to me, barely recognizable through the metal mouthpiece. "She has to die! That's the only way any of this will stop. Don't you see? It's going to be war."

"It already is!" He grabbed her shoulders and she winced in response. "You can't back out now. You know what they do to deserters. Tiny, dirty cells for you and your family to rot in."

She screamed. "Josh died because of her!"

"No." He took her shoulders. "Josh died because of *us!*"

The girl's shoulders slumped over, her legs looked like they'd buckle.

The boy said, "Josh would hate us for this."

She clutched her chest as if she thought her heart was going to crack. Her voice must have lowered because I couldn't hear her anymore. "…don't want this." Then her face darkened and she grabbed the gun and said, "She's not going to make it through the next five minutes. Look at her legs!" She ran a hand over her eyes, the gun passed across her forehead, leaving a shadow trailing her face.

"What did you think was going to happen? I never should've let you out of my sight."

She stared back at him, then at the sky, biting her lip. She shrugged back at the shell of the car. "We can tell them it was because of Michael. He recognized me and there wasn't any other way to keep him down. You know what they say about him. He should have joined us when he had the chance. His kind are everything we're fighting for—"

"Shut up! She can hear you."

"No, she can't. She's barely alive."

They both stared at me—hard—and I did my best to look glazed and not focus on either of them. She'd said something about Michael recognizing her, but it wouldn't matter because Michael was gone. No. *Dead.* I blinked against the burn behind my eyes. The realization that I didn't want him to be dead shook me.

"Well, what are we going to do?"

He shoved his face up into hers. "I don't know! You're the one who blew off her legs. You think of something."

Her tense figure blurred. All I heard was *blew off her legs.* I tried not to react, not to show that I'd heard them when all I wanted to do was scream my lungs out. Air built in my chest, waiting to be released. They had to be lying. It had to be a sick joke. Surely I could feel my toes, perfect and functional like they should be.

Worry raced across the girl's face and that's when she screamed. It was a high-pitched, winded sound like air being forced out of a balloon.

The guy tried to grab her, but not in time to save her from the two arms that crushed her chest. In the next moment, she soared high up into the air, only to crash down onto someone's bent knee.

She dropped to the grass, floppy like a rag doll. Standing behind her, Michael glowed red from the fire. He reminded me of a piece of coal—burned badly, but somehow shiny and new.

I was too dead to care that he was hardly wearing a stitch.

The guy stood staring, tense shoulders squared, knees bent. He looked ready to tackle Michael at any moment.

Michael motioned to the lump on the grass. "You'd better help her. She's going to need a serious recovery dome, real fast."

The guy poised, fixated on Michael. His fists got tighter and Michael's stance became menacing in response.

Michael shook his head slightly. "Don't try it. Not if you know what I can do."

I couldn't see the guy's face anymore, but his shoulders sagged and he seemed to make a decision. He hauled the girl up by her armpits and dragged her down the driveway, across the road, and that's when they disappeared from view.

Michael's torso and then his face came into view as he dropped into a kneeling position beside me. He ran a hand over his eyes. "Oh no, Ava. Your legs."

I tried to speak, but Michael hushed me. He said, "I'm sorry I disappeared for a minute there. But I had to go back … for these." He opened his palms to reveal the two black vials I'd left behind. "I know you're afraid of what could happen, but I don't know what else to do."

He worked quickly, filling a syringe and ramming it into my thigh.

"Listen to me. Don't think about your legs. You're going to be okay." He jabbed a needle into my other leg and sat back on his heels—head in his hands—waiting. "You'll be okay," he said again, but his voice trailed off like he didn't really believe it.

I was ice cold. When he put his hand on my forehead, our skin sizzled. His fingers brushed my cheek, smoothing away my tears, turning them into steam so that little curls of white rose up around my nose and the side of my face. Stabs of energy traveled up to my eyelids and across to my temples, stemming from his fingertips, bleeding into me.

The nectar must have started working because tears ran down my cheeks and moisture came back into my mouth. I wanted to speak. "You're hot," I said.

A quizzical look passed over his face, and he got one of those pretend sexy-boy crinkles in his forehead. "Yeah. I get that all the time."

I rolled my eyes. "Sure you do."

He leaned closer, intent. "At least you're speaking again."

"Seems so." I looked up at the sky, wondering why it was so white. Maybe a cloud had gone over the sun. Perhaps it was about to rain. Then I said, "It's okay."

"What is?"

"About my legs. I wasn't going to dance again anyway. Ms. White didn't want me there anymore."

"Who's Ms. White?"

"She's my dance teacher. She said I had to leave. So I guess that's just as well." Thinking about Ms. White made the sky even stranger. I wondered if she could become her name. The sun had shifted from the edge of my vision to the middle, but it was no longer golden. Big and round, it was a luminescent circle as though it had become the moon in the daylight sky. A white cloud sailed across it, delicate wisps forming into legs, pincers, and a deadly tail. The scorpion-shaped cloud stretched and shimmered across the sky as something white-hot built inside my torso. It spread to my arms, down to my fingertips, a cold heat like the burn of ice.

Michael seemed to be trying to get my attention. "Stuff Ms. White. You can do what you want."

"Don't say that." My voice choked. "My legs are gone."

"Ava?" He squinted as if he was looking into the sun.

"Yeah?"

"What are you doing?"

"Just lying here." I remembered the first time Michael ever spoke to me. I'd slipped on the wet bleachers at school during a rain storm, tripped backward, and would have fallen all the way to the bottom, probably would have broken my neck, except that he was right behind me. He told me to watch out. I didn't remember if I said "thanks," I was so embarrassed. Now I'd give anything to be able to trip again. Even clumsy legs were better than none.

"No, Ava, I really mean it. You're hurting my eyes." His voice jolted through my thoughts. He half turned away from me, reaching back to touch my arm, snapping his hand away with a curse. "Your skin's like ice. And it's glowing. You're glowing. All of you." His words were full of growing panic. He tried to look at me, but winced, his hand going over his eyes.

"Dad used to tell me that I danced like a moonbeam fallen to earth. He said that watching me was like watching moonlight. Shifting. Flying. Floating." I dropped the words into the hollow around me, where the shape of my torso made a shallow crevice in the grass—an indent without legs. I didn't know how, but I realized that if I were really moonlight, then I couldn't break. Light couldn't be wrecked like I could. It was like water. It flowed.

If I became light, my legs wouldn't be gone.

They had never been gone from me. They were with me all along.

Icy white light burst around me, shining from my arms and my torso, covering the ground and sky and everywhere in between.

"Ava! Too bright!" Michael curled himself up into a ball, covering his eyes with his arm. His other hand reached out as though he wanted me to stop.

I held out my own, allowing our fingertips to touch.

"It's okay," I said. "I guess I might dance again, after all."

CHAPTER 14

$\mathcal{B}$RIGHT LIGHT FLOODED over Michael, glowing over the whole front lawn as he hunched over, one arm flung across his face. His bare back glowed, muscles pulled taut as he curled up tight.

"I think you need clothes." I blushed, averted my eyes, and the air around us turned pink.

"Yeah, well, I was kind of in a hurry to get back here." He kept his eyes shielded. "Whatever you're doing, turn it off. Shut it down. I don't know, just make it stop. You're gonna make my head explode." He curled into a tighter ball. "And while you're at it, tell me you're okay."

"I can't turn it off. It's the nectar. How much did you give me anyway?" I patted my thigh. "But I'm okay."

"You're not dead?"

"No. Um. I don't think so."

"Because this is pretty much how I'd imagine an angel. White light, brightest star in the sky, that kind of thing. Look, I can't see a thing. My stuff's back in the house. How do you expect me to find pants with my eyes closed?"

He had a point. I'd have to walk away from him, but first I

needed to check that my new legs were real. "Can you do something for me?"

"Will it make you stop shining?"

"Um. Probably not. Can you tell me if my legs are really there?"

"Ava, if I could look at you, I already would have."

"Here." I sat next to him with my legs stretched out in front of me. I pried one of his hands away from his face, forcing him to press his eyes against his knee. I rested his hand on my calf. I didn't feel any kind of buzz this time, there was barely anything, except a lovely kind of warmth from his skin.

"Tell me if that's real."

His fingers slid down my skin from my knee to my ankle, danced across the top of my foot, and stopped at my toes. The pad of his thumb brushed the ball of my foot and made me shiver. "Feels real to me."

"Okay. So, I guess I'm just going to wander over there for a bit. Away from you. Or something."

He laughed. "Nectar does weird stuff to you, that's what you said. *Um, yeah.* You just grew back a pair of legs."

"Hey, you're the one who walked out of a burning car. After bursting into a thousand pieces, I might add."

"I didn't burst. I just kind of ... moved around a bit. And anyway, you're the only girl who'd complain."

I tried not to laugh. It occurred to me that he really was kind of nice to look at. Actually ... more than just nice. With his shoulders hunched over, his back muscles rippled, moving as he breathed, as though every movement he made had a purpose, a connection. For a moment, I considered fanning my fingers across his skin, over the curve of his shoulder blade. His back was so broad I didn't think the tips of my fingers would even reach the base of his neck. He was all muscle and shadow in my light.

His voice became somber. "Seriously, Ava. I don't think Dad knows nectar can do that. Heal, sure, but regrow a limb or two?

Of course, I mean, I guess nobody's ever had to regrow anything before..."

"Right. Normal people don't need to." *Normal* people's limbs reconnected with their bodies. I tried to keep my tone light, but I was glad he couldn't see my face or the tear that dripped down my cheek. I swiped at it.

I needed answers. I needed to know who I was. What nectar did, helping me heal—no, *regrow*—I needed to know how. "Did you ever take it? Nectar, I mean?"

He shrugged. "I'm not really supposed to know about it. Worst kept secret in our house."

The only way I would ever find out was to hand myself in to Cheyne and let him find out for me. That wasn't going to happen. And nectar couldn't be the answer to my mortality.

"Look, star girl," Michael said. "Why don't you go stand somewhere far away so I can get dressed."

I was glad for the excuse to walk because I needed to escape my thoughts. Focusing on each step, I paced across the road to the house opposite, following the path where the guy had dragged the girl. There was no sign of our attackers. I decided to occupy myself by checking out the street and took off at a gentle jog up the road. I stopped when I reached the cul-de-sac at the end of the road and ran around it a couple of times until I figured that Michael must have had time to get his things and make himself decent.

As I jogged back to the house, the light faded even more. The faster I ran, the quicker it dimmed. By the time I reached him, I glowed like a soft sunset, a distant glimmer, and Michael didn't cover his eyes this time. One hand hovered at his forehead, ready just in case, as I covered the distance between the street and our front door—what was left of it.

He dropped his hand as I approached. "That's better." He'd pulled on jeans and a shirt and found a cap as well. His duffel bag was slung across his shoulder. "We shouldn't stay long. They've had time to get back to base and get reinforcements."

"What about the girl?"

"She'll be fine, you know that. A recovery dome and a flat surface to straighten her spine, that's all it will take."

"Wow, this stuff really doesn't bother you."

He took my shoulders. "Nobody cares, Ava. Why should they? There's no permanent damage. The crazy thing is—this world needs you. It needs people who can die. Because now we might have to care about our lives. Each day would be precious."

He pinned me with his eyes. "The people around us, they've lost their hearts. They just don't know it." He swallowed. "But you and me, both of us, are the end of everything they believe in. Your brother died and I'm the one who killed him. We are a walking reminder that death might not be hundreds of years away anymore—it might be tomorrow. Some people are so sick, they're fascinated by that. Some people are so scared, they'll do anything to make us go away. Then there are other people like the Bashers, who see an opportunity to use you to kill their enemies. If your genetics are the key to figuring out death, they won't stop until they get hold of you."

I stayed frozen to the spot. I could hardly speak. "But, I thought they wanted to kill me because I'm weak." I stared at Michael as he let go of my arms, a chill forming in my heart. "I thought they wanted to kill me because they *could*. Because I'm one weak person they can actually, finally, get rid of."

Michael shook his head. "You're far more valuable than that."

The Basher boy's words rang in my mind. He'd said they wanted me alive. He hadn't killed me even though he had the chance. Cheyne had taken my blood and bone marrow and then let me go. All of them had opportunities to kill me if they wanted to, but they hadn't.

"But that means … If they can figure out a way to use me to kill people, that means it's true what everyone's saying about me. They're right about me." My heart stopped beating and my vision blurred. "I could kill people, Michael. They're right to be afraid of me."

Michael inhaled sharply and suddenly gathered me up in his arms, pulling me close. "No," he said, his voice determined as he crushed me close. "That's not true. It's not you, it's the people who want to use you."

"What about your dad? Is that what he and Cheyne want too?"

"I thought it was about nectar with my dad, but I honestly don't know anymore." His heart beat fast against my ear. "I'm not going to let them get hold of you. Not the Bashers, not my dad." He drew back so I could see his face. "Do you believe me?"

I wanted to, very badly.

"That girl will be hunting you again in a couple of hours." He looked up and down the street, as though he expected the Basher girl to appear at any moment. "We need to keep moving."

"Our ride is gone," I said, gesturing back at the smoldering car.

He didn't seem to care. "C'mon then. Shank's pony."

"What pony?"

"Shank's pony. It means on foot." He smiled for the first time in what seemed like forever as he released me, keeping hold of my hand. "It's something my granddad used to say." Instead of running down the street, he urged me around the side of our house toward the backyard.

"Wait a minute. Where are we going?"

"We have to stay away from the roads. We can cut through your backyard."

"But I have to meet Hannah."

He stopped so suddenly that I smacked into the back of him. The impact zapped me and made my head spin. The nectar was definitely wearing off.

"Explain."

"Hannah called. I arranged to meet her this morning. She's going to lend me some money. We need money..." My voice trailed off at the look on his face.

"Did you tell her where you were?"

She'd told me about spending the weekend at the recovery center. She'd said she wanted to see me. "She asked where I was, and I told her I was at my house."

The expression on his face made me wish I had somewhere to hide. I knew what he was thinking. I shook my head. "No."

"That girl back there. That Basher…"

I couldn't believe that my best friend would betray me like that. "That was not Hannah. She is not one of them."

"She said we'd recognize her."

"No, she said *you'd* recognize her. Not me." I glared, growing brighter with each word. There was no way the Basher girl was Hannah.

It couldn't be her because that would mean that everything about her was an act: the claim that she'd never died before, that she didn't know if she was a slow healer. The look of disgust on her face when she'd talked about the Bashers burying slow healers underground. Then I thought about how easily she'd talked about slow healers, how quickly she'd shrugged off the Basher's hatred. The first time I'd asked my parents about them, Mom had looked me in the eye and told me that some people were raised to hate anyone who was different.

I wondered if the look of disgust I'd seen on Hannah's face was about burying people or about the fact that some people healed slowly. I remembered the way the girl back at the explosion had shouted that the only way for everything to stop was for me to die, that Josh died because of me. That she wouldn't let her family end up in cells.

"If they found out where I was because of that phone call, it's because they were listening in. Not because she told them." My words sounded hollow in my ears. I wanted to believe they were true. I didn't want to believe that Hannah could have hurt me like that.

"I'm sorry, Ava, even if it wasn't her, there'll be more of them." He looked past my shoulder. "They want you alive and they aren't about to give up. Especially not with the Hazards looking for you too."

My skin prickled as his hand snaked around my arm, and we sprinted across the backyard to the high paling fence at the back. He dropped to the ground, bent one knee, and motioned for me to step up.

I eyed the height of the fence as I approached. Even with a leg up, there was no way I could get over it. "I can't fly."

He looked me over. "You're a dancer, aren't you?"

I nodded.

"Then leap."

I took a step back and pelted toward him, aiming my right foot onto the open palms on his knee. I pushed off and felt the extra lift as he propelled my foot higher. Air rushed past my face, light streaked, and I was over the fence. I landed safely on the other side, in a gap between two trees, surprised that I didn't break an ankle. That must have been the last of the nectar working. Wondering if the Hazards had evacuated this side of the street, I scanned the backyard I'd landed in and a flicker at the window told me they hadn't.

I turned to whisper to Michael through the fence and found that he'd already landed on one knee close by. He stumbled a little as he rose, as though he'd hurt something, but in the next instant, he was up and running, calling me to follow. I sprinted after him, dodging around a kid's bike and glancing up at the second-story window. I was sure there was a small face peeking over the window ledge.

"Michael!" I caught up to him at the side of the house. He paused, scanning the street with his keen eyes. In the distance, sirens wailed. "This house isn't empty. There's a kid in there."

"Seriously?"

"I'm sure of it."

"They must have stayed." He frowned. "That's strange—"

We both turned as the sirens became significantly louder.

"Hazards?" I asked.

"Fire engines." He grimaced. "There was a huge explosion, right?" He saw my expression. "Don't worry. It's a good thing. They're with City Council. There'll be questions. Reports to be written. It won't be swept under the carpet."

"Yeah. Maybe." I couldn't help the bad feeling in my stomach as I crept along the side of my neighbor's house, ducking beneath a window. I didn't think the local authorities would have enough clout to get in anyone's way.

Michael tugged on my arm. "I think we should head down there." He pointed to an empty block at the end of the street. There was a walkway through to a park on the other side. I started to nod, but something cold pressed into my ribs. I froze and didn't dare look. "Michael?"

His expression changed from enquiring to alarmed. "Hey, kid. You should put that down."

I swiveled my eyes without turning my head and saw young hands at the end of a long rifle. Energy burst through my system, causing the golden haze around me to brighten, igniting the last of the nectar. My brain told me to freeze, stay still, but my hand shot out, ready to grab the gun.

An older hand got to it first, snatching the gun up high and out of my reach. I followed the line of the rifle to its new handler, taking a precautionary step back as I did so.

The guy held the gun in a tight, familiar grip, hovering over the trigger. He had blond hair in dreadlocks that fell over his face and down his broad chest. Judging by the length, he was at least thirty years old.

With a twist of his lips, he said, "I'm Jeremiah. I've been waiting for you to hop over the fence."

～

He said, "I called the fire brigade. They'll slow that Hazard down—the one coming after you—but he'll be here in no time."

He was talking about Officer Reid.

The younger boy's eyes were huge, glued to the two of us. It didn't seem to bother him that I'd tried to take the gun from him. "We heard the explosion," he said. "The Bashers are after you."

I murmured. "Everyone is." All of them racing to get to me first. The Hazards to keep me out of the wrong hands. The Bashers to use me to kill. And Michael's dad and Cheyne, with Reid doing their bidding, I didn't know exactly what they wanted yet, but for now I had to assume their motives were the same as the Bashers.

Jeremiah cocked the gun, training it on Michael. "I know you aren't afraid of this. My little brother saw you walk out of that burning car, so I know, see. I know I can't touch you."

Michael's eyes flickered as though he was calculating how many split seconds it would take to get in front of me, imagining the impact and readying for the energy it would take to regenerate.

But the guy had already turned the gun on me. He said, "I could blow a good hole in her."

His brother tugged at his shirtsleeve. "No, Jerro. You can't shoot the angel."

The guy scowled, spitting on the ground. "That's no angel."

I wondered how much nectar was left in my system, how long it might last to protect me, help me heal, make me fast. I inched back toward Michael, feeling an intense urge to run. "What do you want?"

Without taking his eyes off us, Jeremiah inclined his head across the fence, back toward my house. "What happened to her?"

I shook my head. "Who?"

"Your neighbor. Mrs. Hubert."

I frowned at him. "She had her final death. It was the same day my brother died."

"No, she didn't." He glared at Michael. "She was like you,

mate." The way he said "mate" scattered shivers across my skin. He may as well have spat at Michael.

Michael took a step back, his face turning a peculiar shade of gray. "What do you—"

"You know what I'm talking about. She couldn't die. She was like you—one of the immortals. So why's she dead, huh?"

"Immortals? You're crazy," I said. "Everybody dies." I turned to Michael. "Right?"

He didn't say anything, just stared at the guy, who demanded, "That Hazard—the one who came here yesterday. He was here when the old lady disappeared."

Michael held up his hands as though he could halt the guy's voice mid-air. "Stop, what are you talking about?" He glanced at me and I could tell that we didn't have much time. The sirens were much closer now.

Jeremiah peered at us between his dreadlocks and I was surprised to discover that he had young eyes, hidden behind his long hair. It was a disguise. He wasn't much older than us.

He glared at me. "It used to be old people—like our grand-dad, and that old woman there—but we've seen things on the news. Homeless people, runaway kids." He leaned in close and there were threads of blood in his eyes, but he smelled like cinnamon, clean. "Your friend took our granddad and now we don't know where he is."

"Why would he do that?"

The fire engine shrieked. A car horn blared and Jeremiah's head snapped up. He shrugged and retreated. "You're gonna have to figure it out for yourself." As he spoke, he pulled his brother with him, backing away.

Michael edged closer to me, turning his body just slightly, ready to jump in front of me if the gun went off. A scowl grew across the other guy's face. Still moving backward, he lowered the gun, letting the tip slide down beside his muddy boots.

Michael gave me a gentle push toward the road. I wasn't about to protest. The sirens were at the end of the street and escape seemed like an impossible dream. The grass fled beneath my bare feet, faster as Michael propelled me away. Glancing back, Jeremiah had his arm around his brother, disappearing around the back of the house.

"What was he talking about?"

Michael shook his head as if he didn't know, but I was sure he did. Now wasn't the time to say so, as we ran for the vacant block.

CHAPTER 15

E REACHED THE path as the fire engines raced past us. Michael pulled me onward. There was no point stopping to see what happened. The further we got, the safer we would be. At least it seemed so. There was a part of me that wanted to run back—as though my world was normal again—and ask the firemen for help. They were meant to rescue people when they were trapped, get cats out of trees, put out fires, save things. Then again, so were the Hazards, but I didn't know how many of them were working with Reid and how many weren't, so for now I couldn't trust any of them. I ran on.

We made it through the park and beyond, and Michael whispered, "Stay cool," as we came out into a busy street. I kept my head down. *Just out for a jog,* I told myself, trying to pretend that I wasn't barefoot and wearing my pajamas.

We ran past a café, slowing to a quick walk along the pathway with tables and chairs on either side and cars cruising the street next to it. The scent of coffee and fruit toast tormented me, but not as much as the gentle buzz of conversation, the people eating, chatting like normal, ignoring the image of my charred house playing on the air screen in the background. Was that Reid, disappearing from the corner of the footage? The screen showed firemen and Hazards everywhere and I couldn't be sure it was him. Then, a picture of me appeared, and under it were written the words:

Suspected Basher.

Stunned, I ground to a halt as the newsreader's voice registered. "Speculation rises as Ava Holland, sister of dead teenager, Joshua Holland, disappeared from her home this morning after a car bomb exploded..."

Michael was a few steps ahead of me, and I wanted to call him back, but my voice wouldn't work. The newsreader continued. "After significant negotiations, we've acquired a still shot of the moment before Joshua Holland died, clearly showing him wearing a Basher uniform." I couldn't look, couldn't see Josh's face before his death, desperation turning to peace. "Which gives rise to questions about his family's involvement with the gangs."

Michael had stopped. He reached back for my hand, his face pale, seeing the footage. "We have to go." He inclined his head further down the road, keeping his voice low. "There's a surveillance drone coming this way. We have to backtrack."

I didn't breathe until we turned into a back alleyway. After a while, the streets blurred and mushed together. I tried not to look at other people as we passed. Michael seemed to know where he was going and sometimes we stopped jogging and walked, other times we flitted between buildings and down alleyways. We climbed a fire escape and crept over a roof. I tried not to think about what they were saying about me on the news or the possibility that Hannah was a Basher, but I heard her voice over and over, asking where I was.

"We should check the news again tonight. We need to know what they're saying."

He nodded but propelled me down an alleyway behind a set of shops. "If we can. Somehow."

Finally, my feet dragged. "I have to stop. Seriously. I'm *starving.*"

He slowed, planting his hands on his waist and shaking out his shoulders as his chest heaved. "Yeah, me too. Let's head down here first. There's a park up ahead. Only the drug addicts go there." He pointed to a nearby street and I realized that we'd left the nice side of town behind us. Hiding in a park with druggies didn't seem safest to me, but then nowhere was safe anymore. The trees might give us some shelter from the drones and at least addicts were less likely to pay attention to our faces.

Michael led me through a crumbling brick archway and into an overgrown area of trees and shrubs. "Park" seemed like the last thing this place was. I spied a filthy syringe left lying on the ground and asked, "Are those dangerous?"

"For you? Probably."

Suddenly my bare feet were a problem. "I need shoes."

"We have to do something about that. This way." He nudged me down the path into the heart of the wilderness and motioned toward a tree that was mostly obscured behind thick bushes. I sank down against it, rubbing my aching calves. It must have rained there recently—or else the sunlight never reached the ground—because the damp seeped through my pajama shorts straight away. I pulled my knees to my chest and tried to ignore it. "You've got food, right?"

He dropped his duffel bag on the ground and laughed. "Because I think of everything?"

"No. I mean … well, yes. At least…"

"Your belief in me is staggering, star girl. But, no, I don't have more food. We ate it all last night."

My shoulders sagged to the mushy earth and he smiled again. "But I do have money."

"Yeah?"

He dropped to his knees beside me and rummaged in the bag, withdrawing a clump of paper notes. "I raided my college fund; a.k.a my dad's safe."

"But … college is important."

"College is for normal people. There's no way I can have a normal life now."

I touched his shoulder. "I can't have a normal life, Michael. You could go home and explain…"

His expression was sharp, determined. "I'm not leaving you." He sighed and his voice softened. "Ava, if I went home right now, the first thing they'd do is pump me for information. They'd use me to find you. And then my dad would pack me up and send me someplace people don't know who I am. I can live the next few hundred years hoping nobody recognizes me. The Attorney-General was right: I killed someone—there's no normal for me anymore." He studied the notes in his hand, as though there was nothing more to say.

Inside his partly open duffel bag, I caught sight of a red cross. "You have a medical kit."

He followed my gaze. "I'm sorry, it's way more basic than the one we lost in the explosion, but there are bandages and plaster." He chewed his lip. "And methylated spirits."

I withdrew as he pulled his bag shut.

He shoved the money into his pocket. "What size shoe are you?"

My voice was small. "Six, but I didn't see any shoe shops along the way."

"I'll figure something out. I won't be long."

He jogged away before I had the chance to say anything else. A half hour later, I was starting to worry. My stomach growled and it sounded too loud in the quiet park.

I jumped at the sound of someone coming along the path, but it was the smell of food that brought me to my feet. Michael appeared with two paper bags full of fries and burgers. I wasn't sure what I was happiest to see—him or the food—especially when he drew a pair of sneakers out of a plastic bag and said, "There's a second-hand shop back there. Sorry it took so long. I had to keep a low profile."

"Thanks." I pulled the shoes onto my dirty feet. I didn't care that they used to be somebody else's if it meant protection from a sharp syringe.

He waited for me to stand up again and handed me the bag. "I got you some clothes too."

I pulled out the jeans and t-shirt and checked the sizes. "Nice guess. For someone without sisters, you seem pretty good at buying girl's stuff."

He shrugged and passed me some food. "Eat first. Try on clothes later."

I crammed the food into my mouth before he'd even finished the sentence. I ignored the growing buzz in my head. I was tired, that was all. When my stomach was full again, I put away the wrappers and tapped his arm. "Where will we go?"

"I don't know."

"Okay, let me rephrase: Where *can* we go?"

"I don't know."

"But—"

"Again with the staggering belief." He shook his head, and I noticed that his hair looked longer than the day before. It cast shadows across his face and his eyes, creating dark pools, making me wonder what was behind them.

"You must have some idea."

"Actually, no. Well…" He ran a hand across his forehead. "I was kind of thinking—"

His words blurred as I peered at his head. The dark strands of his hair looked like threads of ink splattered across his cheekbones. I balanced against the tree as my field of view suddenly swam. So did my stomach. "How fast does your hair grow?"

He stopped and gave me a strange look. "Same as everyone else, but each time I regenerate, it grows a few inches all at once."

"Wow, you must have to cut it all the time."

"Are we really talking about hair right now?"

I held up my free hand, hardly noticing that it trembled.

"Hey, you're the one who bought me clothes without even having to ask my size. These shoes fit, too. Kind of amazing really because everyone has different feet, you know. Some people have really narrow feet and some people—like me—they have wide feet, and some people hate having their toes squished. You know those pixie shoes everyone was wearing a while ago. I hated them! Did you hate them? You must have. Actually, you probably didn't wear them because you're a guy. Why am I talking so much right now?"

I tried to breathe, but my chest constricted.

Michael put down his food, rattling the paper bag, and it screeched in my head. I clamped my hands over my ears, sliding to the ground and ducking my head toward my knees.

"Ava?"

"Stop shouting."

"I'm not shouting."

I squeezed my eyes closed, really tight. I tried to take a deep breath and failed. Something bad rose inside my chest, and my hands shook so much they clattered next to my head. "Something's wrong."

I sensed him move around me and come back. Between the cracks in my fingers, I made out the shape of a jacket. He sat down beside me so slowly and quietly that it barely registered in my throbbing head. He didn't say anything as he lowered the jacket over my shoulders and put his arm around me. I didn't feel any zap when he touched me and that made me shudder.

"You're freezing."

I moved a finger to see a patch of his face—one eye and the corner of his mouth, worried, his lips all pressed together. He said, "I'm sorry I gave you so much nectar today. I wish I'd had another choice, I really do, but you were going to die."

"What's wrong with me?"

"I don't know, some kind of reaction. You can get through it. I'll help you."

I said the first thing that came into my head. "We have to get moving."

"We're not going anywhere right now. We can stay here for tonight. But…" He pulled away a little. "We need more food."

"Don't. Don't go anywhere. I don't know what will happen while you're gone."

"All right, but our dinner will have to be apples and oat bars."

I giggled, and it was a wretched sound. "We can pretend to be horses."

"No." Michael's arm tightened. "Don't do that. Don't pretend. You have to think about what's real. Do you understand? What's real. You're not an angel. You're not made of light. You're Ava. You're the girl who dances and builds walls. You're the girl who picked up the knife. You have to think about all that. Focus on that."

I didn't understand, but I listened anyway. "Tell me."

"You're Josh's sister. You walk to dance class. You're the girl who can die." His voice got all raw and he said only one more thing before he stopped talking. "You scare me."

I kept my head down as his arms remained around me in a solid circle, the only thing that wasn't shaking. I tried to focus on the calm of his words, soak up the new silence. I squeezed my arms against my knees, pulling them into my chest, and smothered my own breathing. He said I was the girl who built walls, so that's what I did.

For the next ten minutes, I built a wall, one block at a time, until it was eye height in my mind. The pressure on my brain lifted a fraction. It was enough for more of his words to register because something struck me as really strange. I unfurled to find him watching me, his arm still resting across my shoulders.

I bit down hard on my lip, not sure if the words would come out straight. "How did you know about the walls?"

It was clearly not what he was expecting, but a small measure of relief passed across his face. "Get better and I'll tell you."

"Tell me how to get better."

"Believe in yourself."

That was it? I tried to shake my head, but it was already shaking, so that seemed pretty pointless. "I have to get moving."

He took my shoulders as if he was going to wrestle me if he had to. "We can't go anywhere while you're like this."

"That's not what I mean." I struggled to make him understand. "Back there. After the explosion, I jogged up and down the street and the nectar started to go away—the effects of it, I mean. Then when we were running, before we got here, I felt okay. Now that we've stopped, it's getting worse. I have to move. I have to shake it off."

"Well, you can't go running laps around here. You'll stir up the addicts." He shot a hand through his hair. The look on his face was scared and worried at the same time. Then his expression cleared. "You could dance for me."

I choked back a laugh that came out as half a sob. "Yeah, sorry, I left my pole back at my burned-down house."

"No, I'm serious. I never saw you dance." He pulled me upward. I dropped his jacket next to the tree as my body lifted, weightless in his arms. He spun me outward, and then back again, as though he'd had dance lessons himself.

I smiled despite myself. "You're kidding."

"What's that look for?" He paused, before taking hold of my waist and moving me backward to the rhythm of a ballroom waltz. "A guy isn't supposed to know how to dance?"

"*You're* not supposed to know how to dance."

"Why not?" He shrugged as he spun me around again. "Mom taught me." He pulled me back against him, but now his face was pensive, the lightness gone. "That was before she left."

His body was warm against mine, his hands as strong as any trained dancer, strong enough to crush me, but his hold was so gentle it brought tears to my eyes. If only I could go back to the moment his hands held the knife and step between him and my brother.

He reached out to stroke the side of my face and I realized that he was wiping a tear from my cheek, his expression as drawn and damaged as I felt. Dancing with him had dulled the buzzing of every cell, the movement lulling me into thinking there was nothing wrong with me.

I pushed away from him. "I can't dance anymore. Why don't you just let me run laps around this tree or something?"

He was back to wary and removed. "Who says you can't dance?"

I scrunched up my shoulders. "Everybody. Ms. White. If I hurt myself..."

He laughed so loudly that it hurt my ears. "Hurt yourself? Ava, your legs were blown off today. I don't think it gets any worse than that."

I looked down at the ground—at my new feet encased in second-hand shoes. They wanted to move, to dance, to *breathe*.

Michael didn't touch me, but his voice was a whisper against my heart. "Nobody can tell you to stop dancing. It's your choice."

CHAPTER 16

"IF I END up with a syringe stuck in my hands, it will be your fault."

"What are you talking about—your hands? You've got shoes on."

"Hah! You were right when you said you'd never seen me dance." Just to show him, I did a standing backflip. It was a stupid thing to do without stretching first, but my body didn't seem to mind. Instead, it felt good, the rush of air and the sense of space—the illusion of control. I expected to wobble and crash on the landing, but I didn't. So I tried another one. It worked and I smiled.

I started to run through one of my old routines—one of the really technical ones where I had to get everything right. I didn't though. I stopped every time I got something wrong and ran over the moves, step by step, again and again. The repetition soothed, the movement calmed. I focused on every bend, every stretch, the finest point of my feet and the broadest span of my arms, the quickest spin, the slowest split. I lost count of the number of times I tempted death-by-diseased-syringe when I planted a part of my body on the ground. I leaped, spun, extended, kicked and twisted my body into a glorious pretzel, only to slide out of it, jump and spin again, sliding through the murky grass as if it was the smoothest dance floor. My lungs pounded out air, but my heart beat slower than I thought possible. I forgot all about nectar and the agitation of running and the horror of losing my legs. I even forgot Michael was there.

I came to a quiet stop and found him leaning up against the tree. I was suddenly transported back to the Terminal, to the Mirror Room. Except this time Michael didn't look bored.

"Your dad was right. You do dance like a moonbeam." He sauntered over to me, pushing my hair out of my face and running his hand through it. "Your hair grew, too."

He let the strands drop over my shoulder and I could see how much it had grown: at least five inches since that morning. A prickle of fear crept up my spine as his hand lingered over my shoulder, not quite brushing my neck. My mouth was suddenly dry, my voice a bare whisper. "Do you think the nectar made my hair grow when I healed?"

He nodded. "Heaps." But he looked at me very intently as if nectar and its effects on my hair were the last thing on his mind. As if he wanted to draw the deepest thoughts out of my head and claim them.

"Ava..." His other hand captured my waist. This time when he touched me, I felt it—the *zap*.

I never thought I'd be so happy to feel that sharp sting. I was myself again. I couldn't help but smile and wince at the same time. He must have caught the wince because he paused, giving me the chance to break away from him.

I took a step back. "You said you'd tell me about walls."

His face fell as if he'd forgotten all about it. As if he'd *wanted* to forget all about it.

"You said you'd tell me how you knew."

"Yeah ... um..." He looked down at his feet, shuffled a bit, and then looked at his hands, not meeting my eyes. "How about you ask me something else instead."

I frowned, not liking the evasion. "Something else? But you promised."

He looked around again as if he'd find something to distract me. He must have come up empty because finally, he met my eyes. "Ask me something else. Please?'

I didn't want to ask him something else, but the look on his face made my think twice about pressing him. He probably thought I wouldn't be okay, that I wouldn't get better, so he'd never have to tell me how he knew what was inside my head. Still, I wasn't about to let him get away that easily. I folded my arms. "All right then, what did that guy back there—Jeremiah— what did he mean about you being an immortal?"

Michael paused, and I glared. "Don't skip out on me."

He exhaled. "Did you know that some ancient Seversandian tribes used to ritually kill their babies?"

"You've got to be joking. That's even worse than Implosion."

"They believed it was necessary to weed out the weak. To guard against extinction."

"Okay. That's pretty horrible, but it doesn't answer my question." I scowled at him. "You can't get out of two questions."

"I'm getting there."

I nodded to let him know I'd listen.

"Those who didn't regenerate fast enough were buried in specially-made tombs and left to fall into a death-sleep."

My eyebrows rose. There was something on the news once about a kid who wandered away from his parents in the national park without food or water. His body had shut down into some kind of preservation state—they called it a coma— not dead, but not alive either. Apparently, he could have stayed that way for a hundred years before his body died.

Michael continued. "Only the fast healers were allowed to live with the tribe. It was survival of the strongest."

"That sounds a lot like the Bashers," I said.

"The Bashers think they're descended from the tribes. They want to recreate a society where only the strongest survive." He slid to the ground and rested against the tree. "Dad used to talk about the tribes. He was an anthropologist before he went into big business. He did his Ph.D. on tribal culture. He even went to Seversand on some international goodwill exchange years ago—some of their academics came here to study how we manage our resources and he got to go there and study their military culture. He was totally into observing the biological basis for killing. It's why he helped design the Terminal. When I was small, he used to call me his little warrior. He called me one of the immortals." He caught my eye. "Crazy, right?"

I knelt beside him and reached out to touch his shoulder, but he shrugged away from me as if he couldn't stand to be touched.

"When I was a kid I thought it was talk. But the thing is … the tribes … with what they did, after a while, there weren't any slow healers left. They got stronger and stronger and people lived for hundreds of years. Not just 400 like most people do. But 700, 800. Nothing made them sick, nothing hurt them. They were the closest thing to immortal."

He picked at the hem of his pants. "The Bashers wanted me to join them, but I said no. As if I would even think about it after what they did to my family. But sometimes I wonder if I'd joined them … maybe I could have protected my brother."

The Basher girl back at my home had said that Michael's kind were everything the Bashers were fighting for. If he was immortal, they would see him as the strongest, the most worthy. And yet, he'd rejected them. "You don't know that. They would have expected you to hurt other people just like your brother."

He shrugged again as if it didn't matter. "Maybe I'll live a long time. Maybe I won't. But that's what Jeremiah meant."

I didn't let him shake me off this time. "It's okay." I met his eyes. "Really." I didn't know how to tell him that he and I were opposite sides of the coin—opposite ends of the spectrum. In a perfect world, maybe we would balance each other out. I struggled for the words and finally found them. "I'm a freak, too."

He looked at me with something dark in the back of his eyes.

His face reminded me of a storm right before the first thunder. Then a spark lit behind his expression and a smile broke through. "We're both just freaks of nature, huh."

I pulled my knees up to my chest. "I feel much better than before. Do you think we should get moving?"

"I don't know, Ava. Let's just stay put for the rest of the evening. Just in case. Okay?"

I stared out at the thick bushes and the cracked concrete pathway running through them. I didn't like the idea of staying. Now that I wasn't out of my mind, the park was beginning to give me the creeps. Before I could say anything, someone lurched out of a bush a few feet away. He had tan arms, a weathered face, and scraggly gray hair, but he didn't notice us as he lumbered past, fixated on something I was sure nobody else would ever see.

I waited for the stranger to disappear back into the trees before I tugged on Michael's arm. "Are you sure we shouldn't keep moving today?"

"We could, but the next safe place is a long way from here on foot. We should start out in the morning."

"You mean there's actually a 'safe' place waiting for us out there?" The corner of my mouth twitched upward, trying really hard to lighten the weight that settled in my chest.

He rubbed his jaw. "Starsgard," he blurted, as though he'd been thinking about it a lot longer than he'd wanted to say. "I think that's where we should go."

I frowned. "Across the border?"

"Nobody can follow us or make us come back. Drones can't enter their airspace."

"But it's…" *So far away.* Even if we made it that far, we had no way of knowing whether they'd let us in. Starsgard was locked down, guarded against Evereach on one side and Seversand on the other. I remembered the picture plastered outside the dance studio, of the towers in the background, so tall they might actually touch the stars.

"We can make it." He took my hand. "We just have to take it one day at a time and we'll get there. I don't know for sure, but I think that's where my mom went. Look." He dug around in his bag and handed me a small square of paper. "A year after she left, I got this in the mail, no return address. My brother was always drawing things—fish, lizards, birds, mountains—I'd know his pictures anywhere."

I studied the simple sketch of a mountaintop covered in snow, a single star drawn in the center.

Michael said, "I've heard of people being granted political asylum there. Not very often, but there was something on the news the other day, some hacker the government wants, but there's no extradition treaty with Starsgard. Once we're there, there's nothing anyone here can do to force us to come back, and if Mom's there, they'll let us in. It's the only chance we have, but it's a good chance. I know it."

"Okay." I turned from the certainty and determination in his eyes, trying to quiet the doubt inside me and failing as dismally as if I'd tried to stop the buzzing of his skin on mine. I stooped to the clothes spread out across his duffel bag. "I'm getting changed behind this tree. Keep your eyes closed."

"Don't stress, star girl. You're safe with me."

We ate oat bars and apples for dinner and I didn't pretend to be a horse. I hung my pajamas out to dry over a nearby tree branch and wondered why he wouldn't tell me how he knew about walls. I guessed I'd never know like so many things in my life. At one point, he collected wood and twigs and set about making a small fire. He produced a bag of marshmallows with a grin.

"And you said you don't plan for everything." I scoffed.

Still, my stomach rumbled louder than I wanted to acknowledge and, after he put out the fire so it wouldn't attract attention in the dark, he promised to get more food in the morning.

"Shank's pony at the crack of dawn," he said, rolling out a sleeping bag.

I eyed the bag. "You got two of those?"

"Nup." Without another word, he shimmied into it, wedging himself back against the seam and leaving a space at the front on the side of the zip.

I put my hands on my hips. "I'm not sleeping in there with you."

"I don't snore."

"I know that already."

He pummeled the ground under his head, as though that would make it more comfortable. His voice got serious. "You're safer in here with me, than you are out there. Plus, the bugs won't bite in here."

"Bugs don't worry me."

"Suit yourself." He started to zip up the bag and I hugged myself, wondering if I could find a blanket in that duffel bag of his. Somehow I didn't think so. I huffed and rushed over before he finished zipping the blanket all the way up. "Move over. Keep your hands to yourself."

He didn't say anything as I slid inside the bag, trying not to touch any part of his body, which was an almost impossible feat. Just when I'd managed it, he reached his arm around me and dropped it over my shoulders. I stopped breathing, tingling all through my neck and back. His hand reached for the top of the zipper and rested there, curled around the metal loop, right at the level of my chest.

I stayed frozen, eyeing his hand with distrust, ignoring the part of me that didn't want him to take his arm away. My voice was sharp. "What are you doing?"

"Have you ever tried to get out of a sleeping bag really fast?"

"No."

"Well, it's super difficult, so don't knock the hand on the zipper."

I snorted, trying to relax. "There's something rude about what you just said, I know it."

He laughed, and the sleeping bag jiggled. "I never say anything right when I'm around you." He took a deep breath. "I'm going to stop talking now."

He did, and I missed his voice.

My arm stung. I tried to swim up, toward the metallic thud that repeated itself over and over again. I couldn't quite locate it—close or far away, up or out there somewhere. All I knew was that it was wrong. That sound didn't belong in a park.

The air went *whoomp* and my back hurt all of a sudden. The cold flooded in. Michael shouted my name.

I was half-crouched, partly out of the sleeping bag. He was on his feet near me, struggling in the shadows. I tried to focus. I thought for a second that I didn't have my eyes open. It was all a dream: the shapes converging on us, whoever had hold of Michael, the elongated, black and gold drone at the corner of my eye.

There was another *whoomp*, much closer this time. It reminded me of the exploding missile that destroyed Michael's car and very nearly destroyed us, too. I expected to see flames, burning trees, the air filled with floating leaves.

The only thing that happened was my back and arm ached, followed by a crawling sensation under my skin and my brain stopped working. I half-turned as Michael kicked his way out of the stranglehold of two men. One of them was Reid.

I tried to get up, to help him, but my legs wouldn't work. I checked them, petrified that I'd lost my legs after all, but I touched them all the way to my knees, my calves—

Then Michael was beside me. He gripped my arm, right where it throbbed, looking from the thing that stuck out of me, up into my eyes. "Oh, no, Ava."

My words slurred. "Something bit me. I thought you said there'd be no bugs."

"I'm sorry, Ava. They've tranq'd you."

"I can't move." I found out how untrue that was when I fell forward onto my face.

He pulled at the dart in my arm, cursing. His hand pressed on my back, right where it ached, trying to turn me over. "There's something else. It's right under your skin and I can see…" His eyes went wide. "I've seen these before. They've given you nectar and it's got—"

Running boots filled my vision. Reid reached us and Michael's hand left my spine.

As the air pumped around me, Reid dragged Michael back, struggling, far away from me, capturing his arms this time and locking them into a glinting restraint.

Michael shouted, "Ava! It's got a tracker!" before they pulled a bag over his head.

Officers swarmed Michael and dragged him with them. Two men crashed down—he must have kicked them—and clambered back to their feet, dragging him to the machine with the pounding rotor blades. Michael shouted, they were all shouting, but his voice became more and more obscured until there was only the thud of metal blades slicing the air. A high-pitched whir shrieked through the park as the helicopter rose up and up, taking Michael away from me. Leaving me behind in the dark.

CHAPTER 17

MY HEAD RESTED half on the sleeping bag, half on the wet ground. My legs had bent into a kneeling crouch under me, arms twisted out at my sides. The night air chilled my skin and the silence chilled my mind. They took Michael but left me behind. I couldn't understand why. Why would they leave me behind? Just like when my parents left, they could have taken me in, right then, but they hadn't, and it didn't make sense.

The rustle of nearby bushes drew my attention. A pair of eyes watched me, the face shadowed. He didn't move toward me, but the more I stared at him, the clearer his outline became until I realized he was sitting cross-legged between the branches of the scraggly bush. For the next ten minutes, he stared as though he was waiting to see what I'd do. Then he rose out of the bush and crept toward me, keeping to the line of trees at first, edging into the small clearing when I didn't respond. *Couldn't* respond.

It was the drug addict who'd passed us earlier, his face shriveled like a prune.

He shuffled up to me, a little bit at a time, stopping and waiting and then moving toward me again until his foot rested an inch away from my face. His boot smelled of sewerage and my stomach turned. He nudged my cheek with a grimy toe and watched me blink.

It was just like when Cheyne had shot me at the recovery center. I could still feel, even though I couldn't move. Michael had dropped the dart right at eye-level, with the end pointing at my cheek. The addict crouched over it, glanced at my face, and whisked the dart up into his palms. He turned it over and over and finally licked the end. He screwed up his face and bent down to examine me again.

I wanted to tell him, *it doesn't have drugs in it. Leave me alone.*

He stuck out his tongue, running it between his teeth as though he'd eaten a sour lemon. "Sweet, sweetie. Nectar. Nice nectar?"

Nectar? How did he know about it? My throat constricted with the effort to speak. *Leave me alone, leave me alone, leave me alone.* He touched my back, plucking at my clothes, as though he'd find some on me. I gathered that he didn't when he gave me a kick in my side. Except that he was laughing, in a weird, excited sort of way.

The air whooshed out of my mouth, but that was the only reaction my body could make to the throbbing that remained after another kick landed in my ribs. To my horror, he lay down next to me, putting his face right next to mine, so close I saw the chip in his front tooth.

"Life is nectar," he said, flapping his hand at our surroundings. "Nectar is tree." He smiled and his swollen gums bulged beneath stretched lips. "Nectar means life." He stroked my hair with his grubby fingers. "No nectar. No life."

Something sharp touched my side. It stung much worse than the dart had. I tried to see what he was doing, but all I knew was his hand was moving.

He said, "Nectar inside. Inside is nectar."

My heart was going to explode. The pounding was too loud

in my ears. He was going to cut me open looking for nectar. *Leave me alone, leave me alone,* "Leave me alone!"

The sharp sting stopped. He jerked away from me, poised with what I now saw was a rusty knife. I was as surprised as he was. I'd spoken. It was slurred, that was for sure, but I'd got the words out. I focused every ounce of energy I had into my mouth. "Get away. Or I will tear you apart."

He drew back into a crouch. The knife trembled in his hands.

I hissed at him because it was the only sound I could make after the effort of speaking. The knife disappeared somewhere on his person. He crouched even lower, reaching out toward me, placating. "Sorry, sweetie. Sorry tree. Nectar is life."

I managed a final shout and put every bit of threat into it. "Get away!" Then my throat closed up, spasms trembling down my neck.

He backed off, scraping his knees along the grass, reaching the concrete pathway that way, where he jumped up and ran into the bushes.

I closed my eyes in relief, but I knew he'd be back. He wanted nectar—somehow he knew what it was—and Michael said they'd given it to me. I had to move. I had to.

I started small, focusing on the first joint of my little finger. It was crushed under me, curved toward my chest. The tip of my finger twitched as I attempted to straighten it. I tried again, and this time it obeyed. I groaned with relief and checked to see if the drug addict was back, but if he lurked in the bushes, I couldn't see him. I told myself to hurry, working through the other joints of my little finger. By the time I reached my hand, the rest of my fingers had released, movement seeping back into my wrist, my elbow, and finally my shoulder. I regained enough control to push up from the ground and stretch my neck, easing it from side to side until I was as certain as possible that it wouldn't seize up.

Resting down again, I hazarded to check the status of my

back where he'd cut me. It was higher up than I first thought. The pain radiated down to my side, but as I ventured up, seeking the spot, I found I could barely reach it. I tried angling my other arm over, but the wound was right between my shoulder blades. With a final determined stretch, my fingertips touched something hard. It was definitely not my bones, but some kind of lump under my skin.

I remembered the *whoomp*, the black drone, and Michael's wide eyes as he checked my back and said they'd given me nectar. He'd shouted something about a tracker. I remembered him telling me his dad worked on tranquilizers and tracking technology as well as nectar. I tried to reach the lump again and managed to touch the edge of it. It was hard, foreign, and as I pressed it, it vibrated under my fingertips as if it was emitting a low-level hum. Could they have shot an ampule of nectar into me? Did such a thing exist? Was the tracker inside it? Maybe I should have let the addict have it...

Something crept through the bushes. The addict was back. The thought of staying made my heart go cold. Even though I wanted the device out of me, he could just as easily slip the knife between my ribs and kill me in the process.

Shaking my legs, I wriggled the feeling back into my toes. The concentration of paralytic must have been in my arms and torso because my legs responded much more quickly. I scrambled to my feet and snatched up the sleeping bag, seeking around for Michael's duffel bag. To my surprise, they'd left it beside the tree. I needed to treat it with suspicion, but right then I didn't have the luxury of time. The shape of the addict appeared around the bushes, startled as I hurled a rock at him. I raced into the dark, my heart up in my throat.

Michael had guided me before. I didn't know this part of the city. I'd never been this way. I didn't even know how to get out of the park, although I was pretty sure I could scale any fence right then, I had enough fear pumping to get me anywhere. The question was where.

I veered across the vacant stretch where the helicopter had landed. Lights sparkled through the branches beyond. The addict might follow me out, I couldn't be sure, but staying in the trees felt like the worst thing I could do.

The sleeping bag slapped my legs and Michael's duffel bag was heavier than I thought it would be, but I ignored them both as I pressed through the nearest break in the tree line. Beyond it, there were more trees. No path.

Tree is nectar. Whatever the addict meant, maybe I could use the trees to slow him down.

Another crash behind me—closer this time—spurred me on through the thick tangle of greenery. Halfway through, the sleeping bag got caught. I tugged hard, something gave, and a branch snapped back—straight into a person-shaped shadow.

At the same time, a creature screeched at my ear and suddenly the air was filled with black, flying things. They whizzed past my face and torso. Sharp things pierced my skin. I tried to shield my face from claws and teeth. The addict wasn't fairing any better, shrieking on the other side of the branches. Desperate to clear the tree, I shielded my face and pushed through sideward, shoving through debris, scraping my arms.

My vision cleared as the flying creatures hurtled up and away. Hundreds of bats circled and beat the air above. Something dropped, thudding onto my foot, and I smelled rotting fruit.

The bats would buy me time. I grabbed the sleeping bag and flung the duffel bag across my shoulder, already running.

A shout behind me told me that, despite the bats, he was way too close.

Something latched onto the duffel bag and yanked hard. "Nectar!"

Without a second thought, I let the bag go and dashed across the grass. The darkness lifted—sunrise was on the way— and I made out the shape of a path. Just as I reached the edge, something slammed into my back and the air left my lungs. I fell, not getting my arms under me in time. Only the sleeping bag broke my fall and stopped me cracking my jaw open on the concrete. The weight stayed on me, shoving down hard as I tried to push up. I rocked and tried to roll my body over, but two grimy hands clutched my neck. The fingers squeezed tighter and tighter. Desperate for air, I forced my arm out from under me and thumped at the knee on one side of me, only then seeing that he'd dropped the knife when he started strangling me.

If I stretched, I'd reach it.

Black spots appeared in my vision and grew. Everything went hazy. My fingers closed over something. I didn't know if it was the knife. I drove it backward, sensing that something connected, but he didn't even react. His hands clenched deeper and deeper into my windpipe. Something ruptured in my throat and I couldn't breathe anymore.

I gasped. My shoulders were numb, my arms dead. I must have dropped the knife, it was impossible to tell. Blackness swirled over me and then there was nothing.

A silence. Not deep, not shallow, not anything.

Every particle dispersed and disappeared. Gone without a single thought or a single sound.

A tiny trickle of warmth drew me forward like a dewdrop warming in the sun.

Consciousness burst back into my body, sizzling through my nerve endings. I heaved upward, thrashing with every part of my body, kicking and punching. I was alive and I wasn't going to let my life go.

He'd released my neck and my back stung again. Catching him off-balance, I lurched sideways. His weight lifted. He thudded and howled onto the grass. "Sweetie!"

The sting left my back—fast. It was the nectar doing its

work, healing me, but I couldn't let him get back up again. I couldn't let him grab me again.

When I was seven years old, I'd taken tap dance lessons. I'd learned to stomp and my legs were even stronger now. I ran at him, kicking straight toward his face and knocking a couple of teeth flying across the grass as he howled. I snatched one up before it could reattach, and at the same time, I sought Michael's bag, lying at the edge of the trees ten feet away, determined to get it back.

"Hey, you!" I shouted, holding his tooth in my fist. "You want nectar, I've got nectar."

He stopped yelling, his hand across his mouth, gray eyes meeting mine.

I inclined my head across the grass, backing up toward the duffel bag. "It's in there. You let me get it, and I'll give it to you. Then you leave me alone. You understand?"

He grinned.

I slid across the grass, not taking my eyes off him. He struggled to his knees, scrambling for his teeth. While he was occupied with fitting them back where they belonged, I risked a glance backward and located the bag. I pivoted back fast and felt for the zip. My other hand clutched his remaining tooth. I wrenched open the bag and rummaged around, panic rising when it took me forever to find that little brown bottle Michael had used on me.

Methylated spirits.

My fingers closed around the cold glass and I resisted the urge to close my eyes with relief. The addict was sitting quietly on the grass, watching me now. One finger prodded a gap in his front teeth.

I lifted the bottle high. "See? Full of nectar." I hefted the bag over my shoulder, wondering if I'd get away with it. I'd have to sacrifice the sleeping bag—I'd never get away with both—but I didn't have a choice. I held up my other fist. "You'll get your tooth back, too. If you stay there. Understand?"

I edged around past him, back to the path. The bats were settling into the fruit tree, their screeches lowering.

When I reached the path and was as far away from him as I dared, I stopped and lifted my hand. He'd obeyed me that far, his face glued to the bottle, eyes flitting to my other hand. The tooth was warm, creating a gentle tingle inside the cage of my fist.

"Catch!" I threw the bottle first and the tooth second. Both in different directions, hoping that it would give me enough time to get away. The addict launched himself for the nectar, catching it before it hit the grass.

Down the concrete pathway, with fruit trees full of bats, I sprinted another two minutes before I shot out onto a busy street.

I skidded to a stop just before I ran out onto the road. A car swerved and beeped. Another raced past behind it. I blinked at the six-lane motorway, trying to place myself. I was sure Michael and I had been heading north, but the motorway led to the inner-city bypass, which led to the Terminal. I didn't have time to figure it out. I ran to where the bushland stretched into the distance, keeping to the tree line to avoid exposure.

A car beeped and there was the addict behind me, swaying at the edge of the road, vehicles swerving to avoid him. He held up the bottle like a final salute to the world and put it to his mouth, gulping it down. Glass shattered around him as he dropped it. His knees buckled and he toppled to the side.

I paused mid-escape, wondering if he was dead. Methylated spirits could very well have been poison for all I knew, and he'd drunk the whole thing in one go. Trying not to care, I sprinted up the road, staying just inside the trees.

The sky lightened as I followed the motorway to a crest that opened out onto a rise with the city in the valley. The Terminal building soared in the middle, all glittering metal in the early morning sun. I shrank back into the trees. I'd definitely chosen the wrong direction.

I didn't want to believe that Michael would have brought me this way—so close to the most dangerous part of the city. He'd said we should go north, to Starsgard. But then I saw the bridge over the river across to my far right. The winding water shimmered behind the Terminal, snaking along behind it and away. Far away. Ferries left the city bridge every hour and from there I could go anywhere, inland or out to the coast, it was my choice. This must have been what Michael had planned.

Scrambling down the road again, I pictured the nearest motorway exit. As soon as I found somewhere safe to stop, I'd figure out how to get the ampule out of my back. If I focused on the gravel and the rising sun, maybe I wouldn't think too much about it. Maybe I could stop the pressing panic. Maybe I could stop thinking about Michael and where they'd taken him. For another twenty minutes, I walked and blocked everything out of my mind, staying in the quiet shadows at the edge of the trees, away from the rushing cars.

Reaching the road that would take me to the bridge, I headed down the slope to a stretch of industrial buildings. I crunched across broken glass to the front of an old motor mechanic's shop. The place was deserted.

Basher graffiti sprawled across the brick fascia in green and black, words obscured but still legible: *Bury the weak.*

Shuddering, I slid behind a concrete pillar in the entrance, the best hideout I could find for the minute. It wouldn't be long before this place was teeming with people and cars. I had maybe a half hour to rest.

The lump in my back was difficult to reach. I had to hunch up my left shoulder and twist and stretch. It was still there, right in the middle between my shoulder blade and spine. It was smooth and at least an inch long, lying parallel with my backbone. I crunched my teeth together. A chill seeped down my back and out to my clammy hands at the thought of digging it out myself.

I tried to control my breathing, clenching and unclenching

my hands, focusing on the ridges of my fingernails. I had to do it myself. I *would* do it myself. Dashing out, I snatched up a piece of beer bottle glass and hurried back behind the pillar. Before I could think any more about it, I twisted and tried to reach the lump on my back.

I bit my lip and hacked at it, and … the edges of my skin pulled toward each other before I'd even finished. I tried again, cutting as fast as I could, but it wasn't fast enough. My skin healed over in an instant, leaving me icy. I dropped into an agonized crouch against the concrete pillar. I didn't know what to do. The ampule would keep me alive, but if they were tracking me, then I was already a prisoner.

At the same time, Michael's bag beeped.

I swung, poised as I realized that I'd forgotten to check it. Another rush of dread washed over me, followed by the same trickle of warmth down my spine that I'd sensed when the addict strangled me. I located it this time, coming from the thing in my back. Nectar. My body knew it was in danger. I stayed, half-crouched, frozen, not knowing what to do as the bag clicked.

There was a pause, so long that I thought about a thousand things—Josh's white lips as he died, the look on Michael's face when he turned to me after the fight, my mom whispering good-bye, Hannah asking me where I was.

One last thought rushed through my mind. Michael telling me about walls, refusing to tell me how he knew.

His bag exploded.

CHAPTER 18

WAVES OF ORANGE HEAT washed over me. The concrete pillar I'd hidden behind fractured. One chunk of rock followed by many more, lit up golden in the fire, pelted the air and my body. My skin split in a hundred different places, a multitude of hairline cracks that closed as soon as they opened. Then more. As fast as the wounds appeared, my body healed them. I didn't know if I was screaming because the world had gone silent. Somewhere inside the building there must have been a gas bottle because a cascade of explosions suddenly ripped through me. More glass. More metal. More blood suspended that never left the surface of my skin.

The roof came down and that was when I made a leap for it. Out into the air, into space, with fire and bricks bursting around me.

I thwacked into something softer than gravel. Someone held me tight.

Michael pulled me down, waiting for the heat to end, for the flames to die. I sought his eyes, holding on to his shoulders, struggling to believe he was there. He came back, he must have escaped, but the look on his face told me it wasn't so. Too soon, he stood up and pushed me away from him.

"Michael…"

"They want you to…" His jaw ticked. "They want me to tell you to come in."

I looked around, ready for uniforms and wasps, but it was just him with that same haunted look on his face that I'd seen a hundred times before, something in the back of his eyes that curled up tight and never let go.

He said, "I'm not alone, Ava. We can't run this time. They want you to come in or they'll take you in."

"Why now? Why not last night? Why not days ago?"

"It took them that long to make the ampule. Once they shot you with it, they planted the bomb in my bag so you'd be hurt and it would trigger the nectar. It's settled into your body now." He took a step toward me, grabbing my arm in a fierce grip. "They'll use it to control you." As soon as the words were out of his mouth, he cried out, his face scrunched up in pain.

"Michael, what have they done to you?"

"Why didn't you get rid of it?"

I wanted to tell him about the addict, but all I said was, "I couldn't reach."

His expression softened and became wry. "Yeah. They think of everything." The pain on his face lessened. "I couldn't reach mine either." He pulled up the back of his shirt, all the way up to his neck. His lump was red and surrounded by scratches and welts. I stared at the implant and the wounds around it, thinking I couldn't be seeing straight. He should have healed already…

I wanted to touch him, but I stopped before my fingers connected. "Why have they given you nectar? You don't need it."

"It's not nectar." He dropped his shirt. "They gave me you. Your mortality."

I wrenched my hand away. "I don't understand."

He shook his head. "I can't even begin to…"

I shook my head, over and over, trying to deny what I saw: the cut on his cheek, the bruise at the base of his eye, the scratches across his arms. He shrugged his shoulders as if it didn't matter.

"Michael." I touched him. No zap. None at all. "That's not possible."

"Believe it, star girl." He winced, tried to smile, an expression that contorted his face. "I'm really sorry about the methylated spirits. I didn't realize how much it kept hurting."

"It's okay. That bottle saved my life. What will they do to you if I don't come in?"

"My dad's not happy. Cheyne said he won't protect me. The thing is, Ava, you shouldn't either. I don't deserve it."

A lump formed in my throat. "Is this about Josh? You know that wasn't your fault."

"No. It's not about Josh." He suddenly gritted his teeth. He was hurting again, I could see it, as though every time he tried to tell me something important he was punished for it. He dropped to his knees—I followed him down, trying to see his eyes, to see what he wanted to tell me—and his voice became a whisper. "It's about the walls."

Then he writhed and screamed and crushed his head between his hands.

"Michael! What are they doing to you?"

He collapsed all the way to the ground, almost in a ball, locked and stiff. He gasped and I ached for him. "Back of my neck."

I pushed aside his hair. At the base of his head, in between the vertebrae of his spine, was a second lump.

He grinned, tears running down his face. "Electrocution. I tried to rip it out, but they turned it on until I blacked out. They attached it to my nerves and told me if I remove it, my legs will stop working. I won't be able to walk again. It's no use. You should get out of here while you—" His voice rose into another scream. He curled tighter, his arms and legs trembling in fits.

"Stop!" I shouted as loud as I could, hoping that wherever they were, they could hear me. "Stop! I'll come in."

Michael stopped screaming, but his body trembled and jolted in the aftershocks. I waited, standing over him, daring them to hurt him again. A truck rumbled in fast from our left.

He looked up at me, his face covered in sweat. There was something new in his expression, a strange mix of disbelief and gratitude. "What are you going to do, Ava?" he asked, his voice low. "Be my human shield?"

He'd spat out bullets for me, walked from a burning car. I tried to smile but failed. I took his hand and helped him to his feet, bearing most of his weight as more tremors racked his body. I sensed the rippling in his skin, a different kind of electricity, not the living kind that brought regeneration, but the bad kind that took life away. It was wrong. It shouldn't be in his body. Just like my own ampule, I would find a way to remove his, too. "If I have to be."

"I don't know how much time we have." His eyes met mine, sunlight reflecting off them. He looked as if he wanted to tell me something, but I hurried to interrupt him.

"Don't say anything else. They'll just hurt you for it."

"It's not something I want to say." He dropped his head into the curve of my neck and shoulder, resting there, and it was all I could do to keep us both upright under his weight. The reversal of our roles shocked me. Suddenly I was the one protecting him. They'd made him like me. To feel pain. To feel fear. Mortal.

He crushed my hand in his. "I just wanted to do this."

"What?"

He didn't say anything, just squeezed my hand harder. "This, star girl." He let out a deep breath. "Because you might never let me hold your hand again."

I concentrated on keeping us on our feet as the roar of the truck came closer. Around the bend in the road, a massive armored vehicle ground to a halt. Then there were men with drones all around us—ten of them all dressed as though they were Hazard officers, but none of them carried a recovery pack, and I was sure they were just like Reid. Black Ops. Not one of them asked questions or hesitated as they dragged Michael away.

He didn't shout or try to resist. Instead, he pulled me with him, not letting go of my hand. One of the soldiers smacked him over the head, telling him to let go, but he didn't. His fingers stayed clamped around mine all the way across the road toward the back of the truck. I stayed close to him until another soldier slammed a metal baton across Michael's forearm with a sickening crunch. I clamped down on a scream. If I fought them, they'd only hurt him more. Michael didn't yell, but his fingers finally unclenched.

I stopped in the middle of the road, standing away from him, not wanting to give them an excuse to break anything else. They dragged him into the truck, his feet bouncing on the gravel.

Someone tapped my shoulder. When I turned, Reid looked grim. "Cheyne was right," he said. "You're ready now."

He seized my forearm and pushed me toward the vehicle, saying, "Michael will die if you do anything we don't like. You know what that's like, don't you? Thinking you're about to die. You don't want him to die, do you?"

I shook my head. "Don't hurt him any more."

His forbidding expression disappeared. He gave me a grin. "We'll see." His grip would have bruised me before. My skin hurt beneath his fingers, but as soon as he let go, the bruise disappeared.

"In here." He motioned inside the truck, at what looked like a cage in the center. Two long benches lined either side, and at the front of the truck was another panel with a door. I didn't see Michael anywhere and I was sure they'd taken him into the front.

I peered into the cage, empty other than a chair with straps on it. Climbing up the ramp, scraping my legs on the metal bumpers, I sat down, letting him restrain my arms and legs.

Six soldiers filed in behind him and lined the area, all of them glaring at me. They were well-muscled, bulky, taller even than Michael, handling their weapons with complete ease, as though they'd been specially chosen for this task.

"I came prepared this time," Reid said, tightening the final strap as one of the soldiers grinned at me. "Just in case we've miscalculated your dosage and given you too much." He tapped my shoulder where the ampule rested and closed my new prison door, padlocking it. "Sit tight. We'll be there soon. In the meantime, you can catch up on the latest news." The doors shut and lights switched on. I clutched the edge of the armrest to keep from overbalancing as the truck headed around the first corner.

Reid clicked a button and a miniature air screen flickered on.

The local news jingle jarred my ears and the newsreader's voice blared in the cramped space. "We have reports of yet another Basher attack this morning, similar to the explosion yesterday that caused the sixth death of eighteen-year-old, Jeremiah Isaacs, and the first death of his ten-year-old brother, Thomas." They cut to a photo of the guy with the gun we'd encountered the day before, and then showed footage of two bodies encased in recovery domes being wheeled away from the front of my house, as though they died when Michael's car exploded.

I tried not to react as I watched the screen. That hadn't happened. We'd left Jeremiah and Thomas alive. I remembered the boy calling me an angel. My jaw ticked, but there was no way I'd show emotion in front of Reid.

The newsreader continued. "This morning's explosion occurred just minutes ago inside a vacant mechanic's shop off the NorthWest Motorway. Hazard Police are on the scene." They cut to an aerial shot showing the truck disappearing off camera. I looked away, not bothering to hear the latest theory about the explosions until I heard my name.

"...missing teenager, Ava Holland. She was last sighted in notorious Bridgefield Park." The screen showed a reporter sticking her microphone in the face of the drug addict who'd tried to strangle me. He grinned. The camera was close enough to see that one of his teeth was in backward. He pointed to the photo of me, nodding and smiling, "Sweetie nectar."

"At this time, Hazard Police advise that Ava Holland should be approached with extreme caution. Anyone with knowledge of her whereabouts is urged to contact police immediately at the number on your screen." The news reporter's solemn face brightened. "On a more cheerful note," she said, swiveling to her co-reporter. "The Terminal has announced its latest experience —a combat room like nothing before."

Her co-anchor gave the viewers a knowing look. "They're calling it 'the Dojo' and it's equipped with the latest technology, even gravity defying fields so you can fight like the ultimate ninja. We can't show you pictures before the unveiling tomorrow night, but we can tell you it is ah-mazing."

The woman said, "All you fans of martial arts out there, don't get too excited, though. Only the best five fighters of the night will be allowed inside the Dojo."

I focused on the floor of my cage and tuned out. I wondered if I should be paying attention to where we were going—the curves in the road, the sounds. The cabin became even darker and I recognized the *whoosh-whoosh* of the inner city bypass tunnel. Five minutes later we hadn't made a turn, so I guessed that meant we were going toward the city. Twenty minutes later I still didn't know for sure because when the truck finally stopped and the doors opened, we were already inside the building.

Keys rattled. Reid opened the cage and put a bag over my head.

~

Half an hour later, the bag came off, but I didn't understand what I was looking at.

My eyes failed to adjust and, at first, there was only my own face staring back at me, reflected in a glass panel. Reid had cuffed my hands, yanking my arms back harder than necessary, especially since I didn't intend making an escape anytime soon. Not until I figured out how to help Michael.

From what I could see, I was in a room without furniture. Just four walls with a door, except that one of the walls—the one facing me—was thick glass and my face, reflected back at me, looked old. Dark under my eyes, cracks in my lips, my hair lank.

I tried to remember the last time I'd had a drink of water. My last meal had been oat bars and apples the night before. I would survive a while longer without food, but I was sure I'd need water soon. I wondered how the nectar would cope with dehydration and whether my body would shut down into a coma like the boy who got lost in the national park. That wouldn't do me any good right now.

Next to me in the glass, Reid's form hovered, a green blur as he spun toward the door. His voice broke my thoughts before I had the chance to look through the panel and see beyond my own face.

"As directed, sir."

"Good."

I looked out of the corner of my eye at the newcomer—Cheyne—Michael's godfather. He seemed to suck all the light out of the room with his big form as he said, "That will be all, officer."

Reid hesitated, looked as if he wanted to stay, but gave a curt nod and left the room. Once alone with Cheyne, I wasn't sure I wanted Reid to leave. At least he was predictable. I didn't like the way my heart rate increased as Cheyne stepped behind me. Up close, he was even bigger than I remembered. Thinning hair in a long braid, sharp hazel eyes. He smelled like tar in the boiling sun, as though he'd ignite at any second and burn me with him. Was he about to grab me? Put my head through the glass? Bitter nectar trickled into my back. Even my body thought I was in trouble.

He ran a hand down the back of my arm and my eyes squeezed shut. There was a click. The handcuffs clattered to the floor.

My eyes flew open and I flexed my fingers, waiting for his next move.

His voice was soft, curling around my ear. "They're not dead."

"Who?" Was he talking about my parents? About Michael?

He gestured at the glass. "We keep them like that because they're useful. Everything you see here has a use. If it doesn't, we get rid of it."

I focused beyond the glass. Before I could stop myself, I drew a quick breath and took a step back, bumping into a muscled arm and thigh.

The bodies in the other room were all lain out on single metal pallets, four of them in a row, their heads cushioned on padded indents. Each one was connected to a separate machine, multi-colored tubes leading to different parts of their bodies.

"I believe that one is your late neighbor." Cheyne leaned against the glass and pointed a thick finger at a bed toward the middle. "She's a fast healer. We needed to test your mortality against the strongest ones."

"Mrs. Hubert." I pressed closer to the glass, putting my hands up beside my face, trying to hide my shock. I scanned the other faces, dreading whom else I might see. In the bed next to her was an older man I didn't recognize. But there was Jeremiah and his younger brother, Thomas, wrapped in white robes with tubes protruding from their feet. They'd ended up there because of me and it made my heart sink.

"Right now, we're trying to identify what part of the body is most vulnerable to your mortality. The armpits seem best so far, but that's hardly practical during combat." He imitated a soldier with a gun. "Hey, lift up your arms so I can shoot you dead." A smirk. "Yeah. Not likely."

"You're talking about me like I'm…"

"A weapon." His keen eyes landed on my face. "That's exactly what you are."

My heart sank. Michael was right… He'd said the Bashers wanted to use my genetics to kill, and now I knew that his dad and Cheyne had the same agenda.

Cheyne circled around me and I cringed as he moved up close. "You're the weapon we've needed for so long. Now Seversand will think twice about attacking us."

I stared at him. "People are saying Seversand will attack us *because* of me. Because I can die."

He shook his head, cutting me off. "What is it they teach you in school about why the world war ended?"

"The nuclear bomb failed. War is pointless."

"My great-grandfather was there the day they dropped that bomb. He said it was the first time he ever felt pain. Seversand split an atom." His expression became incredulous. "They *split* an atom. And still nobody died. So yes, it makes sense to say that war is pointless. But in all the years since that failure, Seversand hasn't stopped trying to find another weapon. They've never stopped searching, infiltrating, threatening us. We even suspect that the Bashers are affiliated with them. But everything changed when the truth about your brother went public."

He stared directly at me. "Our President didn't travel to Seversand to beg for mercy. He went to tell them to back off. Because we beat them to the ultimate weapon and we will use it if we have to. We have you, and now Seversand fears us."

"What about the Bashers?"

"For the first time, we're stronger than they are."

He was triumphant, but the feeling of despair that spread through my body was like nothing I'd felt before. It was so huge and hot and undeniable that I could have withered to a crisp right there. They were going to turn me into something I wasn't, something I didn't want to be.

They were going to use me to kill.

I tried to focus, to get my bearings, there were things I needed to know, answers to questions that had plagued me. "Why did you let me go from the recovery center? You could have kept me there."

He sighed. "We thought we had everything we needed from you to synthesize your DNA into a mortality weapon, and Robert ... he's not a big fan of keeping people against their will unless we have to. It's a particular weakness of his."

I remembered Robert Bradley's name from the news reports. He was Michael's dad.

Cheyne's lips thinned. "But we discovered two things after we let you go: first, the mortality serum has a shelf-life, which means we need you alive to produce more of it. And second, we didn't count on the reaction of the general community. You won't believe me, but we actually hoped you could go back to your life." He held up a finger. "You know what, this is going to be a whole lot easier if I just show you." He smiled as if he was my friend, as he inclined his head toward the door. "C'mon."

He pushed on the metal door and waited for me. It reminded me of the door at the recovery center, right down to the dent in the middle.

He saw me looking at it. "Your brother caused us a lot of trouble too."

My eyes snapped to his, wondering what he meant. I wanted him to say more, but he didn't. I followed him out, expecting to see another swarm of soldiers. Instead, the quiet corridor stared back at me.

"This way." He pulled me to the left.

I could try to run, but it seemed pointless, so, for now, I followed him. He strode on down the corridor, boots thumping, passing five other closed doors before he turned and stopped outside another opening, this one without a door. He gestured inside to a row of chairs and an old wall screen, the kind my parents said they had when they were kids.

He nudged me into a chair facing the screen and stood back as it flickered on to reveal the same green-lit room they'd taken me to at the recovery center. There was a time stamp at the bottom of the screen, seconds ticking over, but it was years ago.

There was a boy inside the room on the footage. He was young, maybe thirteen. He bashed himself against the door.

It was Josh.

As I stared at the footage, a pair of speakers crackled on and I wanted to block my ears as sound filled the room around me.

Josh cried and screamed at the same time, an anguish that wrenched through me. With each impact of his head into the door, a split on his forehead opened, started to bleed, and then closed again. I couldn't see anyone else in the room. The surveillance drone circled, not getting too close.

Cheyne's voice was low, hushed. "This footage is from the day your brother killed that little girl. What was her name?"

I started. Josh killed someone?

He clicked his fingers. "Kristy. Her parents used to work here. They tried to smuggle a sample of nectar out of the country. Their little girl got hold of it and shared it with your brother at school. It was experimental and it gave him some pretty bad hallucinations. He didn't know what he was doing. The Hazards who attended the scene reported the unusual substance and we were alerted as a matter of security."

I tried to remember back when I was twelve. Mom's stricken face. Josh gone all of a sudden. He hadn't come home one night and after that, I didn't see him so often anymore. After that, he was always disappearing on me.

Cheyne pressed a button and the footage skipped forward

three hours and I didn't want to think about how alone and scared Josh was during that time.

The footage slowed and Josh was curled up on the floor in the corner, so still, not even trembling. A man entered the room with a glass of water. His hair had the first hints of gray speckles, reached a little more than halfway down his back, and he wore a beard cut short around his jaw. He looked so much like Michael that it had to be his dad. The older man approached Josh, but kept his distance, telling Josh to drink. Josh unfurled and got to his knees. He scooted forward and snatched up the glass, drinking the whole lot.

The man's voice was gentle. "How are you doing, Josh?"

My brother inched away from the man, shoulders hunched, but he said, "I've been better."

Cheyne bumped my shoulder. "We used to test nectar on homeless people—nobody noticed when they went missing—and we made sure it was safe enough before we tried it on Josh again."

I thought about the homeless addict in the park who'd been desperate to get at the ampule in my back. "Safe enough doesn't mean safe."

He inclined his head. "Over time, we perfected it. We got rid of the hallucinogenic effects, but nothing seemed to change the extra strength it gave him, no matter how we adjusted the formula." His eyes were suddenly hard and piercing. "When we first gave you nectar, it was the raw stuff like Josh had the first time. But you compartmentalized your brain, protecting the part of your mind that controls reason and logic." He tapped my temple before I could shove his hand away. "It's like you built a barrier in there. A *wall*."

Walls. The ones Michael didn't want to talk about.

"Unlike your brother, you stayed aware of what was happening—you controlled the effects and tried to escape. Your strength increased even more than Josh's. That room's made of concrete, Ava. It's twelve inches thick and you put cracks in it. If we'd let you get to the door, you wouldn't have just dented it."

He gestured at the now frozen screen and my brother's small face. "It was only because of Josh's reaction to nectar that we tested his blood and discovered he was nothing like the rest of us."

My teeth chattered. I tried to stop them, but it was no use. They'd known all along about Josh, about his mortality.

"If you had him, why do you need me?"

"You're a girl." His expression was grim. "We tried for years to replicate Josh's DNA, but it was too unstable. We finally realized that the male Y chromosome was making it impossible. We hoped that two X chromosomes would make a difference and we were right: the gene that inhibits regeneration exists on both your X chromosomes. But here's the thing: both genes are active."

I must have given him a blank look because he said, "Usually, the genes on one X chromosome are inactivated. In your case, the additional gene contains the extra information we need to stabilize the formula. Think of it like a bullet without gunpowder. Josh's DNA gave us the bullet, but without the gunpowder it's useless. Even as a mortal, you're a scientific anomaly.

"We always suspected you'd be like Josh, but we didn't want to pull you in unless we had to. Keeping his secret was hard enough, let alone keeping two of you under control."

"And the park? Why did you leave me in the park?"

"For so many reasons. For starters, we needed to give you the nectar ampule and place you in a situation that would trigger it. We could have done that here, as you'll soon see, but we realized something else. Well, Robert realized it. You have a strong protective instinct. We saw it in your brother many times, especially the night he tried to save you. We always thought it was a personality thing with him, trying to help other people. But then we saw it in you too. You remember that little boy who got hit by the car outside your house? I watched you, Ava. You wanted to rescue him."

I remembered the drone that morning, hovering in front of my face, studying me. I remembered his mom calling the Hazards, but hardly looking at him, worrying about being late for work.

Cheyne scratched his chin. "It made us wonder—what else do mortals feel? Could you have instincts, reactions, that we don't have? If those instincts are dormant, but coded into your DNA, then we need to activate them somehow. Your reaction to nectar was exponential and if we combine that reaction with instincts that make you move faster, that cause you to protect people you love, then there's no limit to what you could do." He studied me, a look of wonderment in his eyes. "Boy, you didn't disappoint. That drug addict in the park didn't know what hit him. We left you out there as long as we could, but the Bashers were closing in."

I didn't move. "You gave me the ampule to keep me alive, and then you used Michael as leverage to get me to come in."

"If we calibrate the dose of nectar exactly right, we can give you the gift of healing without the side effects. We did the same for Josh. He went on with his life. If things were different—if your mortality wasn't public—you could have done the same."

The image of my brother bashing himself against the metal door wouldn't leave me. Instead of pulling away from Cheyne, I snatched at his shoulder, pressing my fingertips into him, wrenching closer. "If my brother had a nectar ampule, why did he die?"

Cheyne shouted. "He wasn't supposed to!"

With a shove, he dropped me, and I landed on my knees, barely feeling the bruise before it vanished.

Cheyne towered over me. "Michael thought the final fight was in that room. He was supposed to delay Josh so we could get to you. We were going to run the tests and take your blood during the Basher attack and send you to the recovery center where your parents would be waiting. Nobody was supposed to know about it. Josh wasn't supposed to die. But his ampule wasn't implanted. He didn't take it out himself because that's impossible. You know that already—your skin heals too fast. Someone took it from him!"

I remembered Cheyne pushing Josh over after he died, cursing at the strange, puckered patch of skin on my brother's back, right in the same place my own ampule was located.

My breath hurt. My ears buzzed. "If you knew everything about my brother, how come you didn't know he was a Basher?"

"We knew. We promised him that if he infiltrated their organization and fed us intelligence on their plans, we'd let you both go. When he told us about the planned attack on Implosion, we knew we could use it to keep you alive and get what we needed."

"You tricked him."

"We had to. We needed you. This country needs you."

I gritted my teeth and stared up at him as defiance poured out of me. "I will never participate willingly in anything you do."

His expression turned to rage as I refused to look away. As I refused to give in. He snarled. "You think you don't need us. You think you can survive without us."

He hauled me to my feet and half-dragged, half-walked me out of the room, further down the corridor, until we halted outside another door. I waited for it to open. I wondered if there would be more people laid out on metal beds—if it would be my parents or even Josh's dead body.

Cheyne hissed. "Just remember how much you think you don't need us. Think about that while you're in there. Without this to save you."

His hand snaked out. A knife glinted.

I tried to run, but he grabbed my shoulder, spun me around, and drove the point into my back. I screamed as he angled it, twisted, and pulled. Before I could do anything, something sprang into the air and clanged against the opposite wall. It was a metal cylinder, as long as my thumb and shaped like a golden teardrop.

The ampule of nectar. Etched into it was the outline of a scorpion.

It wobbled a foot down the corridor and skittered out of reach. I grabbed Cheyne, to hit back, but he shoved me into the room and slammed the door behind me.

CHAPTER 19

I LANDED on my hands and knees in the black room, unable to see anything. My back throbbed where Cheyne had ripped out the ampule.

I tried to see where I was, but it was no use. The metal door had sealed behind me, shutting me into some kind of caldron. The only sense I had was that the walls curved because as I scratched at the door behind me, the sound bounced.

My skin prickled a second before pale gray lights flickered on, dotting the ceiling, soaking the room in a soft glow. The room was circular, except that the walls were covered from floor to ceiling in an intricate net, anchored at a multitude of points. The floor was uneven, shaped out of what appeared to be many overlapping panels like a snail shell, or an iris.

If I thought I was alone, I could have dealt with the almost-dark and the not-quite silence, but it was impossible to ignore the sense of being watched.

I blinked, looking for any hint of a shape in the walls behind the netting. If there were cameras or CCTV drones, they were well hidden. I shuffled through the gray haze, trying not to catch my feet on the floor, seeking the nearest wall, but everything curved and I couldn't tell how they were seeing me.

A quiet slither was the only warning I had as the nets began to rise, skimming the walls, inching upward. I eyed the movement, unsure what to make of it, whether it should worry me.

Then the floor creaked.

I wobbled, trying to keep my balance. Panels slid beneath the balls of my feet and an immediate shudder rocked my legs.

The floor was opening. A growing hole appeared at the center of the room, opening wider and wider like a camera shutter. I staggered backward, caught my toes against the edge of a moving panel, struggled to stay upright, and crashed forward at the edge of the hole, my hands gripping it even as it expanded.

Darkness. That's all there was under me.

I gasped, and the sound sucked down and down and I imagined that there was a pit somewhere down there, too far to see. I scrambled backward, scooting on my backside, catching my fingers in the moving panels. It was no use pressing up against the walls. The opening grew and it would expand until there wasn't any floor left.

They wouldn't let me fall. They needed me. I tried to rationalize the situation and ignore the instinct that told me to run. I could stay put and wait for the floor to stop opening.

It will stop before I fall. It has to.

Cheyne had captured Michael in the park and left me there. He'd planted a bomb in Michael's bag. If there was anything I knew for sure, it was that he was unpredictable. He'd pushed me to my limits before and he wouldn't stop now. My instincts won out.

Springing to my feet, there was just enough floor left to jump. I lunged, caught the bottom rung of the net in one hand, swung my other arm up and snatched at it, scrabbling my feet on the smooth walls. I darted a glance below me, but the floor was already gone. There was only an abyss.

I closed my eyes and tried to breathe. The rope netting was rough but thick. I readied myself to push up with my feet, to climb, and just managed to grab a higher rung with my right hand. It was enough to give me leverage. Rung by rung, I progressed upward, pushing my legs against the wall, until I had both feet on the netting. My head was a couple feet from the ceiling. At least the net had stopped retracting upward.

Panting, I clung. For a moment, I breathed, letting the air in and out of my lungs, not looking down into the dark. I decided to wind my wrists into the netting because I'd get tired and I didn't know how long I'd be there, and that way I could rest.

Just as I twisted the rope around my left wrist, there was a snap. I jerked, held on, searching for the source. One of the holds, keeping the net anchored against the wall to my far left, must have broken because a part of the net hung limply further off the wall than the rest.

There was another snap, this time right next to my foot. Then another at my left hand. I jerked backward, clinging, holding on. In quick succession, the net ripped off the wall all around me, my weight forcing it down even further. Like a constant deadly beat, rows of holds across the ceiling broke and I dropped backward, still gripping the net, until I was almost horizontal, the fall sending my stomach spiraling down into the void. The ropes creaked and the sound shuddered through me.

As fast as I could, I wrapped my feet into the netting. There was nowhere between me and the chasm below, nothing to grab hold of or break my fall. My hands and arms were slick with sweat, icy with fear. One of my feet slipped and I stretched my toe, finding the nearest rung just in time, but it wasn't enough. I was going to fall.

At the last moment, there was a whir. At the level of my face, the iris began closing, panels grinding, spinning toward me, faster than it had opened. I was too far down and the iris was going to close around my body. I struggled with the net, trying to pull it taut, yanking on it, attempting to get higher and avoid the crushing floor, but the holds kept breaking and the more I struggled, the worse it got. As the iris closed, I wrenched upward, out of the way, and it snapped shut beneath me, pinning the edge of my t-shirt.

The last of the netting broke free and I thudded against the floor, ripping at my shirt until it tore from the panel, and then I curled up under the rope lattice, chilled to the bone.

I told myself to get up. I had no idea what they'd throw at me next. I forced my shaking legs to function and rose onto my knees. It was all I could manage before the lights came on.

The door swung open. Cheyne dragged the net off me, cutting the tangle from my shoulders and head.

He held out the ampule, the gold metal glinting. "Do you want this now?"

I staggered upward and made it to my feet.

He was offering me the ampule, the one thing that could save me and free me from fear, and it was time for me to choose.

I fixated on the ampule and the scorpion on its surface. If I had it, I wouldn't have to be afraid anymore. I could live without fear of being hurt, without fear of dying.

They'll use it to control you, Michael had said and he was right. My eyes flicked to Cheyne's smug face. They wanted me to need their help. They wanted me to stay willingly, of my own accord because they could offer me the one thing that promised safety.

He hadn't given me the ampule to keep me safe. It was to keep me under control.

They'd done it to Josh and my brother had told me: *Don't let them break you.*

I pressed my palms into my thighs. I'd made my choice.

I refused to give in. I refused to be afraid.

I said, "No."

"Hmm." He looked a bit less pleased. "Well. We'll fix that." He took hold of my arm and pulled me down the corridor again. It curved gently and we passed another three doors before he spoke.

"Do you know what I really love about this place? There are

so many doors. You never know what's behind them. We can keep opening doors all day if you like?"

"Sure, why not?" I said, gritting my teeth, challenging him.

He reassessed me, and I could tell he was thinking it through. "No … I think you've had enough for today. Just one more door."

He stopped and yanked me to a halt in front of a wall. He got out a small electrical device and pointed it at the wall. The shape of a door became visible, sliding back to reveal another bowl-shaped room. He pushed me into it. "Get some rest, Ava."

The door shut and sealed. I dropped my head against it. This room was white and curved up the sides to the flat ceiling. Light came from somewhere, but I couldn't see where. I caught sight of a water jug and raced to it, dropping to my knees and putting it to my lips. I tried to go slowly, afraid that I'd bring it back up if I drank too fast. It tasted better than anything I'd had in my whole life.

Once I swallowed the last drop, I curled up on the floor and listened to the thrumming of white walls vibrating in some kind of tuneless song. It wasn't long before I realized that it was the rhythm of one of my old dances—the one I'd practiced in the park. It made me remember Michael, the way he'd spun me around, telling me I could dance if I wanted to, that nobody could tell me not to. I crawled over to the place where the floor became the wall, leaning my back into the curve and flexing my toes. I was sure the walls were beating. I closed my eyes and let the vibration lull me to sleep.

I woke to more beats, but these were irregular, unwelcome. They ended with a pair of boots at eye level, the only black thing in my white room.

"Get up. It's time for another door." It was Reid and for once I was relieved to see him instead of Cheyne. My relief didn't last long, as he said. "You'll like this one a lot."

I was sure I wouldn't, but I scrambled to my feet. I could see his boots itching to kick me if I wasn't fast enough.

"I need to use the bathroom." I pressed my lips together. I hadn't meant to say it, but there it was.

He scowled. He sauntered across the room, kicked the wall, and in an instant a panel slid away and a toilet rose up out of the floor. He turned to face the other direction and I knew it was the best I was going to get. I shot daggers into his back until I finished. I took a moment to scrutinize the wall. There were two raised bumps. I hit the one that wasn't already compressed and to my relief, a small washbasin extended out of the wall.

"Fine," I said to Reid's back after I washed up. "I'm ready for door number three."

He snickered and grabbed my arm. "I bet you are." Then, "Want your ampule? I have it right here."

I shook my head but took note of where he patted his pocket.

I tried to stay as far away from him as possible as we left the room and headed down the corridor. I tried to imagine how big this place was, since we never went backward, only forward along the curving corridor. The room with Mrs. Hubert and Jeremiah in it might have been a mile back in the other direction or only a few hundred feet, I couldn't tell anymore. I wondered if I was back at the Delaney Recovery Center, but the rooms there had been angular, with straight corridors. There were no corners here, only curves.

I started counting doors since that seemed the only way to tell how far we'd walked. I regretted sleeping. I should have spent the night figuring out a way out of there. I turned my head, trying to ease the stiffness in my neck.

We strode a long way down the corridor before he stopped and pointed. "Door number three."

I didn't move, hanging back, almost pulling away. "You're not going to push me in there, are you?"

"No way. I'm coming in with you. I want to see this. Besides," he continued. "You're going to have questions and I have the answers."

The door slid open. This room was as deep purple as a bruise. It didn't smell right and I put my hand over my mouth to stifle the overwhelming scent of something not quite living.

Reid whispered. "You'll get used to it. C'mon in."

One foot in front of the other. I barely felt the floor, hardly noticed my legs move, aware only of the person strapped to the chair.

CHAPTER 20

THEY'D CUT Michael's hair as short as a child's and it hadn't grown back. No, not cut. Hacked was closer. I bit my lip, glad that he wasn't facing me, so I couldn't see what they'd done to his face.

One of his hands jerked like an impulse against the restraints that kept him in the metal chair. The lump on his upper back was visible between the metal chair rods—the place where they'd injected the ampule that was killing him. The ampule that made him mortal.

The other one at the base of his neck—the one that shocked him—was bright red.

I forced my hand away from my mouth. "Can he hear me?"

Reid strode around in front of Michael. I noticed how similar they looked, so close in age, except that one of them— the one with the power—was warped so badly he couldn't seem to tell what was right anymore.

Empathy.

Cheyne said that I would try to help others. He called it instinct. But I realized it was more than that. It was something most people didn't have because pain and death meant nothing to them.

Reid's voice was strangely gentle, but it was the kind of lulling sound that a predator made. "Michael?"

Michael's hand twitched again, one finger lifting and falling, the only response.

"She wants to know if you can hear her. Why don't you give her a sign?"

Another twitch.

Reid looked at me. "I think that's the best you're going to get, sweetheart."

I tried not to look at what they'd done to him, knowing that I would feel it as though it were my own pain, as though it were my own body. I made it as far as his side, knelt down beside him, and sought his eyes. "Michael?"

He didn't answer. His face was puffy, his lips dry and cracked. I closed my eyes and lowered them to his chest, preparing myself for what I'd see. Puncture marks dotted his torso and neck. A welt as thick as my arm cut from shoulder to hip. I imagined that his eyes swiveled in my direction, and I hoped that he recognized me.

"Let him go," I said to Reid. "You've got me now. You don't need him."

He shook his head. "I can't do that. He knows too much."

"I'm guessing he knew too much before. You let him go then, why not now?"

"Cheyne told you already. We keep things while they're useful."

I shook my head. "How can he be any use to you like this?"

"Because you haven't got your answer."

I frowned. I wasn't sure I wanted any more answers.

Reid knelt down beside me and put his face way too close to mine. I inhaled cigarettes and beer. "He didn't tell you about the walls."

I tried not to react. I'd asked Michael how he knew I'd created walls in my head and he'd refused to answer. I didn't know what that had to do with Reid or my mortality, but something twisted in my stomach.

He gave Michael a poke in the chest. "Tell her about the walls, Mikey-boy."

The sound that came out of Michael's mouth grated like barbed wire. I leaned closer to catch his words.

He said, "I was there."

I put my hand to his arm but jolted away when the mere touch made him wince. My voice was as soft as his. "Where? Where were you?"

His words were slow, laborious. I knew that each one cost him. "When they got you. I was there."

I scrunched up my face, thinking back to the day before when I leaped out of the explosion into Michael's arms. "Michael, I know you were there yesterday. They caught us both and brought us here."

He strained to shake his head. The muscles in his neck looked tight and the pulse in the curve at the base beat faster than it should. "No. The first time. At the recovery center. Cheyne took me down to that room and you were in the chair. He made me watch and I didn't help you. Cheyne told me afterward—he said you made walls. Inside your mind. Walls that let you fight them. They hurt you, and I didn't stop them."

I couldn't move. Everything stopped. My heart, my thoughts. "No. That wasn't you. It was someone else. It couldn't be you. You wouldn't..."

"There were knives everywhere and you were bleeding. And then you were healing and bleeding again. I couldn't stand it anymore. I ran in there, caught you, but I couldn't stop them. He told me afterward I was stupid. You didn't need my help."

I made the mistake of looking at Reid, who perched next to me as if he was ready to pick over our remains.

"He's not really your friend, Ava. He just did what he was told."

I formed the word on the tip of my tongue, but the denial came out of Michael's mouth, stronger than I expected. "No."

My thoughts scattered. The turmoil in my head crashed and banged, I could barely think. "You came to my house because they told you to. You took me to the park. You were bringing me here."

"No." Michael's head jerked as if he wanted to shout but couldn't. "After the recovery center, I swore, Ava. I swore I'd make it right. I'd make amends."

I remembered him spitting out bullets, shattering in flame, sleeping at the base of my bed, making me safe. I stared at him, at his eyes and his bruised mouth. They'd hurt him. So badly. But he'd let them hurt me. Then he ran away with me, away from all that, and he never wanted to go back. I thought about instinct and about empathy and my head cleared. I knew what I had to do.

"I should've killed you when I had the chance." I grabbed his chin as all my emotions boiled. "You brought me here, and I hate you for that. If I could hurt you more, I would."

Reid handed me something and I stared at the small electrical device resting on my palm.

"It controls the charge in his neck," he said, as though he was explaining that the world was round. "Give it a try. It'll make you feel better."

"No. It's not enough. Can I kill him? I want to kill him." My lip curled. "He did this to me. I want to stab him in the back, just like he stabbed me."

Reid handed me a knife. "Sure, Ava. You do whatever you like. When you're done, you can have your ampule back." He fished it out of his pocket and held it up for me to see. It looked clean. A bright, pretty teardrop decorated with a dangerous creature.

Now it was my turn to be the dangerous one.

"We'll put it back in straight away," Reid said. "I promise. Then you'll be safe again."

"Good." I took the knife, rolling it in my other hand. I didn't meet Michael's eyes, but I knew he wouldn't try to protect himself.

I moved to stand behind him, angling the knife just so.

Over Michael's bent head, Reid nodded, encouraging. "Go on, then. Get it over with, so you can move on."

I gritted my teeth. I didn't know how to use a knife, but I was going to learn fast.

~

Michael shouted, drew breath, and shouted again. It was a clumsy cut, but it did what I needed it to.

The mortality ampule hit the wall, just like mine had the day before, another teardrop but this one was made of red metal that looked gruesome in the purple light. It rebounded to the floor and rolled toward me. I withdrew the knife as fast as I could, making sure I didn't touch the electrocution implant, remembering that Michael said his legs would stop working if he tried to take it out. I didn't know if that was true, but I wasn't going to take that chance.

I kicked the mortality ampule away with my foot and held my breath with hope bubbling inside me.

The sides of his skin moved, pulling together. I shut my eyes and breathed again.

He roared—the kind of roar a beast makes when it wakes up. The color came back into his skin. The burns on his head turned pink with new skin. The welts on his arms shrank. His wounds knitted and disappeared. His right leg straightened. His muscles flexed and his head rose.

Reid turned white, a sickly pale color. "Wait ... what did you..."

I dropped next to Michael's feet, hacking frantically at the leather restraint. I had to get him out of the chair before Reid stopped us. He was already beside me, grabbing at my arm. I whipped around and slashed at him, but he didn't even flinch or try to grab the knife. Instead, he drew back his fist to punch me.

The restraint around Michael's leg snapped just in time. He aimed a kick at Reid's ribs and connected with a crunch. This time, Reid howled, hands clamped to his side.

I chopped at the restraint on Michael's nearest arm. Both were still strapped down. If I could get at least one free…

Reid rushed back, ramming me with the full force of his body. I crashed backward as Michael shouted my name. He struggled against the chair, one leg free, while I dodged another hit. Reid went for the knife, trying to snatch it out of my hands as I pushed it upward. It connected, but he ignored the wound, grabbing hold of my wrist.

He twisted. I screamed as pain shot through my arm. The knife tumbled to the floor and I tried to seize it, but it was too far away.

Reid grabbed my head in both his hands and rammed it into the floor. I blacked out and came to a second later. By then, both his legs straddled me, clamped around my torso. He ignored the knife lying on the ground. He thrashed me again, pressing his palms into my temples so that the room spun in a giddy blur of indigo.

In between blows, I thought only about the blade, my fingers stretching and trying to find it. My vision swam as I touched something metallic. I was sure I'd finally got hold of the knife, even though my brain told me something didn't feel right.

I threw a wild punch, trying to unbalance him. As soon as his head whipped back, there was a second of opening, and I stabbed the knife into his chest, right where his heart would be.

He drew a breath. His eyes went wide. He let go of my head and I couldn't stop myself from thumping the floor and blacking out again.

I came back to the sound of his gasp. He blinked rapidly as though he couldn't see anymore, as though his world had gone as dark as mine. I stared at the small thing protruding from his shirtfront, trying to figure out what it was because it wasn't the knife.

It was the ampule I'd ripped out of Michael, its pointed red tip embedded in his skin.

I had only a moment before Reid regained his equilibrium. Struggling against his weight, I shoved and pushed, thrashing from side to side. He slid off, gasping for air, far enough for me to wrench myself in the direction of the real knife.

My hand closed over it and I met Michael's eyes. He watched me and I didn't know what his expression meant, but I knew what I had to do. I didn't have any other choice.

I twisted, the knife in my hand, launching up and over, pushing Reid against the floor. His head hit hard, his eyes glazed, his mouth moaning. I didn't hesitate—*couldn't* hesitate. I wouldn't end up like my brother. I wouldn't let this monster hurt Michael again, or try to twist my thoughts, make me into something I wasn't, kill that part of me that felt what other people felt, kill my compassion.

I drove the knife down.

He looked up at me, right into my face, and I wondered if he saw how much fear I had swirling inside me before he died. The light in his eyes turned glassy, reflective. His lips were white and a last breath escaped, never drawn in again.

A wail broke out of me. There was no way I could find reason in what just happened. There was no way I could ever understand why he'd brought me here, why he'd tried to make me kill Michael, why he hated me. I shook with such violence that my knees knocked against the floor.

Michael's voice barely broke through. "Get me out of this."

I shook my head from side to side, my hands still pressing on the dead man's chest, one leg on the floor, the other pushing on his stomach.

"Ava! Get me out of this. I can help you."

"No." I sobbed. "Nobody can help me now."

"Yes, I can! Just..." He started to swear, kicking and

thrashing against the restraints, hurting himself in his efforts to pull his hands free.

"Michael!" I gasped.

"If I have to cut myself to pieces to get to you, Ava, I will." He gritted his teeth, his eyes wild and dark.

A crazy laugh gushed out of me. "No. Don't." I used the knife to snap the leather around his broken hand.

"I can do the rest myself," he said, taking the weapon and driving it through the other restraint. "Are you hurt?"

I patted the back of my head and rubbed my wrist. "I'm sore. I have a massive headache." My shoulders convulsed. My mouth turned dry. I tried not to think about Reid, except that my nectar ampule was still on him—the one he'd put in his pocket. I dropped beside him, trying to remember which pocket it was in.

Michael was suddenly next to me. He grabbed my arm, dragging me away from the body and up against his side. He crushed me so close that his heartbeat thumped in my ear. It sounded just like the thrumming in the white room, just like the rhythm of my favorite dance. I didn't struggle. I stayed there, listening and trying to straighten out the pulp in my head.

He kept hold of me, pulling me down with him as he knelt beside Reid and reached into his back pocket. He brought out the golden ampule, but he didn't hand it to me. He turned it over to reveal the side with the etching of the scorpion. His hands brushed a little glowing light resting at the tip of the creature's tail.

"Ava, I'm sorry."

Tears fell down my cheeks and I couldn't stop them. "That light in the ampule. That's the tracking device, isn't it?"

He nodded. "I'm not going to tell you not to use this. I know now what it feels like to be truly afraid of death. But if you do, then you have to know, you won't get far." His hands were gentle as he placed the ampule in my palm. "If you choose this, I'll understand."

I stared at it, turning it over and over. Then I put it down, leaving it with the scorpion upturned on Reid's chest. "No. I'm not staying."

"You can survive this. I know you can." He captured me against him, both his arms around me. "I believe anything now because I know you believe in me."

I closed my eyes. I didn't want to talk about walls. "I know they made you do a lot of things. But that night when you came to my house, you weren't there to trap me. You were trying to escape. You weren't lying about that."

"We can get out of here. I can take you somewhere safe."

"Nowhere is safe. There's no way we can make it to Starsgard." I pulled back. "My neighbor's here—Mrs. Hubert—they have her. Same as Jeremiah and his brother. How can we be safe if they aren't?"

"I know, Ava. It was the first thing they showed me when they brought me here."

"Do you know where we are?"

He shook his head. "I guess we'll know when we get out."

When we get out. I clung to his words as tightly as he held me. I almost couldn't breathe, all squished up against his bare chest, but there was a part of me that didn't mind. I said, "That thing's still in your spine." The electrocution device still nestled at the base of Michael's head.

His jaw clenched right next to my forehead. "It can't hurt me now. I mean, it'll hurt, but it won't kill me. Let's get out of here."

There was urgency in his words, but it was like his arms weren't paying attention, still hugging me, spreading warmth through me. I didn't want him to stop, but too soon I found my feet on the purple floor and Michael's hand in mine. He put me to the side and darted to Reid, reaching around the man's neck and pulling out a chain with a key on it.

"I saw them using these keys on some of the doors," he explained, slipping the chain over his own head, but I held out my hand for it.

"It's not exactly hidden on you." I pointed at his bare skin where the key rested. "If it's important, we might want to put it somewhere nobody will see it."

He relinquished the chain and I slid it around my neck and tucked it into my shirt. "Where are we going?"

"There are lots of doors."

By the way he said it, I wasn't sure if that was a good thing or not. He tugged me forward, stopping at the doorway, and ducked his head around it. I half expected a volley of bullets. The serenity was somehow more disturbing.

Michael looked perplexed. "He had to have set off some kind of alarm, but where are they? This place should be crowded by now." He turned his gaze to me. "Unless he wasn't supposed to bring you here."

I shrugged. "Why am I not surprised?"

"They'll figure out you're gone eventually. I think we should go this way to get out."

I put my hand on his arm. "No, Michael. What about the others?"

He frowned, and I reminded him. "Mrs. Hubert? Thomas? You remember that kid who thought I was an angel? We can't leave them here to die."

"I don't think we can save them either."

"I want to try." I was tired and starving, but I couldn't leave them behind.

"No, Ava, there's no way…"

"There has to be." I exhaled, trying to quell my frustration. "What is it with you? You're like this untouchable god, you can survive anything, and yet you're too scared to help them."

"I'm not scared for them. I'm scared for you."

I bit my lip, half out of uncertainty, half because it wouldn't stop trembling. He looked at me the same way he had right before I killed Reid—as though something terrible was about to happen and he couldn't stop it. In the next instant, I remembered Jeremiah's brother, his upturned face, looking at me as if I was a shining star sent to earth.

I said, "I can't leave them there. Just like I couldn't leave you."

His chest rose and fell. "You know, for someone who can die, you are seriously reckless."

I took his hand, forcing him to look at me. "I've only got one shot at this life thing. I'm not going to spend it giving in."

CHAPTER 21

 E CREPT down the corridor with our heads ducked low. If we headed far enough back the way I'd come, we'd reach the room where the people were captive. The streamlined walls formed a long curve ahead of us. Some doors were visible, with glass panels that we edged up to and peered inside, but most were concealed in long stretches of smooth blue wall, the barest outline giving them away. One of them was the room where I'd spent the night, hidden so well I'd never find it again. Further along, we passed the open doorway into the room with the enormous wall screen. After another five doors, I was certain we were close.

Michael suddenly put his hand on my arm. Just ahead, the wall bent sharply and it was impossible to see around the corner. I nodded at the finger he put to his lips. He gave my shirtsleeve a small tug with his other hand and slithered a little further along, pressed up hard against the wall. I followed until I saw the open door.

He stopped again, and I listened for any sign of soldiers. Just when I thought it was safe, I caught a murmur from the room.

Then a louder voice. "How long before the weapon's ready for the drones?"

Michael tensed and I glanced at him.

He mouthed. "That's my dad. I should get you out of here."

I shook my head. Glared. *No.*

Michael gave a silent sigh. He pointed along the corridor and edged closer to the door, checking around the curve. Then he slid to the floor and pulled me with him. I realized why a moment later when I noticed the window ledge above us. The door was a couple feet farther along. We listened again. It was hard to tell, but the voices sounded distant, and I guessed that they were deep inside the room.

Before Michael could stop me, I scooted up and peeked through the window. Not much had changed since the day before. Metal beds lined the middle, and only four of them were filled. Machines rose up behind each one and tubes crisscrossed the bodies like someone's failed knitting project.

Cheyne and Michael's dad stood at either side of Thomas's bed. The boy didn't appear to have any wires or tubes attached. I was sure he'd had a few in his feet the day before. Hovering over him, Michael's dad was an older version of Michael, hair graying at the temples, same jawline, but different eyes—watchful, analyzing—and a short beard speckled with gray. In the next moment, Michael yanked me to the floor, giving me a look that could have killed.

I breathed out. The corridor swam. It wasn't Michael's glare that knotted my stomach. I kept my voice lower than a whisper. "Cheyne has a gun."

From inside the room, Michael's dad said, "How many of these have we manufactured so far?"

"Twenty weapons with one round each."

An exhaled breath. "We need to work faster."

"We're going as fast as we can, Robert."

A growl. "Okay, well, one thing at a time. Shoot the boy, and we'll see what happens."

I wanted to rush in there, but Michael gripped my arm and his fingers tightened. "He'll live."

"Are you sure?"

I could see by the look on Michael's face that he wasn't. This time, it was Michael who pushed upward, peering through the window with all the worry in his body radiating out over me. I joined him, just in time to see Cheyne raise the gun—a small green weapon with gold and brown swirls over it—aim at the kid's leg, and pull the trigger.

The boy's body kicked. He didn't wake up or react in any other way.

Michael's dad remained clinical. "I see what you were trying to tell me: the ampule itself doesn't kill. It only mortalizes."

"Correct."

"Hmm. Is that how you restrained Michael?"

"Yes, but we're using a slow-release ampule designed for a weapon similar to a tranquilizer gun. It's the same system as the nectar ampule. It penetrates the skin, but not the flesh beneath. There's no lasting damage and it can be removed to restore regeneration. Don't worry, he's fine. We'll take it out as soon as he starts cooperating."

There was a pause and a sigh. "Maybe I should speak with him. If I just try to explain everything…"

"Do you think he'll listen?"

Michael's dad shook his head. "Have we heard anything about Seversand's response?"

"They're backing off. For now."

"And the Bashers?"

"We brought Ava here just in time. We need to be prepared, though. They won't give up."

"We can't let them get hold of her. The only way this works is if we have a monopoly on the weapon." He exhaled. "Okay, let's get on with it. It looks like killing is a two-step process."

"Mortalize, then kill." Cheyne looked grim. "It means our soldiers need to be equipped with at least one other weapon. Unless…" He pointed the gun at the boy's head. "They shoot for a vital organ. The ampule lodges in the organ, releases a massive dose of mortality serum, and prevents regeneration. Then the damage becomes fatal."

The corners of the other man's mouth turned down. "We need to test it."

"Are you sure? There might be other tests we need to run on him."

"This *is* the most important test. This is what we're here for. We have to know how it works—and how it can be counteracted."

Cheyne paused. "Which organ?"

"The heart."

I was moving before I knew it, surprised to see that Michael was already ahead of me. He shouted as he ran into the room. At his right, I skidded to a halt before I collided with a table on wheels, covered in neat rows of sharp-looking medical instruments. The table bucked and rolled a couple feet toward the men.

They both leaped upright. Cheyne immediately pointed the gun at us, but Michael's dad stood very still, unmoving, even though his expression betrayed shock.

He drew himself up and he was just as tall as Michael but thinner, lankier. He held something in his hand—some kind of syringe that I hadn't noticed before. "Son?"

Michael came to a halt, six feet away from his dad. "I'm not going to let you kill that kid."

"There are tests we have to run, Michael. It's for the greater good."

Michael shook his head. "No, Dad."

"Sit down and listen, Michael. I need to explain—"

"There's nothing to explain. I know murder when I see it."

His dad snorted and took a step toward Michael, putting the syringe down on the bed, hidden in the folds of material. "Well, I guess you would."

Michael jolted away from his dad. "That wasn't like this! You should have told me about Josh. I never would have fought him."

His dad glanced from me to Michael. "I couldn't, son. I know you think you're doing the right thing here, but the safety and security of our whole country is at risk—millions of innocent people. Seversand wants this weapon—badly. We're in a race right now that makes the nuclear bomb look like a toy. If we don't carry through, our way of life will be destroyed, and you think this kid is worth it. He'll be dead too."

"Nothing justifies what you're doing here. Nothing!"

"You're naïve, Michael." Mr. Bradley's face twisted. "You got that from your mother."

Michael launched himself at his dad, catching the other man on the chin with a ferocious fist. Cheyne waved the gun at them both as Michael's dad hit back, stronger than his wiry frame looked. They banged into the metal bed behind them and I thought it was going to overturn.

Cheyne didn't seem to know where he should shoot. The gun traveled a wild arc from one spot to the next, and there was no way I was letting him hit Michael. Not when *this* gun could kill him.

"Hey!" I snatched up a scalpel and threw it at the officer's round face. It sliced through his muscled forearm as he flung it up to protect himself.

The wound kept bleeding. It took forever for his skin to seal itself.

My eyes widened. He was a slow healer...

I didn't waste any more time. I picked up a pair of scissors and threw those too, followed by a pair of heavy tongs that hit Cheyne across his head and made him yelp.

He trained the gun on me, moving in my direction, but the indecision on his face didn't escape me. He wasn't supposed to kill me.

I waited until he was close enough and then I raced toward him. Surprise broke across his face. At the last moment, I skipped to the side. I thrust my hand out, snatching for the gun. My fingers closed over it.

Cheyne yanked it upward, jerking my arm toward him, so I lost my balance, collided with him, and we crashed at the foot of the kid's bed. The sharp scent of oily tar filled my lungs. I wondered if it would only take one shot to light us both up. The gun jammed between his throat and the crook of my arm.

A *crack* jolted through me.

The sound blanketed everything else. A blur raced past as I tried to raise my head. Somebody running. Toward me or away, I couldn't tell. Cheyne lay partly under and partly over me, a horrifying tangle of heavy limbs, his big body suffocating me. Someone pulled me upward and Michael shouted my name. He hauled me in the direction of the door.

I strained toward the room. "We have to help the others."

"Ava, no. Dad will be back any minute with backup."

I couldn't leave them. I raced to Thomas's bed, assessing the bullet wound in his leg. I figured that the mortality bullet was still stuck in there and it had to come out or else he'd die anyway, or go funny in the head. I snatched up the pair of pliers I'd thrown at Cheyne, wondering how deep the bullet had gone.

The tension in Michael's body was palpable, but he raced over and pressed on the wound. I jabbed the pliers inside it, grabbed something and pulled. The mortality bullet appeared, and I dropped it onto the floor next to Cheyne. It lay next to his face, an empty metal teardrop against his cheek. He remained prone, unmoving, not even blinking, only his chest rising and falling. I wondered if that was what a coma looked like, but right now I didn't care.

"How do we wake Thomas up?"

Michael ran to the head of the bed, pressing buttons. "It's this one." He stabbed at a button on the machine.

Thomas's eyes flashed open, and Michael turned left to free Jeremiah. A shout filled the room as the other guy sat up, punching out, hitting air as Michael ran to the older man.

I waited long enough to see Thomas's bullet wound heal and place my hand on his forehead with a reassuring smile. As he sat up, the syringe that Michael's dad had held rolled off the bed and stopped at my foot. Black liquid like luminescent pearls filled my vision.

It was a syringe full of nectar.

I stared at it. If Michael's dad had nectar ready, then that meant … he was going to give Thomas the nectar after they shot him. He was going to heal him.

I searched around for the cap to place over the sharp tip, and found it in the folds of the bed, then I shoved the syringe into my pocket. This nectar didn't have a tracking device in it.

Then I raced to the next bed—Mrs. Hubert's—punching buttons and pulling out lines.

Jeremiah reached Thomas, picking him up and casting a wild look at us. Michael was busy freeing the older man, leaping out of the way when he woke up in the same way Jeremiah did —with a flying fist.

Jeremiah's eyes widened. "Granddad!" He raced to the bed on the far left, with Thomas clutched tight, reaching the older man in a few strides. "It's really you."

I saw the resemblance immediately—blond hair, broad chest. The older man grabbed Jeremiah and Thomas in a bear hug, his arms going around both of them. Then he shoved his grandsons back with tears in his eyes. "What's happening? Where are we?"

I didn't see how Jeremiah responded because a tug on my arm told me that Mrs. Hubert was free. She wobbled as she sat up, but the weakness seemed momentary. The color flushed back to her cheeks and the strength in her hand was unmistakable as she grabbed my shoulder. "What are you doing here, dear?"

I dropped a quick kiss on her cheek, remembering her old lady scent from another life. There was no way I could even begin to answer that question, so I said, "Be safe."

That was all I had time for before Michael grabbed my hand and pulled me to the door. Behind us, Cheyne was a mound on the floor, and Jeremiah and his granddad were already on the move. They hovered over him and Jeremiah picked up the mortality weapon. He was going to use it, but his grandfather grabbed his hand and took it away, giving his grandson what looked like silent instructions. They strode toward us, Jeremiah with his brother in tow and their grandfather with the gun.

Michael said, "My dad will come back with reinforcements. They won't let you out of here easily. You have to move fast. Can you get the old lady out?"

"Who's an old lady?" Mrs. Hubert demanded. She had a wicked-looking wrench in one hand, tapping it on the other.

Michael shot a look at me, and I shrugged.

"Whatever you are, you should stay away from us. We're..." Michael seemed to search for the right word. "We're targets."

"They won't get us again. Don't you worry about that," Jeremiah said. "I wasn't unconscious for the whole trip here like they thought I was. I know how to get us out. And I will."

"Good." Michael was already pulling me to the right along the corridor and the grip he had on my arm didn't budge. The others disappeared in the opposite direction until I couldn't see them anymore. I was glad we weren't going that way. I never wanted to see that room again, the room where Reid still lay.

Michael didn't look back as he hurried me along, urging me into a jog. His hand was warm in mine, made more so by the constant small tingles of energy rafting from his skin to mine.

"We have to find the right door," he said. "I was blindfolded when they brought me in, but they took it off right at the end. We went through these circular corridors. Kind of like circles within circles, connected by doorways. One of these doors has to lead to a new corridor. Do you still have that key? It'll be a skeleton key."

I touched my neck where the chain rested, trying not to remember the person we'd taken it from, trying not to think of the years he would have lived if not for me. But what would he have done with those years?

Michael ran his left hand along the wall as we walked,

feeling with his fingers and peering at every lump and bump. I slowed down with him, watching to see what he was doing. "What are we looking for?"

"A keyhole without a door."

There were bumps in the wall of the room I'd slept in the night before. Objects had slid out of hidden, seamless openings. I hadn't noticed they were there despite spending the whole night in that room, so I didn't know how we would spot such concealed indentations while running. We didn't have time to look carefully. "We could have missed it already."

"Yep, but if we miss one, we won't miss the next. There has to be a signal of some sort. Otherwise, they'd never find it themselves."

I glanced to the left, to a door with a clear glass panel. My eyes glazed over it. "Nothing here."

"Keep looking."

A crash far behind us made me jump. I wondered if Jeremiah and the others really would be okay. Michael's dad had raised the alarm by now. The determined way Jeremiah had pointed the gun at Cheyne, though, I knew anything was possible. "When we find the right door, we're leaving it open, okay?"

"That's a really bad idea, Ava. The officers will know where we've gone."

"What if this is the only way out? We have to give the others a chance."

He gritted his teeth. Something lit behind his eyes. Worry, frustration, and maybe just a little bit of admiration. "You really care about them."

We passed another door with a glass panel and I glanced inside it. It contained a bunch of computers. "Why don't you?"

"Because I care more about you." He stopped suddenly, looking carefully at a crack in the wall. It must have been nothing because he shook his head. "This is impossible. We're wasting time."

I was still thinking about what he'd just said, that he cared about me. I allowed myself a small moment, a quiet pause where my heart warmed with the thought that this boy standing next to me was my friend. Perhaps the only friend I had.

I tugged on his arm, not wanting to break the moment, but needing to speak. "Michael. Your dad back there. I don't think he was going to kill Thomas. He had a syringe full of nectar in his hand."

Michael stopped, a frown forming on his face.

I said, "I think he was going to bring Thomas back."

Michael was quiet, but he shook his head. "It still doesn't make it right. I saw what that stuff did for you, healing you, but we don't know for sure that it could help someone once they've died. If he was testing it, then he didn't know either, and he was willing to take that risk."

I reached for his hand again. "You said your dad was looking for a cure for your brother. Maybe he thinks this is it."

He shook his head. "I know he's trying. He's been trying ever since my brother was born and when Mom left, it broke him. I don't hate him for that. It's the way he's doing it that makes me sick. Forcing you to come here, using that stuff to try to control you. And then there's all the things he didn't tell me, that he still isn't telling me." He took both my hands in his. "Ava, if he'd told me about Josh, your brother would still be alive. I'll never forgive Dad for that."

I fought the tears burning behind my eyes as I thought of Josh and how hard he'd tried to save me from all of this. "I know."

After that, we walked in silence until another door loomed on our left. This one was glazed and patterned so I couldn't see in.

"There has to be a way that they tell where things are … Wait. Stop." I pulled Michael back to the door with the colored glass and edged closer to it. "Look."

"What?"

"Did you ever see one of those optical illusion images? You

know, there's one with a black and white picture and one minute it's an hourglass, and then it's two people looking at each other?" I tapped the glass panel. "This is a map."

"It's a bunch of swirls."

I jabbed my finger at a particular spot. "It's the curve of the corridor. See this splash. That's where we are. See this other line, stretching perpendicular. It's opposite us." I pushed past him as he peered into the glass with a puzzled look on his face.

There it was, on the opposite wall—a bump. I pressed it and a small, round panel slid open. A lock glided out. I turned to Michael with my best game show host impersonation. "Ta-da."

"Huh. What do you know?"

I turned the key in the lock and pushed. Michael stepped inside and I glanced back at the glass panel. It looked like only part of the map, the beginning of one, but I knew what I was looking for now. We left the door open behind us as we ran down the new corridor, looking for a glass panel with an exit marked on it.

We ran for what seemed like half a mile, the corridor always pulling slightly to the left in the circle that Michael had talked about. We found another exit to a new corridor, and then another, and with each one, the curve in the walls became less distinct, larger as we moved closer to the outside of the building.

Michael pulled me on. "We must be close to the outer corridor."

This time we ran for close to an hour, stopping to assess the glazed panels, which showed the way out always in the same direction, but as we followed the curve of the hallway, I realized that something was wrong. I stopped, puffing, standing outside the latest in a string of panels. "I'm sure we've been here before."

"I'd believe that." Michael had barely broken a sweat.

I frowned at the colors on the glass panel. "I'm not reading this right. All the maps say the way out is this way, but we never get any closer to it. We've been going around and around. Hang on…" I peered at the panel again, following the curves with my finger. "It looks like this is pointing inward again, unless … Oh!"

"What is it?"

I looked up at the ceiling. I pointed.

Michael ran his hand through his hair. "They really don't want anyone getting out of here easy. C'mon. Up on my shoulders."

I bit my lip. "Um…"

"It'll be fine, star girl. Time to fly again." He knelt down and I clambered onto his shoulders, clinging for dear life to his head. I reached upward, touching the ceiling with my palm, balancing there. Little shocks traveled up my legs through the rips in my jeans where his bare shoulders touched my skin, making me shiver. I stretched for the protrusion in the ceiling. "Do you seriously think this is how these guys come to work every day?"

"Not likely. This must be the emergency escape."

I smiled at that. "Do you think they have fire drills?" My fingers found the bump and pressed. It slid open. This time something opened in the ceiling behind us. It creaked and clanged and a pair of stairs unfolded all the way to the floor.

"At least I don't have to toss you up there." There was a grin in his voice. As he spoke, Michael moved, and I lost my balance, the world swung. He caught me—just in time. Right before my field of view filled with Michael's shoulders, I caught a glimpse of something I didn't want to see. A small red light.

I settled down in the crook of his arm, frozen against him.

"Hey," he said. "Don't worry, I've got you."

"No." My breathing increased. I pressed my face into his chest, keeping my voice low, my lips concealed. "They're watching. I've been so stupid."

It took him a moment. He froze too.

"I guess that's why we haven't seen any guards yet." I raised my eyes to his. I ducked my head down again. "I'm sorry. I should have known this was way too easy."

He gave me a single nod. I raised my face to his again. He looked as if he needed to say a thousand things, but they'd see. They'd hear. One corner of his mouth rose. He glanced up at the camera with the strangest look in his eyes. Then he said, "I've been wanting an excuse to do this."

He dropped his lips to mine.

It was so unexpected, I didn't even know how to react. A sharp snap of energy jolted all the way down my neck like a bolt of firelight sizzling all the way to the tips of my toes.

I gasped, and he moved backward, letting me go, as though he was worried he'd done the wrong thing. I pulled him back to me before our lips could part, crushing myself against his chest. My head tipped back as I drank in the rafts of energy coursing from him to me until everything around me blurred and was forgotten, and the electrical pulse between us became a constant thrum that I couldn't live without.

For a moment, I forgot all about running and being afraid, and even the tremors in my body stopped and focused and let me just *be*. And what I wanted to be was there, right then, with his arms around my waist and shoulders, my own around his back, and stillness in my heart.

Too soon, he spoke, his words smothered against my mouth, "Let's go up the stairs. It's probably a trap, but there's no other choice, right?"

"Right," I whispered as our mouths moved apart.

He gave me a crooked smile, with one of those I-kind-of-really-hope-that-was-okay-just-now looks. I grinned back, thinking that it might be the last time I'd have the chance to snatch a moment of happiness, even if it was tempered by cameras and the knowledge that capture was only minutes away.

Michael took my hand and I followed him up the stairs.

CHAPTER 22

E EMERGED into another corridor, only a few feet long, with a door at the end of it. Dim lights lifted the gloom and I ran my hand along the wall, in case I found another concealed bump, but there were no other openings here, no other pathways to escape through. I put my hand up against the door, and Michael rested his over mine, making me feel unnaturally calm.

I leaned in and pressed my ear against the door, hoping to hear something that might tell me what was behind it. I was surprised to find that it wasn't metal, but wood painted black.

I left my face resting there, cool, controlled for a brief moment. Michael breathed out beside me. His hand moved over mine, his fingers wrapping tight. His forehead dropped to the door and my own slumped, until my chin rested all the way on my chest, my hair falling forward. I said, "It's time to go in."

"I won't let anything happen to you."

I didn't quite meet his eyes, turning away from the determined gleam in them. Shivers and knots filled my muscles and made my head swim. When I put the key in the lock and pushed on the door, I moved without feeling my feet.

We heard the fighting before we saw it, but it was the crisp, clean scent of fresh bamboo that overwhelmed me. Two steps took us beyond the short entrance into a wide combat theater. Wooden pillars rose to the ceiling, the floor covered in beautifully woven tatami matting, each wall decorated with swords, knives, and shining weapons.

We were in the Terminal.

Michael pulled me behind a pillar. Three people already battled in the center of the room, whirling in a deadly dance. Not one of them looked to be losing, none of them giving ground.

I expected to see faces in the viewing booths above us, crowds to see the fight. I hoped that maybe someone—anyone—might help us. But the panels were blanked out, shuttered black.

"If this is the Dojo, where are the spectators?"

Michael dropped to one knee, tugging me down with him. "There are drones everywhere. Look." He pointed to the four corners of the ceiling, as well as between each one. Small brown drones blended into the wooden surrounds, barely visible. He ran a hand through his hair, face paler than I thought possible. "Someone's watching us."

My blood pounded, but not with fear. "Then let's take them out."

"Yeah, and then we need to get past those guys."

I forced a smile. "I don't think they're going to let us stroll on out of here."

One of the fighters did a backflip. The other one cast a running jump up one of the wooden pillars and hung in the air, kicking the first one flat, staying airborne for an impossible amount of time.

I remembered the newsflash in the truck. *Gravity-defying fields.* "At least I know how to kill the drones."

I scooted around the edge of the room, aiming for the end furthest away from the fighters. The newsreader had said that only five would be allowed into the Dojo. Either there were two more coming or we *were* the other two. I eyed the weapons on the wall and picked the closest knife with the sturdiest-looking handle. Locating the drone furthest from the fighters, I circled out into the room as far as I dared, knowing the others might see me, but I needed the run up.

I charged at the nearest corner, launched myself at the wall on one side, and felt gravity change, gripping me as if I had a string attached to the top of my head. I bounced over to the other wall and back again, higher each time. On the last bounce, I reached out, plucked the drone out of the air and wrenched it down to the floor, ignoring the whirring blades, smashing the handle of the knife into it. Once. Twice. The glass fell out of the camera and the drone's body cracked, spilling out electronics.

The other fighters seemed oblivious, intent only on each other. I looked to Michael, but he already followed my lead. Within minutes, we broke four of the drones, but as I landed down again, I shuddered to find that the remaining drones circled overhead and the fighting behind us had changed.

The three fighters had separated, keeping a distance from each other, watching us at the same time. It looked like one of them was a woman. The other two were definitely men. It was impossible to tell who they really were because they were in costume. Black ninja garb covered their faces and bodies.

They crept toward us, shoulders hunched, weapons ready. They must have wondered what we were doing there, me in my white t-shirt and ripped jeans, Michael bare to the waist. At least it looked like we'd fought our way in there.

I still had the knife in my hand. So did Michael.

Something about the group changed, their formation altered. I glanced at Michael and he had a look on his face like he'd seen it all before. We were the intruders. The common enemy.

Three against two.

For now.

I figured they were too crazed with battle to recognize my face from the news or else they might have stopped. Maybe asked questions. But of course, they wouldn't. They couldn't die. The idea of dying was impossible to them. They had no war to fight.

I pictured Josh tapping his forehead. *The only war we fight is the one in our own minds.*

Michael moved like a bodyguard, blocking me, but I wasn't going to let him fight for me this time. Live or die. I looked to the nearest wall of weapons, wishing I had something more than the knife, but if I broke off to grab something else, it could set off a reaction from the fighters, and it would leave Michael without backup. The knife would have to do.

One of them headed straight for us, the other two circled, moving in behind. Michael swiveled to the first one. When he fought, before he killed Josh, he was cold and uninterested. The look on his face now was something I hadn't seen before. Anger. So intense that his lips drew back in a snarl.

He spoke to the first one, the woman. "Do your worst."

She raced at him, but instead of meeting her, Michael spun and flung his knife at the man edging up behind me. The guy staggered backward and dropped to the floor. At the same time, the second man lunged for me. Michael brushed past me, snatched the knife from my hand, and the second man went down. The woman changed course and rushed at me instead of Michael. I barely had time to think about dodging when Michael flew back, crashed into her from the side and knocked her to the ground. She rolled to safety.

"They know I'm protecting you!" It was all Michael had time to shout before the woman jumped back to her feet, bouncing up off the wall at him with her weapon ready to cut him to shreds. He didn't move fast enough and she sliced his hand clean off.

It didn't even leave his wrist. The woman's eyes widened and her mouth opened in disbelief. Michael gave his wrist a light touch, watching the woman's reaction with a wicked grin on his face.

Then she charged him again. I sensed movement behind me and I glanced at the other two.

They hadn't stopped watching me while they waited for their bodies to heal. To them, I was the weak one. The one they could get to.

Stuff that.

I raced over to the wall of weapons and grabbed something I could use: a thin ribbon of leather with a serrated edge, about two feet long with a handle at one end. I'd danced with ribbons and I figured this wouldn't be much different. So long as I kept it away from my own face.

The first guy recovered and was upon me.

I swung, letting the ribbon unfurl into the air, arc out, and whip around his upraised arm. He blinked, frozen, but the initial moment of surprise passed. He yanked his hand back, pulling on the ribbon, trying to upset my balance. I braced, held tight, and he roared, his wild eyes the only thing giving away any hint of pain or fear as the ribbon left a gash across his forearm.

He lunged for me again, and I whipped the ribbon his way, missing his face by a scant quarter inch. Up close, I knew I'd be in trouble. I leaped for the nearest wooden pole and shimmied up it. The fighter raced after me, snatching at my ankle with his good hand. He took a second to produce another knife and in the meantime, I'd made it further up the pole. He slashed at me, as high as he could reach, and my thigh stung.

I kicked him hard in the face. He tried to dodge backward, but my foot connected. I was sure I'd broken his nose and it gave me the time I needed to gain another couple feet of height, where I clung with my legs, the task made easier by the anti-gravity. I only had a moment before he climbed up after me. The ribbon was still in my hand, clutched in shaking fingers.

As he spat out blood and wiped his streaming nose, I

dropped my head, arching back and down, still clinging with my legs, controlling the swing just enough to stop before I slammed the back of my head into wood. As the room tilted upside-down, I judged the distance between him and me. My arm snapped out. The ribbon darted like a black snake, winding around his neck.

He forgot his nose and grabbed at the serrated edge around his throat. His eyes changed to something very uncertain. Maybe he even wondered what it might be like to die.

I stopped thinking about it and forced my arms to retract.

He dropped to the floor.

I lifted myself back to the pole, made myself shimmy further up and around to the back and I stayed there with my legs and arms clutching wood as if I could squeeze my soul into it. If I could just see Michael, see that he was okay, then I was sure I'd be okay too. I wanted to bury my head and tune out to the sounds of clashing steel. We hadn't finished smashing drones, but it didn't seem to matter anymore. They'd never let us out. Never.

I touched my pocket, grasping for the only thing that could help us, but all I found was tattered material and a hole through which my fingers poked. The syringe of nectar had to be on the floor somewhere. I dropped to the ground, floating down in the arms of the anti-gravity.

There. The nectar had rolled a few feet away.

"Ava! Move!" Michael's voice shocked me into action. I dropped and rolled without even looking. The air shifted. There was a twang in the pole behind me, a quivering arrow, as the woman ran toward me, notching another one. The last man lunged at Michael as he tried to follow her, forcing him to turn and fight. I sprinted for the wall of weapons, weaving around the pole. Another arrow thwacked wood. There was a clatter behind me, way too close. My hand reached for something— anything—to fight her with.

Something swiped my legs out from under me. I crashed to

my side, the air crushed out of my lungs. She snatched up my arms into a death grip, pressing me into the floor.

Her breath kissed my cheek. "I didn't think I'd dance in the same room with you again, Ava. Not ever."

I struggled, my cheek grazing the tatami floor, the clean musk of bamboo rushing into my lungs. "Hannah?"

CHAPTER 23

SHE PULLED OFF her face mask. Her words washed over me like shock waves. I told myself I wasn't hearing her right, that she couldn't be saying it, that she was my best friend. "You're a Basher."

She planted her knee on the small of my back, pushing my face into the floor with her free hand. "For a while now."

"Why, Hannah?"

"Because the government is creating weapons that kill people. Messing with our DNA. They shouldn't be the ones with that power."

"And the Bashers should? They want to do exactly the same thing. Tell me I'm wrong." I tried to see her face, but she wrenched on my arms.

There was silence, broken only by the distant clashing of swords. Her voice turned to a whisper. "The Bashers want to use you too. They want the blood running in your veins more than anything else. With your blood, they can eliminate the weak once and for all. They can choose who lives."

"Hannah, I—"

"You're nothing to them, Ava. Just like Josh was nothing to them. When they couldn't use him to make a weapon, they took that thing out of his back, took away the only thing keeping him safe because they wanted what was inside it." There was a snarl in her voice. "Nectar. It's just as important as you are. They killed him for it, and they'll end up killing you too."

Her arms trembled and her voice choked. "They asked me to find you. So I did. I found you. And I'm not going to spend the rest of my life buried in a cell." She shook herself before she ground out, "I was glad I blew your legs off. Do you know how demeaning it was to find out I'd been dancing with a *mortal?* Competing with a *mortal?*" She spat the word as if it was a bug that needed squashing.

I twisted my head, trying to breathe. "How are you going to get me out of here, Hannah? There's security everywhere."

"Don't worry, we have a plan."

Running feet drummed my ear. I struggled to raise my head, to see who it was, but Hannah crushed me down, crouching with her back to the wall as if I was some kind of shield. Her left knee still pinned me.

A *snap* made me freeze.

At the same time, she spoke. "Can I shoot him now?"

I pictured the communicator she had hidden in her ear. She must have got the answer she wanted because from beside her right leg, she raised a gun. It was the same weapon Cheyne had shot Thomas with.

It was the mortality weapon.

I gasped. "Where did you get that?"

She smiled, and at the same time, the man I'd killed hobbled to his feet, leaning against the wooden pole several feet away. Golden dreadlocks floated to the floor, chopped short beneath the ragged edge of his facemask.

Jeremiah.

The breath stuck in my throat because I'd rescued him. I'd set Jeremiah free and handed him the mortality weapon.

He gave Hannah a quick salute. He was a Basher all along.

He'd probably got himself caught deliberately so he'd be brought to the facility.

Hannah hefted the gun and took aim at Michael fighting the other man. Her arm was straight, her sight narrow. She was going to kill him.

I arched around her knee and kicked my foot toward my back, connecting with her arm. It didn't have the momentum to hurt her, but the shot went wild. She screamed frustration, her shriek dampened by the wooden walls. I took advantage of her upset balance to kick her again, twisting at the same time, rolling out from under her knee and scrambling to a crouch.

Michael zigzagged across the floor, almost upon us. Behind me, Hannah shouted into her communicator and raised the gun again, but I leaped at her, grabbing her arm and wrestling her back to the wall. Michael crashed into both of us and the gun went off, splintering the ceiling.

I didn't have time to think before soldiers ran inside the room from the far door, ten of them, all dressed in black. Michael didn't seem to notice, pinning Hannah and lifting her up with one hand around her neck, smashing her gun arm with the other. The weapon thudded to the tatami, and I snatched it up, wondering how many bullets were left.

The soldiers raced toward us across the vast room, all of them holding mortality guns.

Their guns were aimed at Michael and Hannah. Jeremiah had disappeared or perhaps he'd been shot, I didn't know.

I screamed at Michael to look out and he whirled, dropping Hannah in a crumple. Without waiting, I threw him the mortality gun and he caught it in one hand, but his eyes went wide when he saw what it was.

He couldn't use it; I saw it on his face. He wasn't a killer and I loved him for it. I wondered if I'd ever get the chance to tell him that.

I shrank against the wall, trying to think as the men sped toward us, twenty feet and closing, training their guns on

Michael. He sought my eyes and touched my hand, folding my fingers into his, and I forgot about the men as the beautiful tingle of energy that rippled through me made me safe, quiet, and free, just for a moment.

He pulled me close. "We're getting out of here. Don't fight, Ava." He gathered me up in the face of the oncoming chaos and held me tight for a moment. His eyes met mine for what felt like the last time. "Don't fight. *Dance.*"

He spun me out, away from him, and released me into the group of oncoming soldiers. I spiraled across the tatami matting. The group of men split in two and, as they did so, Michael opened fire from behind me.

A man to my right clutched his leg, but it was his scream that broke the silence. A wretched sound, his face clouded dark like a shadow passed over him. He wasn't dead, but he was … *mortal.* If he was wounded now, he could die, and he knew it.

In the next instant, a second man plunged, his arm hit, yowling like the reaper had come for him. Someone lurched at me from the right, clutching arms and ruddy face, and I danced into him, spinning like a whirlwind. I flipped and twisted and kicked and jumped my way across the floor. There was a thud, followed by another as Michael shot them, one after the other.

The remaining six soldiers shouted and sought cover behind the wooden pillars. I wondered why they didn't use their weapons until I realized they were afraid of shooting each other by accident.

They were afraid to die.

We had precious seconds before they regrouped, got behind cover, and had a clear shot.

My head whipped around as a soldier broke from the group and blasted toward me, trying to grab me, but he plummeted with what must have been the last of Michael's bullets.

They wanted me out of the way before they fired at Michael. They weren't allowed to hurt me, but I wasn't going to make it easy for them.

I dropped back so Michael caught up to me. He shouted, "Go, Ava!"

"You first! They won't shoot me."

But he shook his head. "No." And I had no choice but to run as fast as I could, praying he wouldn't get shot behind me.

The door was twenty feet away and Michael kept pace on my heels. I didn't have to turn to know he was there. I was as certain as my heart pounded, as certain as if he touched me.

I slammed into the door. Michael planted himself between the soldiers and me. We'd be an easy target now that we were standing still. Panic rose up and threatened to swallow me as I shoved at the etching of a cherry blossom in the middle of the door. The image compressed and the door released.

At the same time, there was a single gunshot, followed by silence.

"Michael!" The room spiraled as I spun back to him.

He doubled up at my feet, trying to stand, the gun at his side. He rose upward, grabbing at something in his chest. Stepping back to cover me completely, he flung one hand back to brace against the wall next to the door.

Another bullet whipped past us and kicked tatami up off the floor. Something nicked my arm. Michael's hand slipped, and I grabbed him around his torso and drew him close to me, plastering his body up against mine. With our body weight, I heaved against the door.

Fresh air rushed in as we fell backward through it. With everything I had, I pushed us back and down, out of the way, crashing to the floor just in time before bullets peppered the wall behind us.

Shouts and blasts and drumming boots muffled and stopped as the door swung closed in front of us. I took deep breaths of air, wondering how much further we'd get. We only had a few seconds before they reached the door and came out after us.

We were sprawled on the floor, his body half over my hips and legs, one of my arms hugging his chest, keeping him close, his head cradled against my chest. He was heavy, a still blanket over me, always a shield. I waited for him to respond, tried to see his eyes, to see if they opened, looked at me. There was blood on his sleeve and a rip in his shirt. I snatched at it, trying to see it better, to see whether it was over his heart.

Please don't let it be his heart. Not with this bullet...

"Michael!" Desperation filled every nerve. He couldn't be dead, I wouldn't let him. I wanted him to hold my hand and run with me as long as we could.

"Ava?" His whisper reached through my despair and I breathed it in, gasping air at the gentle sound of his voice.

He stirred and twisted, drawing upward, raising his face to mine. His eyes were soft, his lips close to my skin. "I think I almost died."

I put my head into my hands, bending over him with tears rushing down my cheeks, my chest heaving with them. "I've had enough of this nightmare."

He stroked my arm. "Time to leave, huh?"

"Please?"

He struggled to his feet, unclenched his fist and dropped a single glittering teardrop onto the floor. I put my hand over his heart, dropped my head there for a second, reassuring myself that it was still beating, and left tears behind when I looked up again.

Yet another corridor stretched out before us, this one lined with sparkling mirrors, the kind of reflections that would puff up victorious fighters ready to enter the Dojo. We'd have to trace their steps backward and I doubted that we'd make it all the way to the entrance. As we paced away from the door, Michael swept my hand into his, amazing me by tugging me into a sprint. "Run, Ava."

He didn't have to tell me twice. My legs pounded a drumbeat down the hallway. We hit the door at the end of the corridor and this one had a panel at the side.

"Let me," Michael said. "I know these codes." He tapped the

panel, the door clicked open, and we ran through into the next corridor.

Michael grabbed my attention. "I know where we are now. This way will get us out of here." He steered me to the left and another door and, as we pushed through, the silence was strange after the chaos we'd left behind.

A hundred steps along, a door at the side opened.

Michael's dad stepped into the corridor, his expression grim. His slim frame blocked the door at the end, his jaw clenched beneath his beard. He held a gun with the same markings as the one Michael held.

Mr. Bradley leveled the mortality weapon at us, but Michael said, "Keep going." He urged me forward, his hand warm and prickling on my arm. "Behind that door is the service area at the side of the Terminal. We can get out that way."

"But it's your dad."

"Just stay behind me."

He walked straight for his dad, getting ahead of me until we were only ten feet away from him. Without taking his eyes from his father, Michael lifted his weapon and sighted down it. I rested my hand on the small of his back, to let him know I was there, that I would do anything to get us both out of there.

His dad said, "You're out of bullets, son."

"Nope. I saved one. Just for you."

Mr. Bradley lifted his own weapon and held it steady, aimed at Michael. "I won't miss."

"Neither will I, Dad. You taught me well."

Taking a deep breath, Mr. Bradley said, "I'm not what you think I am, Michael. I just want a cure for your brother. We're so close with the nectar now. We could help so many people, all the slow healers who are too ashamed or too scared to come forward. Cheyne, your brother. And the mortality weapon can bring the Bashers down. I want your brother to be safe, so your mom can come home and we can be a family again."

I looked between them, father and son, and felt all their

anger as if it was strangling me. There had been enough death today. Reid had died—no, I'd *killed* him. I didn't know about Cheyne. I guessed he was okay, but I didn't know for sure. My hand slipped across Michael's back, absorbing his tense skin and the angry lines of his shoulders. His eyes widened as I stepped out in front of him.

His dad tried to realign his sight, moving his weapon around me, but it was my turn to be the shield.

I walked toward him, sensing every touch of my feet on the cold floor, every movement of air, the way the light reflected off the walls, the absence of cameras. A mere foot away from Mr. Bradley, I stopped, observing the gray in his hair, the tremble in his hands, the beads of sweat on his forehead. "You won't hurt me. You need me."

When he didn't answer, I reached out and took hold of the gun, wrapped my fingers around the barrel, and pushed it down. "I know you didn't intend to kill that kid. You had nectar ready to bring him back."

I remembered how he'd spoken to Josh on the footage, how gentle his voice had been. I wondered how much he knew about what Reid did to me and to Michael, how much of it he sanctioned and how much they didn't tell him. I remembered Cheyne saying that Michael's dad didn't like keeping people against their will, that it was a weakness. But even if he didn't know, he should have. Even if he didn't protect me, he should have protected Michael and put a stop to it.

He studied me, caution painted across his features. "I needed to see if the mortality weapon would work, but I need to know if nectar will counteract it. Every weapon needs a counter-weapon. We can't create something that takes life without knowing how to bring it back. I'm sorry, Ava. I'm sorry it has to be you."

My voice became a whisper. "But I don't want to be anybody's weapon."

He reached for me. "I know it doesn't look like it, but your mortality can save lives, not take them. Seversand has stopped threatening us for the first time in years. We can finally put a stop to the Bashers. How you react to nectar can help me figure out a cure for my son. You're the answer to everything. I need you to stay."

"And what about nectar? Where is that from?"

He shook his head, his expression closing off. "You can't go out there, Ava. The people don't understand what you are. They don't understand that you can help them. We can keep you safe here. And you can help us … like your brother did."

"No," I said. "You won't catch me again."

There was shouting, commotion behind us, and the soldiers had caught up. Feet pounded, and in the next moment, Michael snatched me up as he ran past, bullets pelting around us, hitting the wall behind Michael's dad, striking a dotted line around him like some kind of cut-out character. He ducked, crouched, and tried to stand, screaming orders for the men to stop shooting. I couldn't tell if they were shooting mortality bullets or normal ones.

Michael smashed through the broken wall, pulling me with him, dropping his father at the same time. Debris flew across the floor, but Michael kept going and didn't look back. I touched ground, jumping over the crumpled man on the floor. Mr. Bradley struggled to his knees, surrounded by carnage with his back to us, hunched over his weapon, one hand raised to stop the soldiers.

The thundering weapons faded behind us.

Around the corner, the corridor opened into an arena filled with trucks and machinery, and on the far right was a massive door.

Michael slowed enough to let me catch up. I knew he didn't want to talk about what just happened with his dad and I wasn't going to make him. I pointed at the trucks as we sped past. "Can we take one of these?"

He shook his head. "They're fitted with tracking systems. We have to go on foot. Wait." He veered to the right, to a desk with items sprawled over it and somebody's satchel, tipping out the contents. There was a wallet, and money disappeared into Michael's pocket.

"Whose is that?"

He shrugged and dropped the empty wallet back on the table. "C'mon." He sprinted over to the roller door and thumped on the emergency release. Alarms went off everywhere, but no soldiers appeared.

We waited for the door to rise. It was the first time we'd stopped running since the Dojo. The silence hurt my ears, stillness buzzed like mad inside my head. I looked around the hanger, wondering aloud. "Have they given up?"

Michael shook his head, a deep sadness filling his eyes. "Dad let us go."

He didn't waste another second. He snatched my arm and propelled me through the door and out into the night where fresh air rushed us and our footsteps battered the pavement. We paused at the top of the hill with the Terminal Precinct sparkling below us and the river snaking around it in the distance.

Michael pointed to the far-off boats bobbing like specks of paper at the shoreline. "The river," he said. "We can follow it to Starsgard."

I hardly heard his words as a chasm opened up at my feet. "We're the same now. You and I."

A shadow passed over his face—the memory of Josh, the memory of Reid.

He reached across the black pit of my soul and took hold of my hand, pulling me close and brushing a kiss across my forehead, the lightest touch easing the weight of what I'd done.

He tugged me forward and we ran down the slope.

$\mathcal{D}$RONES HAD been following us for days. Michael kept telling me they wouldn't hurt me, but he sounded less sure each time.

"They could shoot me right now if they wanted to." I studied the bleak clouds where the drones would be hovering, obscured, as the waves around the ferry slapped the side of the moving boat.

"They won't kill you."

"Would they rather lose me? Once I'm over the border, they won't get me back."

Michael shook his head, and I continued. "Or tranq me and pick me up. They could do that."

"On the boat? In the middle of the river?"

"They're bound to have people on this ferry." I eyed the other passengers, about fifteen of them, some sitting, some standing at the railing, watching the coastline pass. We'd ferry-hopped our way a hundred miles upriver and, so far, nobody had recognized us. My hair had grown a lot because of the nectar I'd taken—both when I lost my legs and again at the Terminal. It was past my shoulder blades, making me look twice my age, and we'd lifted sunglasses and black hair dye. The temperature cooled the further north we traveled, so Michael procured a coat for me. The buttons were mostly broken, but it held together with an old brass brooch. I felt bad about stealing, but my life depended on it. The drones would follow us anywhere, always high and just out of sight—we wouldn't escape them until we reached Starsgard— but it was the ordinary people we were really worried about.

A newspaper rested in my lap and the headline asked in big lettering: *Are we safe?* There was a picture beneath it showing a crowd of people holding placards.

One of them read: *Mortals will kill us all.*

The sooner we made it across the border, the better.

Michael nudged me. "What about that old lady?"

I smiled at the woman approaching with the bottle of water. "Maybe not."

Our disguises weren't bad, but it was the rolled-up blanket under my shirt that really kept us safe.

The older lady's long gray plait beat the back of her thighs as she handed me the water and I swallowed it with a grateful look. "Thank you," I said. "I feel much better."

She glided into the seat next to me, disapproval etched in every line on her face. Her glare was for Michael, who shifted in his seat next to me. "You should take better care of her." It was my bare ring finger that she glared at now. "Not everyone's as lucky as you. I couldn't have children."

Michael turned bright red. It was his idea to begin with. *They'll see the tummy and not you,* he'd said. I smiled at him, but my smile slipped as I remembered him being shot, his palm on the wall of the Terminal the only thing keeping him standing, shielding me until the last. "He already does," I said, twining my fingers in his.

The boat turned the final bend in the river and in the distance the mountains of Starsgard shot into the air, looming less than twenty miles away, casting a shadow over the forest beneath them. Cloud cover obscured the tops of the towers built on each mountain peak, extending into the sky higher than the eye could see. I counted at least seven towers, but I was sure there were more.

The river grew visibly narrower to the north and the boats wouldn't travel past the final port. As it approached, the older woman squeezed my shoulder and rose to her feet. "Take care of yourself, dear."

I nodded a good-bye, and we waited for the other passengers to leave. We wandered off last as though we had nothing much to do, all the time assessing our new surroundings and the people making their way up the pier, the bus ready to take them to the nearest town, none of them even glancing toward Starsgard. They were not welcome there.

"How long do you think it will take us to get through the trees to the base of the mountain?"

"Too long." Michael held my hand tighter because he'd seen them too: motley-brown uniforms like dead vines winding through the tree line, waiting for us to reach land. Bashers. I wondered if Jeremiah was among them. Or Hannah, although she'd probably never made it out of the Terminal.

I paused at the end of the pier as the quiet waves lapped the wooden landing. "When will they leave me alone?"

Michael pulled me close, his arms wrapping around my waist. "Guess you're just too irresistible, star girl." His hand brushed the curve between my torso and my hip. "Do you remember your butterfly quilt?"

I frowned at him, wondering how he could think about something so obscure right then. "My quilt?"

"We ended up wrapped up in it."

I remembered bullets kissing the air and launching myself at the medical kit in my bedroom. Michael had leaped from the end of my bed and pulled me down to safety. "I don't think I want to remember it."

He smiled, dropping a tingly kiss on my lips that made me

draw a quick breath. His eyes crinkled up with laughter. "I didn't mind so much."

I couldn't help smiling back at him. There were about a million Bashers waiting for us and we had no weapons, nothing but the trees and the water and a moment to take a breath and breathe, but for some reason, the world could have been as beautiful as Michael's smile right then.

I inhaled and leaned into him. If this was the last time I got to hug him, I wanted to remember it, but I stopped as the hum of drones became more than a distant thrum in the air.

We looked at each other in surprise. I glanced past Michael, to the other side of the river, catching breath as machines flew down on us, racing out of the clouds, maybe a hundred of them, gold and black wasps cutting the air. For a moment, there was only silence and Michael's determined smile as we stood between Bashers and drones, old wooden palings at our feet, gray sky over our heads, and the peaks of Starsgard too far away.

Michael smoothed my hair out of my eyes. "We almost made it."

Except that the drones weren't heading down to the pier. Instead of tracking a descent toward us, they split in two, flying over our heads and heading straight to the trees, firing tranquilizer darts.

A Basher dropped and there was sudden movement everywhere. Men appeared in the trees, driving the Bashers out from their hiding places. The last passengers were still getting on the bus and somebody shouted and then the bus roared into life, speeding away with baggage left on the pavement.

Bullets kicked up dust and rocks. Leaves rained, flicking around the clearing as the Bashers fought back. One of them dodged a drone, zigzagging down the pathway, running toward us with his weapon ready and that was when Michael's hand moved at my waist and I realized what he'd been thinking.

When the Basher was only ten feet away, Michael whipped

the rolled-up blanket out from under my shirt, flicking it open and out at the man. The guy turned to beat it off, tripping, and in that moment, Michael whisked me up with him. I ripped off my coat and flung it aside as we ran for the edge of the pier.

Water engulfed our bodies as we dived in. Darts pierced the space around us, but we swam deeper and deeper, pulling each other down until we reached the bottom and then we swam along it as far as we could before my lungs burned and screamed for air. Still, Michael tugged me along, further than I thought I could possibly go, his wrist clamped on mine as sparkles and light filled my head, and still he pushed me, until the last moment when I was about to pass out. Water rushed over my skin and my clothes dragged in the force of movement as Michael propelled us upward. I gasped, not caring about Bashers or drones, filling my empty chest with sweet oxygen.

"Ava," Michael whispered into my ear and pointed down again. Behind us, the sound of battle was muted, but still too close. The Basher, who'd come after us, was nowhere to be seen, probably taken down by a drone. I nodded and we dived, again and again, over and over, until finally the water was shallow and we surfaced to silence. The river was running out.

I dragged myself to the edge and dropped beside Michael, our clothes plastered around our bodies and the midday sun speckling the sandy edge.

I ran my hand over my eyes, wiping water from my face, trying not to glare at him. "You can't drown, can you?"

"Sorry."

I exhaled, shook my head against the sandy river bank, and pulled air into the bottom of my lungs.

He propped up on one elbow, spreading my hair out across the stones as though we had all the time in the world. "I'd probably pass out eventually."

"That makes me feel so much better." I tried to smile, but I shuddered as I remembered the machines descending from the sky. "The drones saved us back there."

Michael's expression turned wry. "They protected their asset."

I sat up and ran my hand through my wet hair, wringing it out. Droplets ran between the sandy river stones alongside my legs. "How long before the drones reach us again?"

Michael sighed. "They already have, Ava."

I looked up, not seeing the machines, the ones up really high, but knowing he was right. They'd always follow us and they wouldn't stop until we crossed the border into Starsgard.

I dropped my head into my hands. "How are we ever going to make it?"

"It's closer than you think. Look." He pointed to the north and the mountains that towered over us. "It'll only take us another day. We can find somewhere safe to sleep tonight—"

"No." I clenched my jaw. "No sleeping." I hadn't come this far to stop. Not hunger, not fatigue, nothing could get in the way now. "We won't be safe until we get there. We can't stop."

"Okay." Michael pulled me close, nodding his agreement. "No stopping."

We followed the shallow riverbed as far as we could until the trees crowded the way, but there was no danger of getting lost as night fell because the towers of Starsgard shone soft beacons of violet light for a mile around the border—a warning to others to stay away, but a lifeline to us, pointing us in the right direction.

By the time the sun rose over the tops of the trees, my arms and legs were bleeding and scratched and my throat was parched. Vines, branches, prickly leaves, I pushed through them without a second thought, the only thing that mattered was standing at the entrance to Starsgard. The ground began to rise, the trees thickened, and we had to scramble upward, making progress one agonizing step at a time.

A cut on my forearm oozed and I wiped at it with the bottom of my shirt, almost walking into Michael. He grabbed me before I slipped backward down the slope. "Ava. Look."

We'd reached a clearing, only twenty feet deep, that stretched out on either side of us as far as we could see. Michael dropped a warning hand on my arm, making me wince, an apology in his eyes as he lifted my bleeding hand to his lips and kissed my fingertips.

I tried to reassure him with a smile. "I'm okay," I said, before I staggered past him, my legs screaming for rest, the air burning in and out of my chest.

The clearing was cobbled with stone and, on the opposite side, a rock face soared thousands of feet into the air. Hands pressed to my aching side, I craned my neck back. The bottom of a tower was just visible from where I stood, rising so high I wondered how it could be man-made. Bright green moss, about an inch long, covered the rock face, rippling and swaying in the early morning breeze. I inhaled the surprising scent of earth and moisture. I reached out to touch the moss, but Michael's shout stopped me.

The air thrummed and, all along the tree line, drones appeared in a burst of movement.

Michael ran to me, snatching up the nearest tree branch, placing himself between them and me, but the machines halted, coasting the air behind us, not passing the tree line. We backed up, moving along the path, looking for anywhere to run. The mossy rock face stretched left and right as far as we could see. I squinted into the distance. "I thought there'd be a gate."

As we moved, the drones followed, staying close, but never moving past the tree line. In the distance, another sound cut the air: the warble of helicopter blades.

Michael shook his head and gestured at the moss, pulling me to a stop. He peered at the green substance, taking glances at the drones at the same time. "I think I've heard of this." He waved his hand over the surface, not touching it. "It's bioengineered." As he moved closer, the moss straightened toward his palm as though it was straining to make contact. "It's a defense mechanism … something to do with detecting threats." He rubbed his forehead. "I wish I knew more."

"Maybe we should touch it."

"I don't know. It could tranq us." His eyes met mine. "It could kill you." He ran a hand through his hair, frustration radiating off him. "This—all of this—is designed to protect Starsgard from the rest of the world. They don't want people coming in. They have no reason not to kill us first and ask questions later."

"Then, I'll touch it." I walked straight into Michael's protective arm, the worry on his face hitting my heart. I said, "If they identify me, they'll know not to kill me."

"Unless they want to."

I crunched my lip and gestured back at the drones. "They aren't going to grant me mercy, either." There was no other way in. I knew Michael was worried. We didn't know what the moss did, but I couldn't see any other way. The rock face ascended into the sky and stretched for miles. There were no visible openings and there was no movement anywhere, no sign of human life. "Let me do this."

Before he could stop me, I pressed my palm against the soft surface. The moss tickled as it moved around my skin, molding itself to the curves and edges of my fingertips and hand. I braced myself to feel pain, to stop breathing. Maybe the moss would poison me and I'd die. Maybe I'd be tranq'd—or paralyzed.

Warmth spread through my palm like the summer sun, a sensation of something glowing against my skin, and it felt safe, comforting. I suddenly wanted to press my whole body against it. Just as I leaned into it, something flickered at my side. It was an air screen and it showed a woman with kind eyes and a soft smile.

It was the same woman from the air screen at Implosion. Dark hair. Proud face. Full of strength. She ignored the waiting drones and looked right at me, as though she really saw me. She said, "Ava Holland. Speak your purpose."

I remembered the footage of her from the night my brother died, the way she helped her daughter rise from the cracking earth, lifting the girl to her feet, wrapping her in protective arms as flames and debris swirled around them.

"We seek political asylum."

The woman's expression deepened, long hair fanning around her face. "From whom do you seek such refuge?"

I glanced at Michael. He pressed closer to me, watching the drones.

I said, "From the whole world."

The woman paused, assessing me. "That is, indeed, the truth. If we grant you asylum, what will you give in return?"

I blinked. "A bargain?"

She inclined her head. "A contribution. Everyone here gives in some way to our community."

Michael was suddenly in front of me. He said, "My immortality."

"No, Michael." I pulled him aside, lowering my voice. "What are you doing?"

"Even the Bashers don't heal as fast as I do. It's got to be worth something and I'm not going to let them use you—"

"No, not your immortality. Not my mortality. Otherwise, it will never be any different. We may as well go back with the drones, let them lock us up, test us in labs, pit us against each other. We're more than that, Michael." I stood up on tiptoes and kissed him. He was the one who raced into a green-lit room and lifted me away into quiet and calm, the one who danced with me in a beaten-down park, the one who stood with me outside the world looking in. "You're more than that."

Turning back to the woman, I took a deep breath. "I can dance," I said, meeting her eyes, wondering if she could see into my heart from where she was. "I'll teach anyone who wants to learn."

Michael hesitated beside me, then a smile played around his lips. He glanced at me and said, "I know how to stitch people up." He shrugged, his face becoming guarded. "But if that's not enough, I'm good at sports and I can fight."

The woman's face lit with a smile. "We have need for someone who knows how to care for those less fortunate." She turned to me. "And the arts are valued in Starsgard." She lifted her arm and pointed to the rock face. "You are accepted."

As soon as she said it, the drones behind us gave an angry hum, rising up and leaving the tree line. The helicopter was close behind, so close I could see the outline of men and guns. In another second, they would shoot us down.

Michael crouched, ready to spring. I mimicked him, every part of my body ready to respond. As the first drone reached us, Michael swung the tree branch, sending the drone flying. I leaped for the second one, throwing myself across the space and dragging it down, shoving it weapon-side into the rocks, smashing it over and over as it buzzed in my hands. I whipped it around as darts from another three drones shot into it. I threw the dead drone at them, but another five filled their place. Spinning to the woman, desperation forced a scream out of my mouth. "Help us!"

The woman's face was dark, her eyes cold. "Nobody attacks Starsgard."

She lifted her hand. The moss rippled. Something pulsed across the clearing, a thump in the air, a compression of sound so great that it made me slap my hands over my ears, my body fighting against the force that washed the space around us and spread out through the trees.

The drones dropped out of the sky mid-flight, crashing to the ground. The chopper bucked, lurching up and over onto its side, blades dead. Spinning out of control, it plummeted into the trees, taking the soldiers with it. In the distance, crashes echoed, as though a hundred other things dropped to earth one after the other.

A second later, the helicopter hit ground and the shriek of

crunching metal burst through the air. With it, an explosion of flame shot high above the trees.

I threw myself backward, away from the heat and blaze as the trees snapped and crackled, but in the next moment there were a thousand clicks and a stream of water poured from the rock face ten feet above my head. A torrential wave hundreds of feet wide rushed across the clearing.

Michael dived through it, reaching me in the quiet space next to the rock wall. We huddled together as the water drowned out everything around us, hunched against one another, unable to speak. His arm was around my back and my own arms were tangled against his chest. The roar of the water hushed everything.

As the torrent ceased, a final wash of water trickled down the rock face next to us and the scent of burned out smoke hung in the air. We unfurled in the sudden quiet.

The woman appeared next to us, glaring at the fallen drones. "They should know better." She stretched out her arms to me, as though she wanted to help me stand.

Michael walked over to a drone, staring at it. Then he picked it up and threw it across the clearing, scattering metal and wires. He kicked another as though he expected it to wake up. When it didn't, his gaze met mine.

My eyes widened at the metallic wasps scattered across the rocks, drenched and lifeless. "What was that?"

"It was an electromagnetic pulse." She pointed to the rock face. "You'll see very soon."

Two doors slid open, side by side, each revealing a person-sized cavity inside. They were both lined with green moss.

The woman said, "There's only room for one person in each hydraulic elevator. It's a precaution, I'm afraid. You have to come up separately. But don't worry, you'll see each other at the top."

I turned away from the dead drones and the memory of Reid

and Cheyne and even Michael's dad. High above us, the towers glittered, but they were nothing like the Terminal. Far from the glass and steel of Dell city, these were earthy, deep gray like an extension of the rock itself, entwined with green and brown as though the earth stretched upward into the calm of sky and clouds.

"Michael?" I reached for him and he pulled me close. His arms were warm and his eyes told me everything I needed to know. He'd be there with me, no matter what happened.

With my hand in his, we stepped toward the elevators. I knew he wouldn't let go until I was ready.

The mossy cavity waited for me like a soft good-bye to the life I was about to leave behind. My hand, my arm, my whole body buzzed. I wished Josh was with me right now, that he could have made it here, to the only place we could never be followed, never taken away, never forced to be something we didn't want to be.

Michael squeezed my hand. "I'll see you up there, Ava," and the look in his eyes told me he believed in me, that we were two sides of nature, always balancing each other out.

I let go of him and stepped into the lift.

The door closed and, for the first time, I was safe.

Read more in Mortality 2: Beneath the Guarding Stars.

MORTALITY 2: BENEATH THE GUARDING STARS

Read the second book in the complete Mortality series.

Fear is quiet. It waits for me beneath the guarding stars.

Ava and Michael have fought their way to Starsgard, a mysterious and secluded country powered by plant technology. But crossing the border comes with a price and their home country is ravaged by fear and hatred of mortals. They soon discover that peace is an illusion and danger is closer than they feared.

Set in an alternate version of today's Earth where everyone is invincible... but one girl will change it all.

Beneath the Guarding Stars is a full-length science-fantasy romance, the second book in the complete Mortality series.

MORTALITY - COMPLETE

(Science-Fantasy Romance)

Mortality Complete Set: Books 1 to 4

1. Beyond the Ever Reach

2. Beneath the Guarding Stars

3. By the Icy Wild

4. Before the Raging Lion

ASSASSIN'S MAGIC WORLD - COMPLETE

(Urban Fantasy Romance)

Recommended Reading Order:

Assassin's Magic

1. Assassin's Magic

2. Assassin's Mask

3. Assassin's Menace

4. Assassin's Maze

Assassin's Academy

5. Rebels

6. Revenge

The Monster Ball Year 2 Anthology

7. Assassin's Match - Novella

SOUL BITTEN SHIFTER

(Dark Urban Fantasy Romance)

1. This Dark Wolf

2. This Broken Wolf

3. This Caged Wolf

BRIGHT WICKED - COMPLETE

(A Fantasy Romance)

1. Bright Wicked

2. Radiant Fierce

3. Infernal Dark

STORM PRINCESS - COMPLETE

(Fantasy Romance)

Storm Princess Complete Set: Books 1 to 3 (with bonus scenes and a life after story)

1. The Princess Must Die

2. The Princess Must Strike

3. The Princess Must Reign

ABOUT THE AUTHOR

Everly Frost is the USA Today Bestselling author of YA and New Adult urban fantasy and science-fiction romance novels. She spent her childhood dreaming of other worlds and scribbling stories on the leftover blank pages at the back of school notebooks. She lives in Brisbane, Australia with her husband and two children.

amazon.com/author/everlyfrost
facebook.com/everlyfrost
twitter.com/everlyfrost
instagram.com/everlyfrost
bookbub.com/authors/everly-frost